About the Author

Stephen Benatar was born in 1937, to Jewish parents, in Baker Street, London.

Although he started writing when he was only eight, 'The Man on the Bridge' wasn't published until he was forty-four – and even then, if it hadn't been for the kindness and concern of Pamela Hansford Johnson, the novelist wife of C. P. Snow, this might never have happened.

Since then, however, there have been seven novels – one published by a borough council, the first and only time a council has produced a work of fiction. In 1983 he was awarded a £7000 bursary by the Arts Council; and Boston University in Massachusetts is now the repository for all his papers and manuscripts.

He was married for twenty-nine years to Eileen, with whom he had two sons and two daughters – has taught English at the University of Bordeaux, lived in Southern California, been a school teacher, an umbrella salesman, hotel porter, employee of the Forestry Commission – and at long last, in his retirement, has become a fulltime writer.

Having finally moved back to London, he now lives in West Hampstead, with his partner, John.

Stephen Benatar

Letters for a Spy

8.5.2010

For Rachael

Stephen Benatar.

Welbeck New Editions

First published by Robert Hale Limited 2005

This edition published by Welbeck Press 2009

Welbeck Press
4 Parsifal Road
London NW6 1UH
Telephone: 020 7433 8084

ISBN: 978-0-9554757-4-0

Cover design: John Murphy

Printed by:
Broadfield Press Limited
75 Broadfield Lane, London NW1 9YS
Telephone: 020 7482 5282

For John Murphy
(my right-hand man)
And in very grateful memory of Rita Druiff.
Also in memory of
Lieutenant Commander Ewen Montagu –
without whom, obviously, this book could never have been
written.

Laces for a lady, letters for a spy,
Watch the wall, my darling, while the Gentlemen go by!

A Smuggler's Song, Rudyard Kipling.

INTRODUCTION

I was introduced to *Letters for a Spy* when the author sought my help in corroborating details concerning names and locations in Aldershot. Details can create a vivid sense of place and period, and it is those particulars which ultimately are not linked to a character's development, nor have any real impact on the outline of a story, that can make a 'good read' all the better. So to say I was intrigued to see the novel is an understatement – it was definitely one of the more curious requests I've received during my time as curator of the Aldershot Military Museum.

And being someone who deals regularly with the general history of the Second World War, I was looking forward to reading about Britain during one specific week in May 1943; looking forward, too – because I knew the book was basically a detective story – to finding twists along the way and following the steps which would lead to the solving of a mystery.

I was by no means disappointed.

But it's clear that, like myself, there must be many who'll recognize the facts on which the story is based, so it won't be a mystery to everyone. That doesn't matter. This isn't just a novel about warfare; it also deals with the development of a friendship between two people on opposing sides, and with issues, choices and responsibilities that are as relevant today as they obviously were during the nineteen-forties. I don't wish to give away the plot. I shall only say that Stephen Benatar has created something between an espionage thriller and a romantic adventure that delves absorbingly into the complex nature of wartime relationships and into the things we hold as our priorities. It's a love story in which you very much root for the participants.

And even if you *are* familiar with the strategies involved, you'll surely find it fascinating and suspenseful to witness the advances and the setbacks of the novel's hero – a twenty-five-year-old working for the German Intelligence Service – and to follow his steady though, inevitably, stumbling progress. More than that, at this distance in time and between the covers of a book, you will probably wish him well…because, for all his faith in the future of The Third Reich, Erich Anders is a man you cannot help but like. Benatar has drawn him in depth, so that we relate to him as a human being rather than as an enemy agent. For one thing, he essentially lacks confidence – and although he draws strength from the knowledge he was handpicked for this, his first real mission, by the chief of the Abwehr himself, Admiral Canaris, a man he regards as a wise and kindly father figure, he is painfully aware at the same time of his own inexperience…and even of his immaturity.

As I say, you'll almost want him to succeed…well, certainly not to be found out and thereby become subject to the Treachery Act – which was brought in by the government in 1940: anyone convicted of spying faced summary execution. You'll also want to know how Erich's journey of discovery is going to culminate, in the way that we realize it *has* to culminate, in accordance with our history. This is a page-turner of a novel.

But two points arise out of that last paragraph.

The Treachery Act…

Doesn't the very name of it seem slightly unfortunate; there's such a wealth of difference between a traitor and a spy. We British may think that William Joyce – the most infamous of all the Lord Haw-Haws – thoroughly deserved to die; and maybe, from the German point of view, Admiral Canaris did, as well…although emotionally one finds this extremely difficult to accept, for how can you compare the two? Wilhelm Canaris, born in 1887 and chief of the Abwehr from 1935 to 1944 – whose connections to the Resistance were discovered by the Gestapo only in 1944 – was executed alongside the thirty-nine-year-old German Lutheran theologian, Dietrich Bonhoeffer, merely weeks before the end of World War II. The Nazis hanged them both naked.

Yet how on earth could a spy, German and working in the interests of his own country, ever be thought of as a traitor to England?

And my second point: I used the phrase *in accordance with our history*...

But anyone who hasn't read much about the Second World War may believe that the pivot of this novel is just too inconceivable to be true. It isn't. However improbable it may appear, however far-fetched, however incapable of standing up to even the sketchiest of scrutinies, it is still completely true. Every single detail describing it, down to the lost chain attached to a briefcase and the lost aluminium oar accompanying a dinghy, is authentic; and the fact that nearly all the characters are fictional doesn't detract in the least from that basic authenticity or make you want to speculate on how much you can trust.

There's only one thing you may find yourself wanting to speculate on.

In real life – both astoundingly *and* incomprehensibly – the Germans never sent anybody over to investigate...although, during the last half-hour of a film made in 1955, it was suggested (by the novelist Nigel Balchin, who wrote the screenplay) that they did: an Irish malcontent played by Stephen Boyd: it was certainly the film's most entertaining half-hour.

But what would have happened if they *had* sent somebody?

Letters for a Spy sets out to answer that question...even though (unlike, say, Kevin Brownlow's 1963 film, *It Happened Here*) Benatar plainly wants to stay within the parameters of history.

Ewen Montagu's idea turned out to be a stroke of genius; but nothing can disguise the fact that – looked into at close quarters and by someone inclined to be sceptical – it would hardly have survived an hour.

At this point, I feel it necessary to mention something else which has a bearing on this story – and you will see why, when you come to the novel's essentially open-ended (yet wholly satisfying) conclusion.

On August 17th 1943 the following report appeared in the *New York Times*:

The last Axis defenses on Sicily crumbled today as British and American troops met up in Messina, opposite the toe of Italy. The whole of Sicily is now in Allied hands. Long-range guns are already pounding coastal batteries on the mainland, Allied warships are shelling the coast roads out of Reggio, and bombers are harrying targets along the length of Italy.

John Daly, an American broadcaster, was with the first platoon to reach Messina city hall at 8.25 a.m. – fifty minutes ahead of the British. "We did not arrive in style," he reported. "In fact we walked the last seven miles practically on tiptoe, fearing to touch abandoned equipment lest it contained booby-traps. We watched the ground for mines until our eyes ached."

Then, at 9.15 a.m., a lieutenant colonel of the Eighth Army drove up to the advancing Americans. All he said was: "Hello, Yanks. Congratulations."

Daly added: "The city is a complete ruin. Bombs and craters take the place of streets and buildings. The few people are listless and haggard with the horror of what they have been through. But in spite of all this it seems miraculous that Sicily wasn't more comprehensively fortified. Relatively, it was something of a walkover. Just as if the Axis had decided – for reasons perhaps known only to themselves and God – that Sicily was no longer important enough to be properly defended."

*

IV

Against all the odds, then, Ewen Montagu had succeeded.

And possibly the success of Operation Mincemeat was even more far-reaching than initially appeared. The following year a freelance adventurer and opportunist, codenamed Cicero, posing as valet to the British ambassador in Ankara, secured Allied war files detailing the planned D-Day offensive, and sold them to the Germans. When the Germans ultimately dismissed these as being too improbable to be treated seriously, they must surely have been influenced by the memory of how Lieutenant Commander Montagu had – with a great deal of good fortune and a great deal of chutzpah – so cunningly deceived them.

But if they *had* treated those D-Day plans seriously, the consequences for the Allies would have been devastating.

It could easily have meant that the final victory in Europe fell to Hitler and the Axis.

Yet now, in the safe knowledge that it didn't, we can sit back and enjoy, not simply 'a good read' but an excellent one, with lots to think about upon our journey, transcending wartime in 1943 and reaching out to us in peacetime, over half a century later.

Sally Day
Military Museum, Aldershot
Summer 2009

<u>1</u>

"So then, Anders. Current situation in Sicily… Your viewpoint on it, please."

Franz Mannheim was my section head at the Abwehr. The two of us sat facing each other across the desk in his office and my briefing was about to begin. Earlier, I'd been informed of the extreme urgency of this assignment, but knew nothing of its nature.

It was 1943... The afternoon of Wednesday May 5th, 1943.

And, yes, Sicily was very much in the news right now.

But my viewpoint on it?

I picked my words with care.

"Sicily, sir? Well, it's common knowledge we're building up defences there." I didn't add: Even if we *have* left it a little bit late.

Then I groped for an intelligent way to elaborate.

"And especially," I said, "to the south of the island."

But anyway it wasn't the substance of my comment that he chose to focus on. It was the style.

"*To?*" Although Mannheim was speaking in German it had been agreed that all my replies should be in English. "Why *to*, not *in*?"

"I don't know, sir. *To* came naturally. *Towards* the south."

"Please, then, explain the rule governing that particular preposition. If not *in* I should have expected *at*."

But my knowledge of syntax was shaky. "I'm afraid I can't explain. I simply know that it's correct."

This sounded feeble. And what was worse, after a moment I was even beginning to wonder if it *was* correct.

He swivelled slightly in his chair, leaning back as he did so. He had his elbows resting on the arms and had made a steeple out of his stubby, nicotine-stained fingers. His brown eyes gazed into my face. I wondered if he was speculating on why, out of so many others, it was I who had been handpicked for this mission, even though, apart from anything else, Admiral Canaris had a reputation for distrusting tall men – he himself was only five foot three – as well as those whom he considered too articulate (whatever *that* might mean). It was also said he didn't like men with small ears or anyone who was known to be unkind to animals. My own ears were fairly ordinary and I was certainly quite fond of animals. But in any case, if you'd subscribed to merely a tenth of the rumours you heard about Admiral Canaris, you would inevitably have come to see our chief as a laughing stock. In my own view he was so far from being a laughing stock that he was actually one of those people who made me proud to be a German.

Yet so much for paranoia. Mannheim's principal concern at the moment might well have been my grammar.

"Afterwards, I want you to check up on that preposition. Often it's exactly this kind of slip that can lead to somebody's downfall." He waited until I had reassured him that I would. "So then, my friend? Why is it we're strengthening our defences there? Especially" – he gave me an indulgent smile – "*towards* the south?"

"Because, sir, at present the Allies control the North African coast. And having driven us back through Tunisia it must be obvious they'll next want to drive us back through Europe. Well…how better to achieve this than by pushing up through Sicily? Sicily would make the ideal springboard from which to mount an invasion of Italy."

He seemed pensive.

"In other words, the common-sense approach?"

I nodded.

"But somewhat lacking in surprise?"

"Perhaps, sir, in war you can't have everything."

"Yet wouldn't you think that sometimes, in war, an element of surprise might be more effective than mere common sense?"

I couldn't see where this was leading. I answered only in a mumble.

"Well, yes, sir. I suppose that it might."

"Which is precisely what you'll need to find out," he said.

"Sir? Find out? Find out *what*?"

The steeple was finally dismantled. The swivel chair remained stationary.

"We learn there's now a strong likelihood that they don't have Sicily in mind at all," he said. "That they may be aiming for Sardinia."

I stared at him.

"Sardinia!"

"Sardinia," he repeated. Patiently.

"But, sir, that's right in the middle of the Med – slap bang in the middle of the Med! God in heaven! Sardinia's about a hundred miles from Italy!"

I hadn't intended that expletive. Mannheim must have realized. There followed no correction.

Well, anyway, not for that.

"You mean – I hope – more like a hundred and fifty. But even so. We believe that such a ploy could certainly be possible."

He paused; ran a hand over his thinning blond hair.

"And that's going to be your responsibility, Anders. To discover whether it's not only possible – or even probable – but in fact a serious plan, which they are now more or less resolved to implement."

He set about explaining.

2

At some point between the 24th and 26th of April, nine to eleven days ago, an aeroplane belonging to the Allies had crashed into the sea somewhere off Spain. Only a single body had so far been recovered: that of a major in the Royal Marines, whose Naval ID proclaimed him to be one William Martin – thirty-six and born in Cardiff. The card had been issued last February. At that time Major Martin had been working at HQ Combined Operations in Whitehall.

None of which made him very interesting. However, there was something else that did – *extremely* interesting: a black briefcase still clasped between his decomposing fingers. And the briefcase had contained a letter. If this letter had been written by Pope Julius II and been on its way to Michelangelo it could scarcely have occasioned more surprise. In fact, it had been written by Sir Archibald Nye, and was on its way to General Alexander. Sir Archibald Nye was Vice-Chief of the Imperial General Staff; and the letter had been bound for Tunis.

It had been dated April 23rd.

"My dear Alex, I am taking advantage of sending you a personal letter by hand of one of Mountbatten's officers…"

But how, you may ask, had it fallen into *our* hands?

Apparently, on April 30th, maybe as many as six days after leaving England, Major Martin had been sighted by a fisherman trawling out of Huelva. The corpse had been delivered into the custody of the British vice-consul and on the next day, May 1st, had been buried in the local cemetery.

And buried with full military honours. Graveside attenders included both the Spanish services and the civilian authorities – and doubtless even a member or two of that spy ring which had now acquired a nickname: more mocking than affectionate.

Yet certainly on this occasion our 'Hispanic Branch Office' had performed with a competence wholly in line with the parent company. At least one of its agents had got wind of the major's waterlogged arrival sufficiently soon; and thanks to immediate and very effective interception had managed to relieve him of his briefcase…that briefcase which had never in consequence been seen by the vice-consul.

Excellent reproductions had been made of all the papers it contained.

In addition, an inventory of the contents of Major Martin's pockets had been provided – accompanied by photographs. And these, too, had been dispatched to Madrid as speedily as possible.

From Madrid the whole thing had been transmitted to Berlin, with reports detailing the authenticity of the find and the manner in which it had come about.

Berlin had been staggered. Had instantly initiated further enquiries and had considered all the answers supplied by Madrid as being unbelievably sound. Even quasi-miraculous. God *was* on the side of the Axis. (He was, at least, to those who were still happy to acknowledge his existence.)

Sir Archibald's letter, formerly en route to the headquarters of the 18th Army Group, mightn't have been seen, conclusively, as one of those tablets fierily inscribed upon Mount Sinai – but it carried a message practically as life-altering.

Though, granted, a little more informal. Almost gossipy. Containing comments avowedly off-the-record.

Its real point was this: that after mention of an *eastern* Mediterranean operation involving a landing in Greece (which obviously came as a surprise to no one) there followed a similarly casual reference to a hope that the 'Boche' would automatically assume the *western* Mediterranean operation would be in Sicily.

"Indeed, we stand a very good chance of making him think we will go for Sicily – it is an obvious objective and one about which he must be nervous."

There was no allusion at all to Sardinia but what we had instead – in a shorter, accompanying letter – was a joky allusion to sardines, somewhat contrived. ("And the English," scoffed Mannheim, "have the temerity to call *our* sense of humour heavy-handed!") This accompanying letter was addressed to Sir Andrew Cunningham, at the Allied Forces HQ, Algiers.

"Dear Admiral of the Fleet,
"I promised VCIGS that Major Martin would arrange with you for the onward transmission of a letter he has with him for General Alexander. It is very urgent and very 'hot' and as there are some remarks in it that could not be seen by others in the War Office, it could not go by signal. I feel sure that you will see that it goes on safely and without delay.
"I think you will find Martin the man you want. He is quiet and shy at first, but he really knows his stuff. He was more accurate than some of us about the probable run of events at Dieppe and he has been well in on the experiments with the latest barges and equipment which took place up in Scotland.
"Let me have him back, please, as soon as the assault is over. He might bring some sardines with him – they are 'on points' here!
"Yours sincerely,
"Louis Mountbatten."

Although I had been shown this letter before and had been given several minutes in which to digest it, Mannheim now – in heavily accented English – reread to me the sentence referring to the dead man's prophecy. He hadn't needed to. The fact that Lord Louis Mountbatten himself, Chief of Combined Operations, should be tacitly admitting the raid on Dieppe had been nothing short of a fiasco was something which must strongly appeal to anyone here who saw it. And, indeed, by this time word of the admission must surely have filtered through to everybody in Intelligence. Morale-boosting! How the Führer himself must have gone into transports when he heard of it!

"So Anders," said Mannheim finally, "there you have it. In a nutshell!"

Mannheim wasn't known for his levity – well, certainly not at work; certainly not in wartime. But now he added:

"Or should I say, perhaps…in a tin of sardines?"

3

But no. There I didn't have it at all, neither in a nutshell *nor* in a tin of sardines.

"Sir? Going back to the post-mortem for a moment… How reliable would that have been?"

Mannheim shrugged. "The findings were the expected ones…and presumably correct. The man had drowned. He'd been in the sea for anything between four and six days."

The man. For some reason I didn't like the way he said *the man*.

"Do we know if there was any evidence of the impact made on him – made on Major Martin – when his plane came down?"

"None mentioned."

"Isn't that a little strange?" I felt like a detective. (As a boy of thirteen, when I'd first seen *The Maltese Falcon,* I'd decided that in time I should move to Los Angeles and become a private eye. It was ironic: was I now – when I'd nearly forgotten all about this – soon to achieve a small surviving part of that ambition?) "There may not have been any broken bones, but surely there must have been some cuts…grazes…?"

"Must there?" he asked; in truth not sounding very interested.

"And would he have been thrown out of the aircraft – or sucked out – or what? Was he conscious when he hit the water? Can't they gauge such things as concussion in a circumstance like that?"

"Oh well, Anders, you know these Spanish. They quite pride themselves on being slap-happy. But in any case, what difference would it make?"

Yes. I paused. He was right. What difference *would* it make?

7

And while I had naturally hoped my questions might lead on to others more productive, I suspected I had also been firing them off simply for the sake of showing that I could.

Yet, all the same, I felt surprised. Mannheim was generally meticulous.

He must have sensed my reaction.

"Of course, Anders, it's good that you should question. But let's face it: this post-mortem could hardly have seemed *that* important to anyone. And we have to remember that the body was wanted for burial at noon the following day. Besides, we must be fair. The doctor would have had a very clear notion of what he was about to find. The man died when his plane was lost at sea. That's obvious. It's not under debate. Cuts, grazes – concussion – all totally beside the point. Yes?"

"Yes, sir. But why was his the only body? And why no bits of wreckage?"

"The only body *so far*. The others could well have been caught by different currents; may not be found for months, if found at all. The same for any floating debris. I repeat: it's good to be conscientious – incontestably it is – but at present I think you're refining too much on something that doesn't require it. Do you feel in any doubt there was a plane crash? Do you feel in any doubt we have a dead body which was drifting in the sea?"

"No, sir. Of course not." I shook my head, yet at the same time couldn't help but purse my lips a little: a persistent trait my mother used to tease me about when I'd been small and getting ready to be difficult. My English mother, who had died in 1927 – December 1927 – three days in advance of my tenth birthday.

And I was aware that I was beginning to irritate him.

But if so, I reflected, then I might as well make a thorough job of it. Having once begun.

"But if I'm really to be given carte blanche, sir…?"

'Carte blanche' had been Mannheim's phrase. He had already spoken about my setting off for England later that same night and about my being allowed a full week for my enquiries, "if a full week should turn out to be absolutely necessary!" Now he nodded. I thought I must have somewhat overrated my tendency to irritate, for his nod seemed almost avuncular.

"Then where I'd truly like to start, sir – if it's at all feasible, that is – would be with the exhumation of Major Martin's body."

Suddenly no aspect of him seemed even remotely avuncular. (Unless in the manner of Uncle Silas; or of Uncle Ebenezer.)

"Well, you can't!" he snapped. "It isn't feasible; not in the slightest!"

But after a moment he again relaxed. "And what's more – you know it isn't! In Spain we don't possess so much as one *shred* of authority." He smiled. "Well, anyway, not officially," he said.

I accepted such defeat. I had merely wanted to be laying the foundations for my defence – in case the worst should happen, and my eventual findings should prove to be misjudged.

For I couldn't forget that earlier phrase he had employed. It had begun to sound intimidating.

Your responsibility.

He might not have stressed the adjective as now, inside my head, I was hearing it stressed. But I knew the stress had been implicit.

"And even if – officially speaking – we did possess such authority," he went on, "again I ask you, how would it serve, to demand an exhumation? Anders, you need to concentrate on the essentials. You really do!"

I felt that – by this time – he had truly made his point.

"And the essentials are plain. That letter from Nye to Alexander…is it genuine? That letter from Mountbatten to Cunningham? Although if the one is, then undoubtedly the other will be, too. Genuine not simply as regards their having been written by these men, but as regards their having been written by them in complete good faith. That's the first thing. And the second? Well, if all goes according to plan, they will shortly get those letters back – returned to Whitehall by the Naval Attaché in Madrid. *He*'ll have received them from the

9

Spanish Chief of Naval Staff. So, Anders, what *you've* got to find out is whether the British will realize the documents have been tampered with. Or was the resealing of the envelopes done so skilfully that they'll imagine themselves quite safe?"

This secretly amused me. I had a picture of myself strolling into the War Office and debonairly twirling a brolly or a baton. "Oh, good morning, gentlemen! May I put to you a rather silly question?"

The question which I now put to Mannheim, though, wasn't so much silly, I thought, as superfluous. ("Well – *again*!" he might have said.)

"I take it their casualty lists have all been checked?"

"Yes, obviously they have. And he was there all right. In those of last Friday."

And he was there all right. Well, then – in its externals, anyway – the matter seemed watertight.

And in fact I wasn't too surprised about this. Despite my initial astonishment regarding Sardinia.

Which may sound strange...especially on the part of a person expressly chosen to be sceptical. But right from the start I had actually thought those papers likely to be genuine, and for a reason possibly as piffling as Mannheim's concern over a preposition: ironically, a reason also occasioned by an apparent misuse of language. In other words, by that opening sentence of Sir Archibald Nye's – which had *not* been written in good English.

"I am taking advantage of sending you a personal letter by hand of one of Mountbatten's officers…"

Not been written in good English? You could go further. You could say it was written in execrable English. It impressed you as having been dashed off without so much as a second's thought. It gave no sign of being a fair copy. No sign of having been *considered* in a way that surely even the tiniest detail would need to be considered if it were going to form any part of some thoroughly complex stratagem.

So, to paraphrase Mannheim a little, "Often it's exactly this kind of clumsiness that can lead to somebody's belief."

Though, even whilst thinking about it right now, it occurred to me that perhaps I was being naïve. Wasn't clumsiness – or at least spontaneity – precisely the kind of impression they would have been aiming to convey, if this were indeed a subterfuge? An impression of such spontaneity that it amounted almost to sloppiness?

Yes, maybe it was.

No, how stupid of me! 'Maybe'? Quite certainly it was! If this were indeed a subterfuge.

If… But what did I mean, *if*? Again, wasn't I the man who had been detailed to assume duplicity? The man handpicked for the job by Admiral Canaris; handpicked to be a Doubting Thomas, a devil's advocate, a private eye? Detailed to assume that this was quite definitely a trick, and to go back at once to asking questions about the major's post-mortem and about the plane crash and about all other such related issues – no matter how irrelevant or incidental these might for the moment seem?

Not necessarily to be asking them of my section head, but most certainly to be asking them of myself.

4

In the briefcase there had been a second short letter from Lord Mountbatten, this time to General Eisenhower…also, of course, care of the Allied Forces HQ in Algiers. It enclosed the proofs of – and photographs to be used in – a booklet describing the activities of the Commandos. What had been wanted from Eisenhower was a brief foreword so that the book would 'be given every chance to bring its message of co-operation to our two peoples'.

"I am sending the proofs by hand of my Staff Officer, Major W. Martin of the Royal Marines, who will be leaving London on April 24th... I fully realize what a lot is being asked of you at a time when you are so fully occupied with infinitely more important matters... You may speak freely to Major Martin in this as well as any other matters since he has my entire confidence."

And although this third letter was actually of no value to us we were plainly lucky that they had decided to send it with the major: the two normal-sized envelopes could easily have gone inside a jacket pocket, but this one, with its bulky enclosure, had clearly necessitated the carrying of the briefcase. It would have been irksome if our agent in Huelva – or maybe one of his employees – hadn't had something so very official and obvious to attract the attention; the body itself mightn't have been thought sufficiently interesting to merit the complications of a search and the plausible delaying of its progress towards the British vice-consul.

Lucky? Irksome? Good God, it must have been contagious! The *English* were the ones who were commonly supposed to employ understatement.

Actually, in his jacket pockets the major had carried still more letters. But all of these had been personal. One, for instance, was from the head office of Lloyds Bank in London, EC3. Another was from his father, enclosing a copy of something he'd written on his son's behalf to a firm of solicitors. There was even a communication from that same firm of solicitors, dealing with another matter and dispatched directly to the son.

Additionally, there were three receipts: one from the Naval & Military Club covering the two nights prior to April 24th; one from Messrs Gieves Ltd, a gentlemen's outfitters in Piccadilly; and one for a diamond ring – Major Martin had recently become engaged: a fact that compounded this tragedy of war still further. If such a thing were possible.

Also, there had been a packet of Player's...with only seven cigarettes remaining out of twenty – I found it faintly surprising a number could still be determined upon. A box of matches, a bunch of keys and a pencil stub. Two ticket counterfoils for the Prince of Wales Theatre, dated April 22nd. Two bus tickets. A half-crown, florin, three shillings, a sixpence, threepenny bit and five coppers. A five-pound note, twice folded, which had now, of course, completely lost its crispness. A couple of pound notes – one with a tear across its top right-hand corner.

These last had been in his wallet, naturally…along with a snapshot of his fiancée (incidentally, a photograph far better preserved, just by reason of its being inside the wallet, than those intended for General Eisenhower) and two letters that had come from her, likewise better safeguarded than the remainder of his mail. The wallet had further contained a book of stamps – of which three had been used – an invitation to something called the Cabaret Club; his CCO pass and Admiralty Identity Card (these two kept together in a little cellophane folder); and a St Christopher medal…which clearly hadn't done him an awful lot of good.

Major Martin was evidently a magpie. His uniform, even supposing it hadn't been in the water for six days, could hardly have retained its original immaculate appearance.

Otherwise about his person the dead man wore a wristwatch, and a silver cross upon a silver neckchain. He also carried two identity discs. These were attached to his braces. 'Major W. Martin, RM, R/C.'

The inventory Madrid had sent us appeared to be exhaustive; the photographs supporting it, a bonus. My eye was drawn back time after time to those two ticket-stubs. I couldn't forget that only forty-eight hours before his plane crash – maybe even fewer – the poor fellow had been sitting in a theatre in London's West End: a district still quite glamorous, probably, despite the blackout.

I assumed that he had been with his fiancée.

I could only hope their evening had been a very special one. In every way. A fitting culmination.

13

5

Her name was Sybella.

(This resonated. My mother's name was Penny, but up to the last moment she might well have been christened Sybil.)

"And I should strongly suggest," recommended Mannheim, resuming the briefing after we had stopped for coffee and, in his own case, for a couple of chain-smoked cigarettes, "I should strongly suggest that your investigations begin with her. *Cherchez la femme*, as Monsieur Dumas – Monsieur Dumas père – once famously advised."

I wouldn't have known the source.

"Or, indeed, to quote him more accurately, *cherchons la femme. Cherchons, cherchons.*"

That was unfortunate. It immediately set up a rhythm in my head as insistent as train wheels and it made me think of Walt Disney. '*Cherchons…cherchons…*it's off to work we've gone! We work all day and get no pay, *cherchons…cherchons, cherchons, cherchons…*' I was aware it wasn't appropriate. I picked up the facsimile of the young woman's snapshot. She looked nice. Not just pretty; wide-smiled – warm-eyed – *nice*. The sympathy I'd felt towards her fiancé extended now towards her. The song subsided.

"For it's perfectly possible," Mannheim continued, "that if this whole business *is* a hoax then Major Martin could have been a party to it. 'I think you will find Martin the man you want.' 'You may speak freely to Major Martin in this as well as any other matters.' And if he *did* know what was going on, if he *did* know the nature of the letters he was going to be entrusted with, I also consider it perfectly possible that in a particularly unguarded moment or during a particularly…intimate one, let us say…well, that he might unwittingly have revealed something secret to the woman he loved. I mean simply the odd word or so, but maybe that odd word or so could prove to be illuminating."

He dropped onto the desk the two letters he had quoted from, having briefly looked at each for perhaps the twentieth time that afternoon.

"And, of course, it's more than probable," he added, "that she wouldn't even have understood their significance. Still doesn't, in fact."

When he tested me like this I found it hard to conceal my impatience.

"But it could scarcely be a hoax," I said, momentarily forgetting my role as devil's advocate. "If that air crash hadn't happened, how on earth would they have got all this information through to us?" I indicated the desktop.

"Yes, exactly," he agreed.

It seemed I had supplied the answer he wanted. But I felt less gratified at my success than offended by his implication of possible failure.

We were silent for a moment. Then he shook his head.

"In fact, Anders, do you know what I think? That in sending you to England we're wasting your time. Wasting *our* time, too. *And* all the manpower involved in getting you out there and getting you back…to say nothing of our other highly valuable resources!"

Well, privately I agreed – although I would have refused absolutely to admit this. (Apart from all the rest of it, I *wanted* to go to England.) But even in spite of what I had recently admitted to, I tried to view the matter with complete distrust. Yes, it *was* a hoax. Of course it was. It was the most arrant form of deception imaginable. How it had been brought about – or *would* have been brought about – was basically beside the point.

"For, Anders, can we really believe the British would sabotage one of their own planes, and sacrifice one of their ablest men, purely on the off-chance of these papers eventually finding their way home to us? End justifying means? Can we really believe the British would ever stoop so low as that, even in the interests of the greater good?"

A Freudian slip, maybe. I imagined he meant only the greater good so far as the *British* saw it.

"Yet isn't it conceivable," I said, "that the operation simply went awry? That there may have been some sad – no, totally unspeakable – error of judgment?"

"In what way?"

"The major may have made his jump before he was supposed to. Much too far from land."

Mannheim thought about this. "And what became of his parachute?"

"Well, naturally he didn't die at once. He had time in which to sink it." I added: "For all the point there would then have been to *that*."

"The pilot having just gone off and left him?"

"But what else *could* he have done?"

That was true – I didn't see what other choice the pilot might have had – and I may even have sounded fairly calm whilst allowing it. But I was still a long way from feeling calm. The idea of Martin struggling to stay alive, then finally realizing he hadn't got a chance, that even the plan he was about to die for would probably prove abortive, the briefcase entirely lost…all this made me practically as angry, inwardly as angry, as if the scene I was envisaging had been an actuality, not merely a hypothesis.

Strangely, it was Mannheim who now employed that word. Albeit in German.

"Interesting hypothesis," he said. "Although I would suggest not really a practicable one. You're forgetting something. If the jump you propound had been successful, how would our sympathizers ever have got hold of that briefcase…with a live major most tenaciously attached?"

"The live major could easily have feigned unconsciousness. Could have come to, maybe, only after they had got him into hospital."

"Having given them enough time to duplicate documents, write out inventories, take photographs, reseal envelopes and get the briefcase comfortably back into his possession before he *did* come to? Hmm. I don't know why but perhaps that does strike me as a *shade* optimistic."

"Yes, sir – in all honesty – it does me, too." It also struck me just how little I really knew my section head. His response had been pleasant…humorous…not in the least judgmental.

"Though I admire your inventiveness. So does the Admiral, plainly." In fact, it was well known that Canaris and Mannheim were friends.

"Thank you, sir."

"But only think of it!" He absently reached for his cigarettes; then presumably remembered that smoking on duty was officially discouraged. "My God! Only think of it! If what *appears* to be the case actually turns out to *be* the case…"

"That's why I can't accept it, sir. That's why I *won't* accept it." I felt almost guilty. I had never seen him so expansive.

"Explain," he said.

"Well, it's simply too good to be true."

"And aren't things ever allowed to happen that seem simply too good to be true? Is there some ordinance, or law of nature, which categorically forbids it?"

All expansiveness now shrivelling up – *fast*.

"But anyhow, Anders, I feel this is hardly the moment to be comparing our philosophies."

We set aside those philosophies.

Set them aside in favour of a brisk and exceedingly businesslike summation.

"So, then, Sicily or Sardinia? Sardinia or Sicily? That's the crux of it. And I can't say this to you too often. Sheer speed is henceforth of the essence. For it's unquestionably a complex, a *colossal* operation – the work of the very devil – to stop concentrating on one place, start concentrating on another. Making plans, laying minefields, setting demolitions, building defences – moving armies – none of this can be accomplished, you understand, in the odd free hour or so. Moreover, the enemy won't just be standing still all the while, even if he *does* think that he's caught us with our pants down!"

He said this as if my agreement, or disagreement, might radically alter the circumstances.

"Well, then," he went on, abruptly – no doubt to illustrate that time was truly of the essence. "What further questions do you have?"

I felt I should have had a hundred further questions, all of them probing and insightful. Instead, the relatively few I could muster appeared more or less inept and had mainly to do with practicalities.

So it was little more than a half-hour later when he shook my hand – wished me Godspeed – and solemnly acknowledged my salute.

6

I left Berlin that night. A lone passenger in a Fiesler Storch. We flew over Belgium and France, avoiding the English Channel and avoiding, equally, any English fighters. The trip was uncomfortable but passed without incident – not even any turbulence to speak of. I was deposited in Dublin in the small hours; then slept fitfully until about six on a wooden bench in a garden of remembrance – mercifully, a garden both unlocked and empty. Afterwards, a little bleary-eyed, I sailed on the first crossing to Holyhead. In Holyhead I was conscious of committing a transgression. ("You need to concentrate on the essentials, Anders! And the essentials are plain.") For it would never have occurred to me to visit Mold if one of my fellow passengers on the crossing hadn't mentioned that she'd been born there. She now lived near Holyhead but still saw her parents every fortnight, catching a train to Chester at 7.30a.m., and – barring holdups – making a first-class connection: Mold at two minutes past eleven. Prior to this I had been planning to travel straight to London.

So, to some extent, it was only a spur-of-the-moment thing. Mold had no real relevance to my mission; was merely the small Welsh town where the major's father had been staying when he had written to his son. I didn't even think of this as a coincidence: consulting my atlas during the flight I had noted that Mold was close to Holyhead – noted it, but certainly not lingered over it.

Yet the very fact of my having been sitting beside this woman on the boat made me feel that I was being guided; that I had just been offered a sign – along with a timetable. The major's father had written:

"My dear William,

"I cannot say that this hotel is any longer as comfortable as I remember it to have been in pre-war days. I am however staying here as the only alternative to imposing myself once more upon your aunt whose depleted staff & strict regard for fuel economy (which I agree to be necessary in war time) has made the house almost uninhabitable to a guest, at least one of my age. I propose to be in Town for the nights of the 20th & 21st of April when no doubt we shall have an opportunity to meet. I enclose the copy of a letter which I have written to Gwatkin of McKenna's about your affairs. You will see that I have asked him to lunch with me at the Carlton Grill (which I understand still to be open) at a quarter to one on Wednesday the 21st. I should be glad if you would make it possible to join us. We shall not however await luncheon for you, so I trust that, if you are able to come, you will make a point of being punctual.

"Your cousin Priscilla has asked to be remembered to you. She has grown into a sensible girl though I cannot say that her work for the Land Army has done much to improve her looks. In that respect I am afraid that she will take after her mother's side of the family.

"Your affectionate
"Father."

It had been addressed from the Black Lion Hotel, Mold (telephone number 98), North Wales.

And dated April 13th, 1943.

19

I didn't think I should care much for Mr Martin. 'We shall not however await luncheon for you, so I trust that, if you are able to come, you will make a point of being punctual.' This, to a man who had been commissioned in the Royal Marines and, on top of that, had been so warmly endorsed by Lord Louis Mountbatten. And there was nothing like: 'How is everything? I hope you're well. This comes with lots of love.' No best wishes, even. No mention of Sybella. To me, he sounded both pompous and imperious.

Cold.

And the enclosed copy of what he had written to the solicitor – although of course that was a business letter and couldn't be so readily assessed – did little to soften this impression.

"My dear Gwatkin,

"I have considered your recent letter concerning the Settlement that I intend to make on the occasion of William's marriage. The provisions which you outline appear to be reasonable except in one particular. Since in this case the wife's family will not be contributing to the Settlement, I do not think it proper that they should necessarily preserve, after William's death, a life interest in the funds which I am providing. I should agree to this course only were there children of the marriage. Will you therefore so redraft the Settlement as to provide that if there are children the income is paid to the wife only until such time as she remarries or the children come of age. After that date the children alone should benefit.

"I intend to be in London for the two nights of the 20th & 21st of April. I should be glad if you could make it convenient to take luncheon with me at the Carlton Grill at a quarter to one on Wednesday 21st. If you will bring the new draft with you we shall have leisure to examine it afterwards. I have written to William & hope that he will be able to join us.

"Yrs. sincerely,

"(Signed) J.G. Martin."

Addressed to F.A.S. Gwatkin, Esq., McKenna & Co., 14 Waterloo Place, London, SW1. Written on the 10th of April and clearly marked 'Copy'.

I could almost *hear* the man saying: "I should be glad if you could make it convenient…!"

And what a fibber! It had occurred to me yesterday, on my second reading of these letters, that in fact he *hadn't* written to William – and wouldn't indeed be doing so for a further three days. But, again, this had appeared to me such a piffling point that I hadn't even mentioned it to Mannheim. At twenty-five, I had no wish to sound as fussy as the old fellow I was finding fault with. (I assumed Mr Martin to be well into his sixties.)

But now, come to think of it, wasn't it perhaps slightly surprising that he had allowed himself this small inaccuracy? Small, yet so unnecessary. Didn't it seem to go wholly against type?

And I didn't much like the way, either, that he referred to 'the wife' both times, rather than attempting to personalize things by using Sybella's name – although maybe this was more or less standard practice between a client and his solicitor.

But would it have been standard practice, I wondered, even when the client and the solicitor were on sufficiently friendly terms to be meeting each other for lunch?

On the other hand, however, at least he had written *William's* marriage, *William's* death. (Which succinct phrase, 'after William's death', repeatedly gave me pause. The sanguine expectation would have been of something approaching forty years. The cruel reality had turned out to be a mere fortnight. That made me feel – but only temporarily each time – almost as sorry for the father as I had felt for the son, and for Sybella too. I had the idea that Mr J.G. Martin was a widower, and that William must have been his only child. The old man became less cold and imperious, therefore, and more simply a suffering human being, whenever I paused for a moment to think about the full picture.)

The hotel in which these letters had been written was Georgian. It stood in the High Street and had an ivy-covered portico. On coming out of the railway station, I had found myself in New Street, which was only a short distance from the Black Lion.

There, I pressed the bell on Reception, put down my suitcase – a large blue leather one of my mother's – and rested my trilby near the handle.

The woman who answered my summons had greying hair pulled back in a bun. She wished me good morning and asked if she might help.

"Yes. Thank you. I'm wondering if you have a Mr J.G. Martin staying with you at present?"

On the way, of course, I had worked out what line I would follow if she answered yes.

"No, I'm afraid we haven't. Nor are we expecting anyone of that name."

I smiled. "Well, I recognized it as a long shot. But he stayed with you last month, you see, and therefore I was hoping…" My query petered out when I noticed her expression.

"Really?" she said.

Before this, I had been tired, aware of how very little sleep I had procured either on the plane or in the garden of remembrance.

But now – suddenly – I was awake.

"Excuse me?"

"I think, sir, you're mistaken. I don't recall any Mr Martin staying with us last month."

Just then, not even the Admiral at his most mistrustful could have considered me *too* articulate.

She added: "This isn't a large hotel and I'm thought to have a good memory."

"But I mean…"

She waited.

"I mean, it just never occurred to me. I felt so certain that…"

"You're sure it was the Black Lion?"

"Yes. Quite sure. Positive."

The hotel register lay on the counter. I watched her run her finger down the two appropriate pages. Even at such a time as

22

this, it struck me that her pink nail polish seemed at variance with her scraped-back bun and with her lack of make-up.

"No," she said. "No, I'm afraid not. Nothing."

Naturally I had facsimiles of the two letters Mr Martin had written. Facsimiles of the facsimiles. I reached through my raincoat and extracted these from a pocket of my suit. The woman studied them.

"Yes, those are ours, all right. And April 10th, April 13th – there's no mistaking the dates. But just the same… I really don't understand it."

"Perhaps you could take a look through March? Maybe he simply got the month wrong? Wrote April when he meant March."

"What – and did it twice? With a gap of three days in between? *I've* never done that. Have you?"

"No."

"And in any case," she repeated, "I should be certain to remember him; we're not quite the size of Claridge's, you know." Nevertheless – though with a faintly disapproving air – she did turn back a further page.

"You don't suppose, do you, he might have been travelling incognito?"

She answered me in the same dry tone. "Well, if he was, one can only hope his ration book was also travelling incognito."

I bit my lip; abandoned all flippancy.

"But there's another thing. He's clearly stayed here in the past." I read out the sentence about the hotel's being less comfortable than he remembered it from pre-war days. "I'm sorry about that," I said.

"No need to be. The same must be true of almost anywhere."

"May I ask: were *you* here in pre-war days?"

"Yes, I've been here since 'thirty-two." Frowningly, she absently scratched at some imperceptible mark on the counter before she looked up. "You know, there's bound to be a very simple solution to all of this. Do you mind waiting here a moment?"

Thereupon she went into an adjacent office to check through the hotel's filing system. On her return she enquired whether I actually knew the person we were searching for.

I slowly shook my head. "Why?"

"I was only wondering if you might have misread the signature…is there any chance of that, do you think?" There was a note of apology in her tone which further belied her appearance of severity. "We have a Mr Barton who visits us regularly – also a Mr and Mrs J.Wharton. And on several occasions we've had a *Miss* Martin staying here."

But when I again handed her the Gwatkin letter she smilingly conceded the surname couldn't be anything other than Martin; and that the initials J.G. couldn't really be twisted into standing for Edith Mary Rose.

Indeed, for a couple of preposterous seconds I *had* actually played with the notion that we might have got the sex wrong. Could we only have *assumed* the major's parent was male? But Edith Mary Rose, although she might well have sent her son a little more in the way of love and tender reassurances, would scarcely have signed herself 'Your affectionate father', nor would she – in all probability – have registered as 'Miss'.

I asked: "How hard would it be for someone to acquire samples of your stationery?"

"Not hard at all. There's always a supply of paper and envelopes on the writing table in the lounge – as well as a few sheets in each of the guests' bedrooms. Even now," she added, with some pride.

"And the firm of printers which you use? I suppose that virtually any one of its employees…?"

I hoped I wasn't alarming her. But her reaction was to laugh.

"Oh, the plot thickens! I can see we'll have to call in Scotland Yard!"

"Absolutely!" I thanked her and picked up my hat and suitcase before it could occur to her to pursue her own line of enquiry.

Out in the street again, however, my bonhomie vanished. I reflected on how unfortunate it was that already I was faced with an obstacle of this size. Hell, it looked as if I'd need to get in touch with Berlin a lot sooner than any of us had expected. The Abwehr hadn't used me a great deal up till then. Wouldn't it seem a little unimpressive to have to go running back at such an early stage in search of further guidance? Please help me, Uncle Franz.

And rather more important – no, *altogether* more important – I didn't mean to go calling into question the Martin papers until I knew that such an act could be fully justified. Even if my superiors *had* sent me over here to play the devil's advocate I'd still have to be extraordinarily cautious with regard to that. Obviously.

Although, on thinking about it, how much justification did I reckon I was going to need? It was a truism, surely? If you couldn't trust the messenger you couldn't trust the message. End of story. Nothing more to say.

All right. I understood that. But…oh, for Pete's sake! The *father* of the messenger?

I knew it was inconsistent of me to be feeling so frustrated by this odd behaviour of the parent. I had come to Mold entirely of my own volition and practically *despite* my section head's instructions – and if it hadn't been for that woman on the boat I should never have set foot inside the Black Lion.

But all the same.

From now on, was our trust in the messenger truly going to have to concern itself with genealogy?

I hurried to the public library.

7

There was no J.G. Martin included in the Cardiff telephone directory. No J.G. but certainly no shortage of others – which would be relevant if I had to ring them at any stage to enquire about unlisted relatives. So I went between two high and well-stacked bookshelves to tear out the requisite pages (coughing to cover the sounds of my defacement) and told myself I shouldn't be surprised that William's father wasn't on the phone: in Germany there'd been extensive waiting lists even before the war so why should it be different here? Anyway, he sounded very much a fellow of the old school who might still regard this modern means of communication – well, relatively modern – as just some new-fangled nonsense, loud and peremptory and often inconvenient.

Of course, on the other hand, it was also conceivable that he no longer lived near the city in which his son had been born. A person could many times move house over a period of thirty-six years.

Also… Sitting at a table in the reference section of the library, with a large English dictionary opened randomly in front of me, I managed to formulate a theory which might (just) explain his non-appearance at the hotel. As I say, I had been assuming he was a widower. He could have been deserted or divorced but the main point was he seemed to be alone. So might he not, despite his age (and unappealing personality), have been conducting a clandestine love affair? Staying at the home of some woman whose good name had to be consistently protected?

An Agatha Christie sort of scenario, but I thought it might be possible. Not perfect – did the pilfering of hotel stationery tie in with a developed sense of propriety? And still it left that allusion to pre-war visits unaccounted for. But I felt the first *could* have been inspired by a sudden attack of bravado, and the second by a simple striving after authenticity. It *was* possible.

Yet, damn it, if he'd had even the slightest consideration for either poor Hercule Poirot *or* poor Erich Anders, he would at least have given a name to William's aunt, who evidently lived here in the neighbourhood but 'whose depleted staff & strict regard for fuel economy' had driven her brother, or brother-in-law – yes, brother-in-law, *much* more likely – into the greater, though sadly diminished, comfort of the Black Lion Hotel.

Except that, of course, they hadn't. They might have driven him somewhere, but not into the Black Lion Hotel.

However, I came out of the library feeling better. I stood for a moment in the sunshine – by the statue of a local nineteenth-century novelist and tailor named Daniel Owen – and then made up my mind.

Went back along the High Street.

Turned in through the ivy-covered portico.

"Excuse me for bothering you again. But may I just ask? In this part of the world…is Priscilla a very common name?"

"No. I wouldn't have thought it was a very common name in any part of the world. Why?"

"Mr Martin has a niece here called Priscilla."

"In that case I'd suggest you try the post office. If Mrs Griffith can't help you, then I don't think anybody can."

But Mrs Griffith *couldn't* help me; nor could the postman she obligingly summoned from somewhere at the back.

Nor could the woman in the library.

Nor yet the buxom young assistants working in the town's two small and spicily aromatic groceries. As far as either of them knew, they had no registered customer called Priscilla.

"But, then, if it was me," declared one of them cheerfully, with an assertive toss of her bottle-blonde hair, "I'd either change it fast or else make blinking sure I only put down my initial. My own name's Jean," she added, with an unmistakably come-hither glance.

The other said: "Or maybe the family prefers to do its shopping in Wrexham?"

Even the pair of glowingly red-faced women labouring in a nearby field (but thankfully – from my own point of view – within easy hailing distance of the road) couldn't come up with any likely candidate. It seemed that Priscilla of the Land Army was going to prove just as elusive as her uncle of the Black Lion.

Clearly, elusiveness ran in the family.

I said as much when I *again* returned to the hotel – this time to book a room.

I was requested, in a wryly humorous tone, to sign the register.

I wrote my name as Eric Andrews. Gave a genuine address in Chorleywood. Handed over my ration book. This was heavily blue-pencilled in some places, and neatly cut away in others – every bit as well prepared as my apparently long-held identity card.

I was also sympathetically quizzed – as I had feared might happen – on why I had been making those earlier enquiries. But I laid a finger against the side of my nose and tried to sound like George Sanders, or some other equally suave and elegant bounder:

"Annoyingly hush-hush, my dear! Quite frankly, I should have liked nothing better than to be able to take you into my confidence!"

And she both smiled at the joke and took respectful note of its underlying message. "Just something to do with very boring business," I added, more prosaically.

"I think you mean," she said, "as I was consistently taught at school: ask no questions, hear no lies!"

"We must have gone to the same school," I told her. "My grandmother's the principal."

I put away my fountain pen. Was glad to hear that dinner would be served from six. (It was now about a quarter to.) My last proper meal had been in Germany. As I made my way upstairs, carrying my suitcase – for apparently the hall porter, poor man, was again laid up with his arthritis – there was already the sound of laughter proceeding from the taproom. I thought it might be amusing, later on, to come down and investigate.

Yet in the meanwhile I had a telephone call to make.

No 5 was on the second floor. Not very large, but bright. Quite sunny still. I removed my raincoat and hung it behind the door, then sat cross-legged on the bed. Picked up the receiver and asked my friend on reception to get me please – or ask the operator to get me please – a number in Ogbourne St George, in Wiltshire.

Ogbourne St George 242.

I was advised it might take twenty minutes. Which would mean – what? – that the call would probably come through at dinnertime…since lots of people these days, both in England and Germany, were eating their dinner so much earlier than before. And dinner-time, my English grandmother had always told me (and told my grandfather, and told the dog, and told anybody else who might be sitting round the table) was decidedly no moment at which to be making any phone calls – not if you claimed to have been properly brought up, that was, or to possess the tiniest crumb of consideration. My English grandmother defied the stereotype: was even more strong-willed than my German one; and I didn't think it was only my recent mention of her which had now brought this to mind.

But she was the grandmother I loved.

Indeed, I loved both my English grandparents better than their German counterparts. And several of my English aunts and uncles, too.

Naturally, however, I had never been able to let on about this. Not at home. And even less so, of course, after I had applied to the Abwehr. At the Abwehr I had needed to feign complete indifference. Indifference, moreover, bordering on contempt.

Yet I still hadn't believed I was going to be accepted. Such assets as I had, or thought I had (the ability to speak English without a German accent; to show initiative; be analytical; box well), none of these would have counted for a thing if there'd been the least suspicion of any conflict of loyalties. And afterwards I had felt astonished that my examiners could ever have allowed themselves to be so thoroughly deluded.

But at the same time, since I could truthfully say that I loved both my father and my Fatherland, and had seen very clearly where my overriding duty lay, perhaps in fact they hadn't been. Well, not so unreservedly, I mean, not so *thoroughly*, deluded.

My initial application to the Abwehr had been made six years ago, long before I had last seen my British relatives. The fact of my being able to resist telling them about it, when it had then been by far the most exciting decision of my life, had furnished irrefutable proof to myself, though naturally to very few others, that I was indeed worthy to become a secret agent.

I had been thinking of all this while I partly unpacked my suitcase and afterwards shone my shoes; wondering how much of that initial excitement I had managed to retain. (Not a great deal, I suppose – yet wouldn't there have been something a little wrong with me if I *had* managed to retain it?) The telephone dispelled this reverie. I was astonished to discover how swiftly those estimated twenty minutes had elapsed.

The operator announced that she now had my call on the line. Another woman's voice then said pleasantly, "Hello...?" My pulse rate, which had been speeding up somewhat, immediately began to calm.

"Oh, good evening," I said. "I do hope I'm not interrupting your meal – if I am, I can easily phone back." I could hear myself sounding slightly too formal; not quite a hundred per cent English. "My name is Eric Andrews and I'm wondering if Sybella is there."

"Good evening, Mr Andrews. No, you're not interrupting us one bit." (I wished I could have known *her* name. I only knew its first letter...assuming, of course, that she hadn't remarried. The engraving on Sybella's engagement ring, work which – according to the jeweller's bill – had cost the major ten-and-six, had provided me with that. 'S.S. from W.M. 14.4.43.') "But I'm afraid," she said, "that my daughter isn't here right now. In fact, she's not been home for several weeks. As I'm sure you must know, she works for Ensa. Are you a friend of hers?"

"No, actually we've never met. I happen to be a friend of a friend." Clearly, it worried me I should have no idea what Ensa was (surely it couldn't be a *who*?) or more probably, I thought, ENSA; obviously I couldn't ask. "But is she on the phone," I went on quickly, "or could you give me her address? I'd really like to get in touch."

"Yes, of course. She lives in London – shares a flat with two other girls – although I don't think she'll be there at present. But I imagine either of them could easily tell you where she is." She added, "Or failing that, the head office of ENSA is in

Drury Lane. At the Theatre Royal, naturally. But hold on. I'll get you the girls' number."

When she returned she gave me the ENSA number as well.

This was more than I deserved. During her absence I had grown furious at my own stupidity. In Sybella's second letter there had been a plain reference to things theatrical, but for some reason we'd assumed, both Mannheim and myself, that she'd been speaking only about *amateur* theatricals. Yet how crazy – how totally inexplicable! I saw now that her mention of spending just one night in Wolverhampton should instantly have set us right. Damn! What sort of a detective *was* I?

An overhasty one, plainly. And possibly more akin to Captain Hastings than to Hercule Poirot.

But as soon as I had jotted down the two numbers – *and* on a sheet of Black Lion stationery, to boot – Sybella's mother enquired:

"Do you mind my being inquisitive? Who is this friend you have in common? I'm curious to know whether it's somebody I might have met."

Her question was by no means unexpected. I answered conversationally:

"Well, I very much doubt that you would have met him, because as a matter of fact…"

And then I broke the connection.

I was sorry to be discourteous; but I thought – and hoped – that she would only blame the vagaries of the wartime telephone system.

Indeed, my plan had been a simple one. If Sybella had answered, or her mother had asked me to hang on while she went to fetch her, I should merely have placed my finger on that bar a lot sooner – and then taken a train first thing in the morning to Ogbourne St George and spoken to Sybella in person.

Or, anyway, as first thing in the morning as possible, allowing for probable complications – although there was a railway station at both places and the distance in fact wasn't that great.

But at least such complications would have given me enough time to think up a good story.

Sybella's mother had sounded animated. I didn't believe she could have heard about the major's death. Which meant that in all likelihood Sybella herself hadn't. But, whether or not this proved to be the case, that story would obviously have *needed* to be good.

Wrong tense, though. Made it sound as if, the way things were, the story was no longer going to be required.

And before I went down to dinner I spent several minutes standing by the window and gazing out – somewhat blindly after a while – at the pleasant view before me. At the mountains in the distance.

But I had known beforehand that my mind wouldn't be dwelling solely upon features of the landscape.

Thy will be done was what I finally came up with. I did my level best to mean it.

8

After I had eaten I went back to my room and decided to lie down for a while. Stretched out contentedly, my hands clasped beneath my head.

Contentedly? I wasn't sure that I had much business to be lying anywhere contentedly. Not with the world being as it was.

Yet at any rate – although tired – I was now feeling pleasantly fed and comfortable and free. That last word caught me slightly by surprise. But the reason for its being there was this: that for the moment I was completely my own boss. Most nights at this time I would be sitting over supper with my father and my stepmother, and although I was fond of my father – and, yes, fond of my stepmother too – I suddenly realized just how inhibiting they both were.

(In fact, I wasn't nearly so fond of my father as I once had been...not since our falling-out in the days after *Kristallnacht*.

It was true, of course – just as he had claimed – that every nation did indeed have its share of hooliganism and thuggery. But that we ourselves could so effectively have cornered the market…! Our dispute had been bitter, and was unresolved.)

Anyway, it was ridiculous. I was clearly regarded by the Abwehr as being adult enough, responsible enough, to be sent on a mission of no small importance to the future of Germany. Maybe to the future of the world. And yet here I was, still living in my father's house and being expected to account for almost every minute of my spare time. My stepmother was well-meaning but inquisitive.

I had complained to my father about this. He had spoken simply of a need for greater tolerance and understanding.

Though just on my own part, it seemed. Not on hers.

I recognized that the war was principally to blame: the housing shortage in Berlin. In peacetime it would all have been so different.

No. In peacetime it was all *going* to be so different. I smiled, unlinked my hands and stretched my arms towards the ceiling. Here in a tiny town in the north of Wales, on Thursday 6th May in the year of our Lord 1943, with the last of the sun slanting across the floor and highlighting the dust motes and gently catching the bottom of the bed, it actually felt, right now, pretty much like peacetime.

It was even good to think that I myself, in some small way, could possibly be bringing it closer: the end of the war.

This brought a comforting association of ideas. My jacket was on the back of the chair by the bed and I was suddenly inspired to reach across. Although Mr Martin's letters were both in a side pocket, I had been carrying Sybella's two in my wallet. I knew (nearly by heart) everything that she had written; and yet – still – I took them out again.

It was the second I had been meaning to reread. But I became distracted, and gave further thought to the address – which was only on the first of them. In the original, it had been embossed.

33

The Manor House,
Ogbourne St George,
Marlborough,
Wilts.

My goodness, talk about idyllic!

In fact, it sounded *so* idyllic it almost teetered on the verge of parody: rural England at its most gracious and romantic. In a mere eight words it managed to pay homage to an illustrious ancestor of the present Mr Churchill, to the national patron saint, the legacies of the feudal system, and even to an especially stirring chapter in the military history of – I smiled – this dear, dear land, this scepter'd isle, this blessed plot. Yes, *there* lay the only wonder: that somehow it hadn't managed to make room for Mr Shakespeare. But even so. Not bad.

Yet following on from all this high romanticism and happy pageantry…what?

Merely a telephone number and a date.

Sunday 18th April.

Then straight into the letter.

"I do think dearest that seeing people like you off at railway stations is one of the poorer forms of sport. A train going out can leave a howling great gap in ones life & one has to try madly – & quite in vain – to fill it with all the things one used to enjoy a whole five weeks ago. That lovely golden day we spent together – oh! I know it has been said before, but if *only* time could sometimes stand still just for a *minute* – But that line of thought is too pointless. Pull your socks up, Syb, & dont be such a fool.

"Your letter made me feel slightly better – but I shall get horribly conceited if you go on saying things like that about me – they're utterly unlike ME, as I'm afraid you'll soon find out. Here I am for the weekend in this divine place with Mummy & Jane being too sweet & understanding the whole time, bored beyond words & panting for Monday so that I can get back to my crowd of silly females, not always *that* sweet & not always *that* understanding. What an idiotic waste!

"Bill darling, do let me know as soon as you get fixed & can make some more plans, & dont *please* let them send you off into the blue the horrible way they do nowadays – now that we've found each other out of the whole world I dont think I could bear it –

"All my love,
"Sybella."

And, as had happened on every single occasion I had read the letter, I thought it odd about the lack of apostrophes in certain places and about the way she always used an ampersand. Could she honestly believe that it saved time? Perhaps in England this represented a revived style of letter-writing. Mr Martin had adopted it, as well, although I couldn't see William's father as being someone generally influenced by fads – nor, indeed, very much aware of them. But actually *he* had used an ampersand both in his personal and his business correspondence. (Lord Mountbatten hadn't; nor had Sir Archibald Nye; though was this because typewriters had been to the fore here, rather than plain fountain pens?) And I supposed, of course, that you could always put it down to mere coincidence.

Yet that sounded grudging – and why, all of a sudden, should I have chosen to sound grudging? Good heavens, wasn't I well aware of the astonishing frequency of this kind of coincidence? How often had I come across a word or a name unknown to me on one day, and then, in some wholly unrelated context, heard it again the very next? Ironically enough, the word ampersand itself was an example. At least temporarily, therefore, the Sybella and J.G. Martin thing could be filed away – without too much fret and too much fuss – under the codename: Ampersand.

In fact, just had to be.

For how could they possibly have influenced one another? I acknowledged that they *might* have corresponded – once, perhaps? – but even this I somewhat doubted; and, anyhow, just a single brief exchange could hardly have accounted for it.

Instinctively, I didn't believe that they'd have met. Not that, if they had, meetings were in any way germane to writing styles, unless they had actually sat down together and zealously drawn up guidelines on how to achieve epistolary excellence in six easy lessons.

Which – I had to admit – didn't seem likely.

Otherwise, we were back with coincidence.

Or, maybe, with just one last tenuous option: Bill Martin as common denominator?

Because if the major himself had employed such a style of writing, wasn't it feasible that both his father and his fiancée, whether consciously or unconsciously, should at some stage have fallen in with it? Out of sheer admiration and a wish to emulate. Possibly unrecognized.

And out of affection, too, of course. Out of love.

But then I was struck by something else. *Could* Sybella and J.G. Martin have ever met? I still strongly doubted it, but how long did you normally delay a meeting between your fiancée and your father? Weren't you rather keen to have it happen? At the very least, wasn't your *father* rather keen to have it happen? And that engraving on the ring revealed, incontestably, the date of the engagement. 14.4.43.

Which led us on to another point. Mr Martin had written to his solicitor on 10th April. "I have considered your recent letter concerning the Settlement that I intend to make on the occasion of William's marriage." Which definitely suggested, didn't it, that he must have contacted Gwatkin on the subject at least five or six days earlier?

Yet that either meant his son had confided in him some considerable time before he had actually proposed and been accepted – which, to my mind, seemed improbable – or else that we were now up against a *further* very odd coincidence. (No! "Since in this case the wife's family will not be contributing to the Settlement..." Things had all too clearly been discussed.)

I continued to lie on the bed; told myself that for the time being I must file away the Settlement in the same pending folder as the ampersands. Told myself that nothing could have thrown me quite so forcibly as Mr Martin's disappearing act – and yet look at how quickly an explanation for even that had come to light. I told myself that if I slid down any further into this whirling mass of inessential detail I should soon be incapable of making out a single thing...the wood for the trees, the words for the letters.

So what should I do? Plainly this. Take a deep breath and relax. Bid a final farewell to pedantry. To pedantry and to an attitude that warned inexorably of Jack declining into dullness. (I could now hear the sounds of a piano and of singing floating up from the taproom.) Bid a final farewell to...

Well, to downright perversity, why not? For when was I *ever* going to learn? Just because Sybella's mother had said, "She's not been home for several weeks," and just because Sybella's letter had been written – from home – on Sunday 18th April, I was *already* seriously debating whether two and a half weeks could properly be described as several. Having – only ten seconds ago – declared my fixed intention to reform!

(And perhaps from the viewpoint of a doting mother two and a half weeks could certainly be described as several. Possibly to a doting mother seventeen days could appear as practically interminable. "Good gracious!" she might have said. "Seventeen days? Is that all? I must be a *much* better parent than I realized!")

So there you are, then. Maybe, in that case, *not* downright perversity after all. There could still be hope.

I turned to Sybella's second letter.

This one had been scrawled on lined foolscap, torn from a student's notepad.

In fact, the writing hadn't started out as a scrawl; but it had rapidly degenerated.

Once more, no salutation. The only form of heading was the date.

Wed, 21st.

"We've been given half an hour off – oh, blessed dispensation! – so here I am scribbling nonsense to you again. Your letter came this morning just as I was dashing for the coach – holding everybody up, *as usual*! You do write such heavenly ones. But what are these horrible dark hints you're throwing out about being sent off somewhere – *of course* I won't say a word to anyone – I never do when you tell me things, but it's not abroad is it? Because I won't have it, I WON'T, tell them so from me. Darling, why did we go & meet in the middle of a war, such a silly thing for anybody to do – if it weren't for the war we might have been nearly married by now, going round together choosing curtains etc. And I wouldn't be sitting here in Wolverhampton – Wolverhampton for one night only – though of course we will be coming back – yes, I *know*, you dont ever need to tell me, doing the thing which normally I love the best but which at the moment seems really to be getting on top of me – it may be doing something (one prays!) to slightly sweeten the war for some lucky few (what impossible arrogance!) but it isn't doing anything actually to *shorten* it. Is it? Whereas what you're doing…

"Dearest Bill, I'm so thrilled with my ring – scandalously extravagant – you know how I adore diamonds – I simply can't stop looking at it.

"I'm going to a rather dreary dance tonight with Jock & Hazel, after the show of course, so I'll only have to stay there for an hour or so. I think they've got some other man coming. You know what their friends always turn out to be like, he'll have the sweetest little Adam's apple & the shiniest bald head! How beastly and ungrateful of me, but it isnt really that – you know – dont you?

"Look darling, I've got next Sunday & Monday off for Easter. I shall go home for it, naturally, *do* come too if you possibly can, or even if you can't I'll dash up to London & we'll have an evening of wild gaiety – (By the way Aunt Marion said to bring you to dinner next time I was up, but I think that might wait?)

"Oh dear. Here comes our 'Lady Producer' who feels by rights she should be directing Thorndike & Evans & Ashcroft rather than the likes of little old us – although actually she's quite sweet, quite long-suffering, we really shouldn't bait her as we do.

"So masses & masses of love for now & a wholly tremendous kiss from

"Sybella – your very own Sybella, who adores you."

I returned both letters to my wallet. *Your very own Sybella, who adores you…* And I switched my thoughts back, abruptly, to the one sentence which I always found particularly encouraging. "But what are these horrible dark hints you're throwing out about being sent off somewhere – *of course* I won't say a word to anyone – I never do when you tell me things…"

Indeed, I had once again found this sentence so highly encouraging that as a result I remained more or less conscious of it during the whole of the time I later spent in the taproom…where I passed an enjoyable couple of hours amongst roughly a dozen welcoming people, including the receptionist, who were grouped convivially about the piano and belting out such songs as 'Louise' and 'Thanks For The Memory' and 'See What The Boys In The Back Room Will Have' and, perhaps a little more surprisingly, 'Lili Marlene'. However, I warned myself not to set too great a store by it, that long and reassuring sentence – our lives, of course, were full of disappointment.

(Yet I hope I didn't actually think of it like that! Not simply because of the sentiment's banality but because I was aware that my own potential disappointment could be as nothing compared to that of others.)

Whatever the reason, though, Sybella plainly hadn't managed to return home for Easter. But at least, I assumed (and surely *some* assumptions ought to be permissible), that she had been able to dash up to London for that evening of wild gaiety – and probably much sooner than expected: the Prince of Wales theatre tickets had been for the second house on Thursday 22nd, the very day after she had written from Wolverhampton. The very day prior to Good Friday. And only two days before her warmly adored and professionally up-and-coming fiancé – who wrote such heavenly letters and was so scandalously extravagant and who might have been going around choosing curtains by now if he hadn't met Sybella in the middle of a war – only *two* days before her warmly adored fiancé was either drowned or drowning, or about to be drowned, in a cold and clearly unadoring sea.

9

I didn't like loose ends. I arrived at the Carlton Grill shortly before two. It wasn't a good time to have chosen. The obsequious maître d' – smilingly effusive to those who had reservations, or even to those who hadn't but might still be hoping for a table – was merely irritated by somebody who only wanted to ask questions: namely, about whether a certain booking had been made for a date over two weeks earlier and, if so, whether or not it had actually been taken up. He coolly enquired whether I was a plain-clothes policeman. I said, no, I was simply a private individual attempting to trace the movements of a missing relative. He hardly troubled to hide his exasperation; brusquely dismissed me with a sop – i.e., a reluctant suggestion I should come back after four.

So, from the grandeur of the Carlton Grill, I crossed the Haymarket to a snack bar, where I had a sandwich and some not very good minestrone.

But then a speedy return to grandeur. Across Pall Mall and into Waterloo Place.

No 14 was an impressive mansion built of Portland Stone. But here the magnificence was principally external. Although one of the original functions of this house had no doubt been to provide a sumptuous ballroom, lit brilliantly by chandeliers, now its meanly partitioned pokiness wasn't even enlivened by a solitary low-wattage bulb.

Yet, dim as its interior was, and far removed from the heady days of Beau Brummell and of the present King's somewhat unstable forebear, there was still enough penetration of daylight, just, to enable visitors to read the nameplates near the entrance. And I saw that McKenna & Co., Solicitors, had their offices on the first floor.

The staircase itself remained imposing. But in place of a footman to announce my name and a fashionable duchess to receive me at the top, there was now only a shabby green-painted door with, beyond that, a motherly-looking typist who sat at her desk before a switchboard.

She clearly doubled as a secretary. When I went in she was trying to transcribe something from a folded-over notepad; my first glance had taken in a perceptible frown. But then she looked up and gave me a friendly smile.

"Good afternoon. I suppose you wouldn't have a talent for reading back shorthand? *My* shorthand?"

"I'm afraid I wouldn't have a talent for reading back *anybody's* shorthand."

"What a shame! Even so. May I help you?"

"Yes, I'm here to see Mr Gwatkin."

"Mr F.A. or Mr L.G.?"

"Mr F.A."

"Which is just as well," she answered lightly. "Mr L.G. is away for the moment, sick. And *your* name, please?"

"Andrews. Eric Andrews."

She consulted a diary that lay open on her desk.

I said, "No, I'm sorry. I wasn't implying that I had any appointment. Although if he *could* fit me in...? It's extremely urgent – and it needn't take long!"

"How long? Fifteen minutes?"

"I'd happily settle for ten. Or even five."

"Then I'll see what I can do. No guarantees, mind." She was putting on her headset. "May I ask about its general nature?"

I gave her a brief outline and presently she was passing on what I'd said. But it obviously wasn't a good connection: there were several things she needed to repeat. And it seemed that for some reason Mr Gwatkin was being obstreperous. The woman looked startled – she even flushed a little – cast me an agitated glance.

"Yes, very well," she said. "Very well. Yes, of course, Mr Gwatkin. Yes, I will." She nervously pulled out the jackplug.

"I'm sorry," I murmured. "Have I got you into trouble?"

"What? Oh, no. That was something else entirely." But she was now finding it difficult to look at me and I felt convinced I must have laid her open to some form of reprimand.

(I could certainly see why Mr Martin would have chosen Mr Gwatkin. Plainly they were both sticklers; plainly carved from the same block of granite. Granite, I thought, because it was grey rather than hard.)

She rallied, though. "No, Mr Gwatkin says he'll be quite willing to see you. But at present he has a client and hopes you won't mind having to wait. Perhaps you'd care to take a seat?"

There were some armchairs, a small sofa, and a low table bearing copies of *Punch* and *Picture Post*. I took off my raincoat and settled on the sofa – beneath a large framed photograph, in colour, of the King and Queen.

"He should only be a short while." Her manner was nearly back to what it had been. (Yes, she was indeed motherly-looking.) "In the meantime, would you like a cup of tea? I was just about to make one."

I declined, with gratitude.

"Or perhaps you'd like some coffee? It's only Bev, of course."

"No thank you. Nothing."

"Then if you're quite sure…? I shan't be long."

It seemed slightly strange that, in a firm of solicitors, tea or coffee wasn't made for everyone at once by an office boy. That's the way it would have worked in Germany – or so at least I imagined. Possibly the war had made a difference.

Or was it perhaps Mr Gwatkin's tetchy reaction on the phone which had meant she couldn't wait?

Be that as it may, though, when a few minutes later she returned, she hadn't got her cup of tea.

"My," I said, "you must have drunk that fast!"

She looked puzzled.

"Your tea," I reminded her.

"Oh, yes, of course! How silly of me…I forgot."

That sounded ambiguous.

But then she started putting through an outside call and became wholly taken up by the demands which this imposed. I noticed, with a gentle smile, how relieved she appeared when she got hold of the person she was after – maybe her telephonic skills were every bit as shaky as her shorthand.

Her typing seemed more competent. After transferring the call, she rattled away at a speed I wouldn't have expected. And apart from pausing for the brisk removal and replacement of paper, or to deal with the occasional terse requirement of the switchboard, she kept up her momentum for a good half-hour…the good half-hour that went by before Mr Gwatkin was able to see me. During that time, to my surprise, no departing client had passed through Reception. But there was probably a back staircase.

So I was into my third copy of *Punch* when she spoke to me for the first time since the commencement of her typing.

"Oh, Mr Gwatkin says he's ready now. If you'd like to go through the door at the end of the passageway, his is the second on the left."

But she still seemed preoccupied; and her expression was still quite strained. What had happened to the relatively calm person I had encountered on entry? No longer especially friendly, and certainly not in the least bit motherly. Even her silence while I got up from the sofa and walked towards the passageway now struck me as being hostile.

Mr Gwatkin, as well, belied my first impression – or, rather, my preconception. I had expected somebody ill-natured and

43

aggressive. He seemed so far from being either that you might have thought him timid. His manner appeared hesitant.

Also, he was younger than I'd anticipated. Much. Maybe thirty-five, with thinning, gingery hair and a vaguely undernourished look. I wondered if he wasn't in good enough health to have been called up or whether law was classified as a reserved occupation – like banking amongst other things. But, whatever the case, I couldn't seriously imagine him as being a bully to his secretary. I could imagine him as becoming excitable, yes. But not as behaving badly. Not with intent.

"Mr Andrews, is it? Sorry you've had to wait."

"No, it's good of you to see me."

His handshake felt clammy. His forehead *looked* clammy – in fact, within the next couple of minutes, he would actually need to wipe it. Twice.

"And…er…please, won't you take a seat? And let me know how I can help you."

As if he hadn't already been informed about that! Painstakingly.

"Well, I don't think I can add a great deal to what I heard your secretary telling you. I met Mr Martin about a fortnight ago. I'd just had my pocket picked and would have found myself in a very awkward situation if he hadn't been kind enough to lend me thirty shillings. Naturally, I wish to return this, yet now discover that I've lost his address. I should hate him to view me as dishonourable."

"Yes, yes, of course." The solicitor had sat down and was now moving papers around on his desk. But if he was meaning to tidy things he was hardly making a good job of it. "Er…Mr *John* Martin, I think you said?"

"Mr J.G. At least I remember that much."

"Yes, indeed." He laughed nervously – as though he thought I'd made a joke. "But how…? Well, how did you know that Mr Martin was a client of McKenna & Company?"

"Just lucky, I suppose. We'd been chatting over a glass of sherry when he suddenly realized the time. He told me he had a luncheon appointment with his solicitor which he couldn't afford to be late for."

"Oh, that sounds *exactly* like Mr Martin! How many others do you meet who still say 'luncheon'?" He nodded, and appeared better pleased with himself – as if merely knowing that we were speaking of the right man considerably increased his confidence. "And he does so enjoy his little glass of sherry! Was it Bristol Cream?"

This artless enquiry produced an odd effect. It brought back a memory of my childhood. Of how, after a long period of having dared myself, I had finally dived off the second highest board, and become so pleased with myself that I had straightaway graduated to the highest. I had forgotten to go home for lunch, and Gretchen, my stepmother, had been obliged to come to the baths in order to fetch me. (Had done so with her usual mien of bubbling good humour.) That evening, in celebration, my father had opened a bottle of sherry.

I replied, "Yes, I think so. Bristol Cream. And I told Mr Martin that – as it happened – I myself was in need of a solicitor. He recommended you without reservation. Said his son was also a client of the firm and was always more than satisfied with the way you managed his affairs."

"That was kind of him. Yes. William," he said. "Major William Martin. Of the Royal Marines." He still spoke slowly but now I got the impression he was feeling less shy of me and that his hesitancy had more to do with his concerns over how much he could ethically divulge. "For many years we have been privileged to handle the business of the entire family."

"Oh, really? You make it sound as though it's a large one. I never pictured it like that."

I thought for a moment he seemed taken aback by what I'd said but then he mumbled something about Mr Martin's deceased father. "Which was all a bit before my time..." Again his thin and protuberantly veined hands embarked upon a mission of introducing order to the world of stationery. He straightened his blotter and placed two fountain pens in careful alignment, as well as a propelling pencil, a stick of red sealing wax and a bottle of Parker's Navy-Blue Quink.

"Look, I'll tell you what we can do," he offered, at last. "If you give me the thirty shillings and a short covering note I'll see that they're sent off to him this afternoon. Registered."

"But the thing is – I'm afraid I shan't have an address until tonight and I was particularly wanting to ask him something."

"Oh?"

"The name of a hotel which he mentioned in Mold in North Wales."

"Ah well. As it happens, *I* can help you there." He now spent a moment settling back in his revolving chair and swivelling slightly – perhaps he, too, would soon erect a steeple? "It's called the Black Lion. And its address, quite simply, would be the High Street, Mold. Yes, I know he'd recommend it. He's stayed there often and has always spoken of it in the very highest terms."

But I somehow think that the receptionist, a woman who has worked there for eleven years and who in addition has a very sound memory, might really need to be convinced of that.

I wished I could have said it. And seen what would result.

Then something wholly unexpected happened.

The solicitor laughed.

Admittedly, he hastily suppressed the sound, as though it were something which was neither quite appropriate nor even quite natural, but the fact that it had happened at all provided me with a new angle on him. I wondered if this sudden spurt of amusement could have been occasioned by the thought of Mr Martin's being a compulsive recommender (whereas up to now I might have thought of him as being more of a compulsive bellyacher) or whether there could indeed follow some much funnier explanation.

(Also, I wondered if Mr Gwatkin were married and had children. For an irrelevant second or two I tried to envisage him at home.)

But if there *was* some other explanation it appeared I wasn't going to hear it. My look of enquiry was ignored.

46

At first, that is. After a while, the solicitor relented.

"I'm sorry," he said. "I was reminded of a recent practical joke which Mr Martin had played on his son. Concerning that hotel. I'm not sure I ought to tell you."

"A joke?"

"Completely harmless, of course, but I suppose it's just the idea of Mr Martin playing any sort of joke on *anyone* ! You see, he wanted William to believe he was putting up at the Black Lion because... Well, because if he'd told him where he was *actually* staying, it would have spoilt a little surprise he was planning for the boy's next homecoming..."

The rush of words halted. So – for the time being – did that perceptibly easier manner. Mr Gwatkin had remembered something. When he spoke again his tone had lost its energy.

"But in fact, Mr Andrews, there isn't going to be any next homecoming. Not now; not ever. William was on his way to North Africa when his aeroplane crash-landed in the sea."

"Oh God!" I stared at him. "Poor man!" He would probably have supposed I was meaning William, but for once I was thinking more of the father. Of the father devising some little surprise for the son who would never return to enjoy it. Or appreciate it. I had been forced to acknowledge – *yet again* – just how judgmental I was capable of being. "I'd imagined I would be sending my thanks – not my condolences."

He nodded.

I asked if William had had brothers or sisters. No; none. And I learned that his mother had died more than twenty years before.

For some ten seconds I hesitated.

"You say you were surprised by his being a practical joker? The father."

"Yes, I was," he answered.

"Me – much as I liked him – I should never in a hundred years have taken him for that."

"He was a complex individual."

"Was?"

"Is."

47

"Complex in what way?"

The solicitor paused – evidently deliberating. He took out his handkerchief again and wiped his brow.

"Oh, I feel certain he wouldn't mind my telling you. You see, in so many respects, Mr Martin presents the image of a typical old fogey. But I have to confess to something. In one area I've been guilty of misleading you. More than that – of telling you a barefaced lie. The Black Lion in Mold? I'm sure it *is* very good. But Mr Martin's never stayed there in his life!"

"What!"

"No, I'm afraid not."

"But…?" I was suddenly experiencing a sense of disorientation which – almost literally – was rendering me a bit woozy. "Then I just don't understand. Why did he…? Why did *you*…?"

"Do you happen to know *The Importance of Being Earnest*?"

"I've mostly forgotten it," I replied – in a voice that sounded suddenly and alarmingly disembodied.

"Well, one of its protagonists, Algernon, claims he has a perennially sick friend who is constantly summoning him to his bedside. But Mr Bunbury is pure invention: just a convenient alibi to escape social entanglements with – for example – Algernon's Aunt Augusta. The Black Lion, of course, is neither a person nor an invention but it provides Mr Martin with a very similar sort of cover."

I still felt numbed; my voice, apparently, still originating from somewhere across the room.

"A cover for what?"

"Well, in the main – and I suppose there simply isn't any way of my disguising this – for a succession of lady friends."

Oddly, it gave me no satisfaction to learn that my theory of the day before hadn't been so very far removed from the truth.

"And also," said the solicitor, "Mr Martin suffers from frequent bouts of depression." For a moment I imagined there might be some connection here with Mr Martin's pretence of a hideaway in Mold. Then I realized it referred back only to that statement about his complexity.

"Bouts of depression?" I repeated. "Dear Lord! And now he has to deal with the death of his son!"

Again we were silent.

"And what makes matters even worse," said Mr Gwatkin presently, "William had recently become engaged. The last time I saw him – would you believe it? – I had just drawn up a marriage settlement."

I nodded in sympathy but said nothing.

"And if we're talking about irony," he added, "it doesn't even stop *there*." He leant towards me, confidentially. "William had finally got around to making out his will! How's that for a nice, neat, tidying-up sort of touch? Special timing or what?"

"Well, it just seems so…so monstrously unfair," I answered. Lamely.

And I shook my head in expected disbelief – although in fact I already knew about the will. Presumably William had seen to it because he *had* so recently become engaged. I didn't argue the point but I actually thought the timing of the will was less ironic than that of the engagement.

Because I remembered the letter:

"Dear Sir,

"Re your affairs

"We thank you for your letter of yesterday's date returning the draft of your will approved. We will insert the legacy of £50 to your batman and our Mr Gwatkin will bring the fair copy with him when he meets you at lunch on the 21st inst. so that you can sign it there.

"The inspector of taxes has asked us for particulars of your service pay and allowances during 1941/2 before he will finally agree to the amount of reliefs due to you for that year. We cannot find that we have ever had these particulars and shall, therefore, be grateful if you will let us have them.

"Yours faithfully,
"McKENNA & Co."

"Yes, you're right," said Mr Gwatkin. "Monstrously unfair! And shall I tell you something still *more* unfair? The Inland Revenue! Quibbling to the last over what's deductible! It hardly matters whether people have just become engaged or made out wills or are off to sacrifice their lives for King and country…just so long as, *first*, they've shown their hearts to be truly in the right place – by way of filing their income tax returns! Now, doesn't *that* make you meditate for a while on some of life's priorities?"

Gracious! Was this the man I had started out by thinking timid? From reticence to rhetoric, from shyness to superfluity! He was like someone called upon to give an after-dinner speech, suffering initially from nerves but growing garrulous as he became emboldened. I might like and respect him all the more for this abrupt outpouring of humanity; yet even so…quite suddenly I'd had enough.

It was time for me to go.

And he must have sensed my discomfiture. Greek tragedy reverted to something a little more sedate – possibly something set in a drawing room, a drawing room with French windows. *The Importance of Being Earnest*? Mr Gwatkin took a single sheet of notepaper from one of his desk drawers and offered me a fountain pen. I preferred to use my own. He then provided a file for me to rest my paper on; and whilst I considered what to write he made out a receipt. (I had wanted to include the cost of postage but he was adamant in not allowing this.)

I finally wrote:

"Dear Mr Martin, we've never met but I wanted to say how sorry I was to hear about William. If there's to be a memorial service may I ask you to buy some flowers with the enclosed or – if not – to forward the money to a favourite charity? Both you and William are greatly in my thoughts."

There seemed no point in saying more. I simply signed it, folded the sheet over – having visibly inserted the three ten-shilling notes – and watched Mr Gwatkin place the paper in an envelope. He licked the flap; then sealed it with the red wax.

Obviously he would already have sent his own condolences. Therefore, with any luck, it could be some time before he again needed to get in touch with Mr Martin. If such *were* the case, would it be possible – even probable – that whenever the two of them next got into contact they might have forgotten about myself? Dear God. Oh, *yes*!

I stood up. Mr Gwatkin came around the desk.

"Are you in town on leave, Mr Andrews?"

I nodded.

"Which branch, may one enquire…?"

"R.A.F."

"It seems to have been a long leave."

"Convalescence. Unfortunately, they had to whip out my appendix."

"And then – how unfortunately again – you had to have your pocket picked! Were you in uniform when that happened?"

"Yes."

"You wouldn't think any Englishman could ever be so vile."

I smiled. "Couldn't it as easily have been a Welshman or a Scot? A Canadian or American or Pole?"

"No. I wouldn't believe that. Not in wartime. The only kind you could really believe capable of such despicable behaviour would be a Kraut – one of your filthy, low-down, nauseating Krauts."

I felt a hot surge of anger but managed to keep my answer cool.

"Oh, I don't suppose there'd be too many of that kind over here right now."

"Well, you mustn't sound so sure! The bastards could be anywhere. I know what you mean, though. You'd think you'd be able to smell them, wouldn't you, like rotten eggs or sewage?"

There was a pause. I knew I had to get away.

"I wonder what you'd have done if you hadn't met Mr Martin?" he went on.

51

"Gone to the police," I said, abruptly.

"Didn't you do that, anyway?"

"What? For the sake of just thirty bob?"

"You know…I'm really surprised Mr Martin didn't mention it when he arrived at the Carlton Grill."

"Sometimes a person doesn't like to advertise his good deeds."

It was inane: for a split second I considered this as yet another point in favour of Bill Martin's father.

"By the way," asked Mr Gwatkin, "why were you wanting a solicitor?"

For a moment I was caught off guard.

"Oh…for something which eventually blew over, thank heaven."

"Good. Well, let me show you out, then." Mr Gwatkin opened the door and preceded me through it.

"No – please. I know the way and I've already taken up enough of your time." I held out my hand. "Or is there a rear exit? That could suit me even better."

But Mr Gwatkin – now resolutely heading down my original route, back to the reception area – punctiliously ignored this. As we walked along the corridor, the firebreak door we'd just come through was pushed open again, somewhat jerkily. We continued our journey to the rattling accompaniment of teacups on a large tin tray.

10

Obviously I didn't need to go back to the Carlton Grill. I tried to ring the Theatre Royal but the number was persistently engaged. I gave up. Yet when I pressed Button B for the final time, returned the pennies to my pocket and left the current kiosk – it was the fourth I had been into – I happened to see a scrawny individual whose hat looked grease-stained and whose dirty raincoat couldn't hide the fact that his trousers were too short, revealing holey grey socks above brown, unpolished brogues.

In fact, it wasn't the first time I had noticed him. He had caught my eye some forty minutes earlier, when I was re-emerging into sunlight, after leaving the solicitor.

Then the man had been chatting to a newspaper vendor. Now he was looking into a shop window.

But all right, I told myself – all right! Don't start imagining things. From Waterloo Place I had descended the steps to the Mall, turned left towards Trafalgar Square and then gone right, past Charing Cross and along the Strand. Owing to those abortive phone calls I hadn't come any great distance – hadn't realized, until much later, that I had been almost within *hailing* distance of the wretched Theatre Royal – so why was it remarkable that someone else should have been heading gently in the same direction: someone who might have started out either a short time or a long time after I had? Of course, if I had been weaving my way through a labyrinthine network of side streets and alleys…well then, yes, okay. But this was clearly a main route.

Besides, why the hell should anyone be following me?

However, I surreptitiously kept him under surveillance; and before long I saw him turn to the right and head towards Waterloo Bridge. (Waterloo Place to Waterloo Bridge? There seemed a symmetry about his journey.) Afterwards, I was endlessly scanning the crowds in search of a replacement.

Until at last I told myself – told myself again – to *stop* being so imaginative. I carried on to Fleet Street, attempting not to look back. (I looked back only three times; it could have been much worse.) Halfway down Fleet Street, on the left-hand side, I came to the shiny black wall of the *Express* building. All glass and chrome and black reflection.

I had chosen the *Express* for reasons that weren't perhaps the most scientific but seemed at least as good as any other: it was the newspaper my grandparents had always read and therefore the only one in this country for which I felt affection – Rupert Bear had played a major part in my development.

Now I walked into the paper's spacious lobby and learnt that I shouldn't, after all, be in need of its back-numbers department. Not for any date as recent as last month. I was shown a couple of enormous binders that sat side-by-side on a display stand.

My search began with the issue dated Sunday April 25th. There was no report in it of any Allied aircraft being lost in the Atlantic but I should have felt surprised if there had been. Supposing the crash had happened on the 24th it would surely have been too new for even the stop press. Particularly if it had happened *late* on the 24th.

But after skimming the actual news I started to read an article purporting to be about my boss at the Abwehr. Yet it was all so ridiculous I could barely make myself continue. The piece had been headed: 'MAN WHO WAS AFRAID TO BE PHOTOGRAPHED. Hitler's Number 1 Spy.'

"Only half a dozen men outside Germany have ever met Admiral Canaris, the mysterious chief of the German Secret Service, who is reported from Stockholm to have been dismissed at the demand of Himmler, head of the Gestapo…"

Well, now, who'd have thought it? The admiral dismissed, indeed…and at Himmler's instigation! How strange that no word of this had yet filtered through to Berlin – or, anyway, hadn't done so by the time that I'd departed. And all the more remarkable, of course, when London's *Sunday Express* had known about it for practically a fortnight. My, my! How remiss of Stockholm! Such laxity in keeping us abreast!

"In the years leading up to the war Canaris began to work on undermining the countries scheduled as the future victims of Hitler's and Germany's world-conquering ambitions.

"To Canaris was entrusted the work of infiltration, corruption and demoralization. He marked down the future quislings of Europe. He sent hundreds of his handsomest agents, men and women, to corrupt some of the most influential figures – social, political and financial – in the lands to be invaded..."

No, why was I even troubling to read it? Further down the page there was something of far greater import. The latest film reviews.

(*Mademoiselle France*. Joan Crawford playing a selfish Parisian dress designer asked to help a stranded American flyer get out of Paris during the Occupation. This pilot was John Wayne so she obviously fell in love with him and became a very much nicer person. Bully for Joan.)

And while I was on the entertainments page I looked to see what show Major Martin had taken his fiancée to (had presumably taken his fiancée to). It was advertised as George Black's *Strike A New Note*. Starring somebody named Sid Field. I recalled that they had gone to the second house. Second house at five-thirty.

Then I glanced back at the article on Canaris and acknowledged my debt to the writer: "At least you signposted the way to Joan and John and Sid. You mustn't feel your efforts were entirely wasted."

I moved on to the Express of the following day, Easter Monday. But it carried no report of any air accident affecting the Allies.

Nor did the issue of the 27th.

On the 28th, however...if not an accident, at least an incident:

"Three U.S. planes, flying from England to North Africa, force-landed at Lisbon airfield yesterday through lack of petrol. The crews were interned – Oslo radio."

Yet that was absolutely it. The closest thing you got. I even checked the 29th and 30th and then went back to the 24th...all of which was patently absurd. But I now felt obsessed, driven...quite incapable of giving up the search. And there was nothing. Not on any of those dates. Nothing – nothing – *nothing*!

Amongst other things, though, I read that at the moment (if you were lucky) you could find a little liver in the shops; that the nation's milk ration had lately been cut to half a pint per day per head; and that Clark Gable, without the slightest show of side, had been found drinking beer in a pub in Lincolnshire – "Just think of it, Clark Gable came to Scunthorpe!" was the proud comment of the publican. Said his wife: "I'd never seen a film star! Now I've seen the best!"

But nowhere, nowhere, was there anything to do with any aeroplane – British, American, Lilliputian – which, between April 24th and April 30th 1943, had come down off the coast of south-west Spain. And at last I really had to face it – there was simply no alternative.

That plane crash hadn't happened.

11

So where in heaven's name did that get us: a body floating in the sea without any apparent means of reaching it?

It had to be a set-up.

Yes, in some mysterious way, it just had to be a set-up.

And I should have felt pleased. I should have felt exuberant. Discovering the truth – wasn't that the very reason I was here? To sniff out duplicity and guile, to sniff out that one small unimportant detail which they might have overlooked? To show that the magnetically seductive music we had listened to was nothing but the song of the Lorelei, and that what we needed was a pair of earplugs, not a massive redeployment of troops?

Therefore – a job well done; one that would maybe save my country a defeat, maybe even save it from the ultimate defeat, who knew? I should have been happy and excited and celebrating my pride-inducing moment of success.

Why wasn't I?

Because, basically, I still couldn't believe it; couldn't believe I'd got it right. For if I had…what would it mean? That we were now back with some elaborate plot which had simply gone haywire. Needlessly and horrifically haywire. Back with that wildly botched compass reading; back with that situation where – surely after long weeks of preparation and refinement – no one had even thought to supply a life belt. Nor a Mae West. Nor a rubber dinghy. Nor anything to assist the survival of either the messenger himself *or* of the message which he carried. Nothing but a feeble expectation of complete aircrew accuracy.

Yes. That was the crux of it.

Back with the pilot incompetence theory. Pilot or navigator.

And in all honesty it wasn't much of a theory. I already knew that Mannheim hadn't accepted it. I didn't believe Canaris would, either.

For they could hardly have *wanted* him dead. In no way would they have set out to betray him. Not the British! Any other nation…well, perhaps…but certainly not the citizens of the Land of Fair Play. Again, I agreed with my section head.

Nor would they have allowed him (as the Japanese did, with *their* heroes) to choose to make a sacrifice of his own life, no matter how willingly he might have done so. Almost, they would have preferred to lose the whole war.

No.

I wasn't – not in any way – celebrating my moment of success.

Instead I went into a Lyons teashop near Lincoln's Inn and had a cup of tea; also a slice of very dry and excessively yellow cake. I had hoped that these would help my brain to overcome that vital sticking point. Given the facts, what explanation could I find to fit them?

But soon my brain had grown as stale as the Madeira cake. And it was informing me, reliably, of only one thing. That I just couldn't risk, on my own, furnishing the wrong explanation.

Therefore I saw only one course open to me: that same line of action I had refused to follow yesterday because it had appeared to contain such a shockingly feeble admission. Confess my inability to solve this riddle. Send home for assistance.

Sherlock Holmes would never have countenanced such a course. Nor Hercule Poirot. Nor Sam Spade.

But even so.

It was my sole remaining option.

12

Paradise Street was a misnomer if ever there was one. A slummy side road running off Marylebone High Street, it was short, narrow, grey. Its single redeeming feature seemed to be the fair-sized recreation garden at its further end. This looked both tranquil and green when viewed from the corner halfway down, on the right-hand side, where the newsagent's shop stood.

The shop was run by an old woman dingily headscarved and cardiganed, with dusty smears across her forehead and a wooden leg (a detail disclosed to me towards the end of my briefing) concealed at present by the counter.

I entered the place a minute after six and was immediately advised – as presumably anybody else would have been advised – that I could count myself lucky. Because, she said, if only she'd had sufficient energy to stir her stumps (an impressive bit of so-called cockney humour here) the door would have been bolted by now, the window shuttered.

The woman and I were on our own in the cramped and murky interior. It couldn't have been much murkier, I thought, even if the window *had* been shuttered.

"Mrs Smee?" Before I asked the question, I removed my hat.

She looked at me with dark suspicion and didn't answer straightaway.

"Yes, that's right. And who's enquiring?"

But I took almost longer to identify myself than she had. Standing as I was within easy reach of the door, I slid the bolt home for her.

"I've heard that *Lady Precious Stream* is being performed near here. Can you give me the details?"

"No, I haven't seen it," she said, slowly. "It's playing in the park."

"Queen Mary's Garden?"

"Open Air Theatre – yes."

I laughed. "What a load of nonsense this all is! I'm Erich Anders," I said. "And I need to see your son."

By now she was on her feet, had put down the copy of *Film Fun* she'd been reading – Oliver Hardy gazed up at us reproachfully – and lifted the counter flap. We shook hands.

"I'll take you through," she said, the inch of smoky cigarette still held between her lips.

The room she took me into was divided from the shop by heavy curtaining. It was a surprisingly colourful room: attractive and comfortable-looking. To our right – rising discreetly out of the near corner – was a steep and narrow staircase. The woman stood at the foot of this and called up: "Visitor!" Which evoked a practically instantaneous response. "Coming!" Both words spoken in English: the former in a convincing cockney, the latter in something much closer to the King's. I heard a door open.

The step on the bare wooden stairs was light; the middle-aged man producing it, somewhat plump. But he wore slippers rather than shoes – tan leather slippers which toned in with his herringbone tweed suit, beige shirt and knitted yellow tie. Heinrich Buchholz had curly brown hair, striking blue eyes, a countenance you might have called cherubic. Yet his handshake was a long way from being cherubic – so far as one could guess.

"Come upstairs," he said. "Mother will be wanting to make herself presentable."

They seemed an unlikely pairing; I wondered what his father had been like.

"Then we'll go down later and you must stay and take pot luck." He turned back, briefly. "Eh, *Mutti*?" From the minimal hesitation, I sensed that generally he might not have used the German.

But the woman who was still standing at the bottom of the stairs gave him only a dour nod. In view of the dourness, I was about to decline, yet her son soon cut me short.

"Don't worry," he said, after he had closed the door behind us. "It invariably takes her a while to readjust and to step out of character."

Also, he assured me, he always kept in his room an interesting bottle of some kind…God willing.

"No, let me rephrase that, hastily. Not so much God willing, as Fred willing. I fear Fred dabbles in the Black Market." He gave a tsk tsk.

The current interesting bottle was Johnny Walker, which took pride of place on a chest of drawers that also bore a soda siphon. But for the time being I turned down his offer. "Because," I said, "I want to keep a clear head to tell you why I've come."

I sat in the room's only chair, by the grubbily net-curtained window (plainly meant to tone in with the neglected air of the façade), while my host reclined on the bed, his back supported by an array of large and brightly coloured cushions. Underneath the bed I could see part of a brown suitcase, and wondered if it were here that his transmitter was being stored.

Which was what had brought me into Paradise Street in the first place. Naturally.

"All right; you keep your head clear," said Buchholz, sipping pleasurably at his own half-filled tumbler – but after those initial sips merely cradling it against his chest.

I began: "I've just been paying a call on the *Express* newspaper office." A delaying tactic. I obviously felt reluctant to come directly to the point.

Buchholz said nothing.

"And, incidentally, while I was there I chanced to be reading an article published on the Sunday before last. And how do you like this? That, on the orders of Himmler, Admiral Canaris had recently been dismissed. Wherever do they dredge up such a load of garbage?"

"My dear friend. You mustn't let it rankle. I saw that article, and found it quite amusing."

"I admit – it does rankle."

"But why? There are always *reasons* for the things they put in their newspapers. And also for the things they leave out. I should have thought you'd be aware of that."

"Yes, I suppose so." I gave a shrug; and then, almost unwillingly, produced a smile. "Well, anyhow, you and I…we're two amongst those hundreds of his handsomest agents sent out to corrupt and demoralize! In this case, to corrupt and demoralize all the most important in British society!"

"Mmm, that's something," he agreed. "And Mother is, too, of course."

He made this addition without the slightest hint of irony. I half-wondered whether Buchholz saw it as some part of his mission to discourage vanity in freshly met young upstarts.

Yet then his sense of irony *did* show through. Though not unkindly.

"Yes, ever since reading that," he said, "it's inspired her to put on at least twice as much lipstick!"

I smiled again – this time, ungrudgingly. But still I hesitated. Idly, I lifted a corner of the net curtain.

Two little girls were drawing chalk marks in the road. On the further pavement a wiry black mongrel was sniffing at a paper bag. Nearer the High Street, a man was lounging against a barber's shop, the sole of one shoe resting on the brickwork immediately below the window. He was holding open an *Evening News*. The smoke from a cigarette, partly obscured by

61

the newspaper, trailed up beyond his hat brim. I turned my eyes back to the figure on the bed.

"Have they told you anything of why I'm here?"

"No," he said. "And naturally I hope you're not going to tell me anything, either. Clearly, the less I have to know, the better! For all of us."

For all of us, I thought, except for me – because firstly it would have been useful to give him my account and maybe clarify my own ideas concerning it, and secondly I should have welcomed the input of somebody new to the subject, somebody who might have noticed things which I myself had either overlooked or else been looking at too closely.

But I was aware that if I tried to express this, he might have perceived it as a weakness.

"Okay, then." I took the plunge: I *had* to master my reluctance. "So what you'll need to tell Berlin is this. It appears that no Allied plane was lost over the Atlantic on April the 24th or April the 25th. Nor yet on the 26th or 27th."

I glanced back at the man with the *Evening News*.

"And then you'd better add that in the absence of a crash I haven't been able to work out yet what happened, but in my own mind the whole situation is suspect and should be viewed with extreme caution."

It must have been clear I had finished. Yet Buchholz passed no comment for maybe as much as half a minute. And neither, stubbornly, did I.

"Sounds intriguing," he said, at last. He stared into his whisky glass and now gave himself the luxury of a further sip. "But am I to understand that the credence attached to this important matter, whatever it may be, finally rests or falls on the strength of whether or not a certain plane came down in a certain area on or around a certain date? Is that what you're telling me?"

I hesitated. "Yes. I suppose so. Basically."

"And that the occurrence or non-occurrence of this plane crash is really the prime factor? One that effectively provides either a veto or an all-clear?"

It was essentially the same question but while he rephrased it he looked up from his tumbler and transferred his coolly contemplative gaze to me.

"Yes," I said again. "In this case – a veto, more like. But of course that's for our superiors to decide."

"Yet do I get the feeling that otherwise the issue is clear-cut? And one in which nobody seriously foresaw any impediment?"

I gave him a slow nod.

He smiled.

"Which is maybe why they sent an agent so relatively young and inexperienced?" This might have been rhetorical, yet his eyebrow remained raised and seemed to be demanding of an answer.

The answer broke my series of affirmatives.

"I think that's uncalled for," I told him, coldly – and if my words sounded pompous...well, then, too bad...so be it. "You know nothing about me."

But he didn't seem abashed.

"And, on all those days you checked, how many aircraft would you say were recorded as being missing – or destroyed – in toto? Even if such losses occurred in parts of the war zone not of any immediate interest to yourself?"

"As a matter of fact," I replied sulkily, "none."

"None?"

"No."

"But, my dear boy, doesn't that strike you as unusual?"

"No, my dear boy, it doesn't – not really."

Buchholz grinned.

"I'm sorry if I've upset you; but this is far too important for anything like that. I believe I've got tidings which should now compensate a little."

"All right," I said. "Apology accepted." But I still sounded sulky.

"Fine." He swirled his whisky gently round the glass. "So you told me you had checked through four whole days of news?"

Now I did smile again. Ruefully. "Only because I didn't want to admit I'd actually checked through *seven* whole days of news!"

"My word!" He returned the smile. "*Seven*?"

"There are times when – just possibly – I do get a fraction carried away."

"Or else you simply don't like having to give up?" Hereafter, he would probably treat me a shade more diplomatically. "Well, that's altogether to your credit, plainly. But more to the point at present: are you honestly suggesting that no Allied plane, not one, was shot down anywhere over Europe during the course of an entire week? Not even one?"

"There were three that ran out of petrol and had to land on Lisbon airfield."

Quite properly, of course, he ignored this.

"Because I'm perfectly willing to bet," he said, "that there were plenty of *German* planes which were. Shot down," he added.

"I honestly don't know. That's not what I was looking for."

"I'd still be willing to bet on it."

It hadn't occurred to me that such an omission might merely have been a question of keeping up morale. Evidently it should have occurred to me. Perhaps this showed him justified in declaring that I was young and inexperienced.

"So…?" he continued, after he had briefly surveyed me once more in silence. "If previously you had reasonable evidence to suggest that a plane crash did indeed happen, then I'd be inclined to say you mustn't stop believing in this, simply because you haven't read about it in the British press."

"Nor yet the German."

"No, but it's idle to pretend that every Allied plane which comes down does so as a direct result of enemy action. Accidents still take place, even in wartime. Why?" he asked, abruptly.

"Why what?"

"Why hasn't it been in the German press…when the Abwehr obviously knows all about it?"

"Not *all* about it. In fact, there's very little that's so far been confirmed. As yet, it's nothing but guesswork."

"And why should you think that *that* would stop anyone? Our own propaganda machine is at least as efficient as theirs, in terms of what it puts in and what it leaves out."

I paused. "Though, anyway, it may well have got into the German newspapers by now. Yes – thinking about it – I'm almost sure it will have."

Because, I thought, if the whole thing were a trick, wouldn't British Intelligence be keeping a lookout for some mention of the accident, no matter how pared down? And if, on the other hand, it *weren't* a trick, wouldn't they still be expecting to see the crash reported…once, that was, they had received their letters back from Madrid? It again annoyed me that there could be points like this which I had missed.

I informed Buchholz that I had changed my mind – for the moment – in regard to his having to make contact with Berlin.

"Good," he said. "Quite excellent. So long as you feel happy about it?"

"Yes. Completely."

"In that case, now accept the whisky you wouldn't have earlier on and let us drink to the fact of your feeling happy. And also to the fact of *my* feeling happy. Even one less message out – and one less message in – can make a big difference to the safety of our sanctuary here."

He glanced about him, sardonically.

"To its safety, if not to its splendour!"

We went downstairs a short time later. Before we did so, Heinrich changed into his shoes.

"As you can see, my dear…we like to dress for dinner!"

His mother did, certainly. Frankly, that lady wouldn't have been recognizable. She had washed her face and removed her scarf and cardigan; had put on a floor-length dress in Cambridge blue, which so intensified the colour of her eyes that they became fully as piercing as her son's, setting off in turn the snowy softness of her hair. And she now wore make-up. Even her delivery had changed. Although she unfailingly kept to English, her voice had shed its London accent, along with all the stridency going with it.

"I give them what they expect," she said, "and in Paradise Street, poor devils, with the workhouse just around the corner, what else can they expect?"

When I asked where she had ever learned such skills, she told me that a dozen years ago she had appeared in *Der Kongress Tanzt* with Conrad Veidt and Lilian Harvey, and in *Die Dreigroschenoper* with Lotte Lenya, and that after the war she wanted to return to acting.

"If they make a film about Methuselah I shall campaign to play his mother."

I said that as part of my assignment I was hoping soon to meet an English actress. Wouldn't *she* be impressed to hear I knew someone who had once starred with Conrad Veidt and Lotte Lenya?

"No, 'starred', unhappily, is putting it *far* too strongly. And, anyway, wouldn't it be slightly safer just to mention Lilian Harvey, who was – still is, of course – so prettily and sweetly and respectably English?"

"Oh," remarked Heinrich, "Conrad Veidt's okay. Nearly a British institution, he's been working over here so long. But I doubt that Eric is really going to mention you at all."

He looked down at his nails.

"Wouldn't it be fascinating, though, to hear how English actresses in any way fit in with the current preoccupations of the Abwehr? Yet sadly, Mama, for the moment that's a pleasure I fear we must forgo."

He smiled.

"But after the war, Erich, after the war…"

13

I felt that I was back in business.

Following a meal that was both tasty and companionable I left the Buchholzes, went into the first telephone box I came to and dialled the Knightsbridge number I had now transcribed into my book.

But I had probably picked a bad moment: nearly nine-fifteen on a Friday evening, at a period when London social life was reputedly at its zenith. Why in heaven's name hadn't I thought to do this before supper? Now, most likely, I should have to phone again tomorrow and in the meanwhile resign myself to a complete waste of time that might have been avoided. Oh, damn it! Why was I so foolish?

Yet on the sixth or seventh ring somebody answered.

"Reggie, you beast! You'd better have a pretty good excuse!"

I pressed Button A.

"The best excuse in the world," I replied, easily. "This isn't Reggie." But bless him, I thought: he had caused me to feel instantly at home.

"Oh." A sharp intake of breath, a nervous and embarrassed giggle. "Then all I can say is – whoever you are, you have had a *very* narrow escape!"

"Thank you. I'd better be fast, though. He might be trying to get through even as we talk."

"Well, in that case, let him sweat! Serve the fellow right!"

"Okay. Point taken. By the way – am I speaking to Sybella?" I knew very well I wasn't.

"No, I'm sorry. Sybella isn't here. This is Lucy."

"Oh, right – how are you, Lucy? This is Eric. Sybella's mother didn't think Sybella would be in town, but knew you'd be able to tell me where she'd gone."

"Ah! Not too sure about that. Depends on how carefully she's filled in the calendar above her bed."

She went to look. I felt anxious; offered up a prayer. I couldn't afford to lose the whole weekend – it seemed unlikely I'd be able to raise the ENSA people until Monday. Again, why hadn't I worked at it with greater resolution on leaving the solicitor's? She came back.

"Tonight, Biggin Hill; tomorrow afternoon and evening, Aldershot." The relief was palpable. For once, I remembered to say *thank you*.

"Oh, great! Do you know where in Aldershot? And will that be only for tomorrow or will it also include Sunday?"

"Where? Well, I'd suppose at the garrison theatre, wouldn't you? And then she'll obviously be spending the night on camp – lucky girl! – and I imagine they'd be likely to move off straight after lunch on Sunday. Oh, drat, I forgot to check their next date. I'm afraid you'll have to hold on again."

It was that 'lucky girl' which did it.

"My God," I exclaimed, before she'd even had a chance to lay down the receiver, "then you can't have heard the news about Major Martin!"

I had to blame it on the Scotch, of course, and on that bottle of red wine which had accompanied our *Sauerbraten* and vegetables – "Eric, my dear boy, well naturally we must! How often do we have a visitor?" – blame it more on those things than on the simple shock of Lucy's bubbly and facetious comment.

But whatever I might choose to blame it on, how could I – how *could* I – have let it happen?

Yet I knew the thought which had betrayed me. Tomorrow a whole week would have gone by since the funeral. And I was now aware that William's father had been told. Therefore Sybella, as William's fiancée, must also have been told.

She *must* have.

So I had obviously assumed (definitely *not* a permissible assumption) that Lucy would have known as well. But 'lucky girl' wasn't the phrase of someone who had known. And, if it hadn't been for the whisky and/or the wine, I would have registered that fact roughly three seconds earlier than I did, and reacted accordingly.

Only three seconds earlier!

And now, of course – only *three* seconds later! – I perfectly well understood why Sybella hadn't passed on the information to her flatmates. Quite simply, she hadn't felt up to it. Not yet. Who would have?

But the question which faced me at present – clearly – was how to set things right. Lucy would say, "Received *what* news about him?" And I couldn't possibly tell her; not when Sybella herself hadn't done so.

Yet Lucy's reply was marginally different from the one I had expected.

"The news about *who*?"

"Major Martin."

I repeated it distinctly, for by now I had managed to gather my thoughts and I guessed that in retrospect she would already have caught on – I couldn't run the risk of giving her another name. (Besides, what earthly good would that have done?) Because of a strange and rather difficult hiatus I even expanded on it.

"Bill Martin. Her fiancé."

But, in any case, the name wasn't important. It was the news itself which was going to prove the problem. (Oh, perhaps – after all – not so terribly much of one. "I'm sorry," I should have to say. "I've just remembered that I gave my word to keep this thing a secret.")

Yet the woman I was speaking to – Sybella's flatmate, Sybella's close friend – now broke her silence with a gasp.

"Oh, come off it!" she exclaimed. "Who *are* you? You're only pulling my leg – surely?"

"What?"

"You're pulling my leg, aren't you?"

"No," I answered, stiffly. "I am not pulling your leg. Why would you think that?"

None of this was real. Indeed, it was almost *surreal* – like at the solicitor's. No longer just a matter of not telling somebody about somebody's death, it was now more a matter of…well, I wasn't sure of what, exactly. In one way it was possibly similar to riding on a roller-coaster: alternately up high, enjoying the view, full of confidence – then back at ground level, moving through mist, having to re-explore absolutely everything that I encountered. I said: "Are you telling me, then, that Sybella didn't recently become engaged? To a man named Bill Martin? A major in the Royal Marines?"

"Well, I'm telling you that if she *did* it's the very first *I've* heard about it! Or about him, either, if you really want to know."

"Yes, I see," I answered slowly – totally the opposite of what was true. "Then I suppose I must have been mistaken. Sorry. You'll have to ignore everything I've just said."

"Ignore…?"

"And in any case, we've quite forgotten Reggie, haven't we? He must have sweated long enough by now. Isn't it time you showed a little mercy?"

But my heart wasn't in it any more. My tone sounded leaden.

"Anyhow, Lucy, I appreciate your help."

"Gosh, but – well, you can't simply tell me to ignore it and then leave it at that! The treacherous little minx…oh, you just wait till I catch up with *her*! But you know, Eric – is that right: Eric? – I can't believe there hasn't been some monumental mix-up…that this isn't something which will soon have all of us in the most terrific gales of laughter…"

I could tell: she had now begun to come to terms with her astonishment, her natural curiosity was about to reassert itself. Therefore I spoke firmly; even abruptly.

"Good night, Lucy – thank you – it's been good talking to you!" Before long I should be getting quite used to cutting people off.

But when I'd put down the phone I stayed on a further minute in the booth, just standing there and staring through the glass. The High Street was dark, of course, yet even in broad daylight I probably shouldn't have noticed much.

However. At least my brain was gradually – very gradually – resuming operations. Just like Lucy's.

So Sybella hadn't told her, then, about Bill Martin?

Yet evidently she had told others. "By the way, Aunt Marion said to bring you to dinner next time I was up, but I think that might wait?" And it sounded as if Bill had certainly met Jock and Hazel – and most likely more than once: "You know what their friends always turn out to be like…"

Therefore, I could take comfort; she hadn't kept him entirely to herself.

And fairly soon I began to feel better. Heinrich Buchholz had suggested I should contact a Mrs Hilling, who had a lodging house in Abbey Road: "a nice enough Englishwoman," he had said, "who will do her best to make you comfortable." So I first caught a taxi to Euston to collect my suitcase and then took that same taxicab back towards St John's Wood.

All right. Sybella had definitely kept quiet about her engagement. But was that really so difficult to understand? For one reason or another, people often preferred at first to be secretly engaged. (I remembered Jane Fairfax and Frank Churchill in *Emma* – which made me smile a little: I was only, approximately, a hundred-and-thirty years behind the times.) On the other hand, she had also kept quiet about having Bill Martin as a boyfriend, let alone as a fiancé. Not everywhere, thank God, but in certain quarters, manifestly. That one was perhaps a little harder. When you were in love didn't you want to advertise the fact and throw the name of your beloved into nearly every sentence?

But, naturally, I didn't know how Sybella might feel about Lucy. Just because they shared a flat didn't *necessarily* mean that they were close – bosom pals – confidantes. No. Sitting in the taxi as it went up Baker Street I reminded myself that I knew next to nothing of the status quo.

And then a short while later – we were now in Lisson Grove – I asked myself what difference did it make. (I could hear Franz Mannheim posing precisely that same question.) Why should it have dismayed me even for one minute? We *know* Bill

Martin and Sybella were engaged, whether secretly or not – and yes, okay, let's admit she did behave a bit strangely in keeping his existence hidden from her flatmate, hidden from her other flatmate too, presumably, but so what? Am I now becoming such a die-hard cynic that any new revelation must automatically set off warning bells? Purely on account of its being unexpected – well, isn't that the whole *point* concerning revelations? And warning bells alerting me to *what*, for heaven's sake? That the man floating in the Atlantic, bearing letters to General Alexander from General Sir Archibald Nye – and to the Admiral of the Fleet and to General Eisenhower from Lord Louis Mountbatten – was in some sense not so real, not so trustworthy, simply because his girlfriend hadn't rattled on about him? Well, didn't that in fact render him *more* trustworthy? Perhaps Sybella hadn't bandied his name around for one perfectly good reason: she'd known about the nature of his work and had been terrified of endangering him in some way. In a climate where everyone was persistently being urged to refrain from careless talk, should it even strike me as surprising that a responsible person had done her best to follow a responsible instruction?

No, it should not. Not for an instant.

(But actually, I thought, for someone in a situation like mine, it was no bad thing to be hearing warning bells. Even to be hearing them at every turn. All I had to guard against, however, was taking them each time for an injunction to jump ship.)

And, anyway, I must continually hold fast to that all-important possibility which had just re-occurred to me.

She had known about the nature of his work.

14

The previous day's train journey from Mold to Euston had been a relatively easy one, notwithstanding its couple of time-consuming changes, but this morning's journey into Hampshire was an altogether different matter.

As soon as I came up from the underground at Waterloo and emerged into the mainline station I received warning of how it was going to be. The crowds appeared impregnable.

And almost at once I gave up any attempt to penetrate them. My suitcase in itself would hardly have allowed it. Mrs Hilling had wanted to lend me an overnight bag and look after the rest of my belongings until I came back, but since I had neither known how long I'd be away nor whether, in fact, I should be going back, this was an offer I hadn't accepted. So now I found myself with an encumbrance which seemed doggedly insubordinate and which banged continually against both my own shins and other people's. I was repeatedly needing to apologize.

Yet, on the whole, everybody remained calm-tempered. Perhaps this was partly a consequence of the music being piped over the public address system. Good and lively. Or perhaps it had more to do with the traditional British mentality: accustomed both to muddle and to muddling through. ("Oh, things will work out, eventually. Somehow. We always land on our feet and come up smiling." Many Germans, indeed, found this attitude contemptible, quite beyond their understanding.) But I heard a lot of laughter in the shuffling crowd. I also heard a lot of grumbling. Yet it was grumbling laced with humour.

And in the end even my suitcase proved a blessing. For if I'd left it in London not only would I have had nothing to sit on myself but obviously shouldn't have been able to offer anyone else a seat – that 'anyone' being a pretty redhead serving with the Wrens, who had been some half-dozen places ahead of me

73

in the queue and whose hair I'd been sporadically admiring. Throughout the journey she chatted to me so entertainingly, and was so philosophical about all the servicemen and civilians and railway officials who were forever squeezing past us, that her company appeared to reduce our travelling time by half.

Actually I had felt tempted, as we were pulling into Aldershot, to invite her to the ENSA show. But fortunately I'd decided against this even before I saw her being exuberantly embraced by a large and handsome staff sergeant.

And the warmth of their reunion gave me such a pang! I left the station rather hurriedly.

Yet in any case, after I had found a B and B and had also stopped for lunch, I was too late for the matinée I'd half hoped we'd be attending.

Still, I then bought my ticket for that evening's performance. It cost me three-and-six. I could have got one for as little as two shillings but I wanted a seat in the front stalls. I had expected the garrison theatre to be inside the camp. Tonight, for some reason, the Theatre Royal – in Gordon Road – would be filling in.

The playbills all told me what ENSA stood for: Entertainments National Service Association. Yet none of them clued me in on Sybella's surname. They didn't list performers.

The woman in the box office said, both to myself and to the corporal in front of me – she must have been repeating it to everyone:

"You do realize, don't you, that it's a play, not a concert party or revue? For that kind of thing you'd need the Hippodrome. Don't fret, though: the cast here is composed entirely of ladies – sixteen ladies – so none of you boys should find yourselves with any grounds for complaint!"

Nine Till Six. Last week at some camp in the Midlands a group of soldiers – "a little bit under the influence," she said – had thought that it was going to be a girlie show. They had stormed out, "behaving rather rudely as they did so," and could easily, it seemed, have been court-martialled as a consequence.

"But luckily," she added, "they were let off with jankers, or put on fatigue, and I think they had to apologize. My point is…it's a very serious play."

And at any rate, when here in Aldershot the time arrived, no one appeared to have misunderstood; she had clearly performed her job well.

It seemed a quietly anticipatory audience. After the curtain went up, there was a round of clapping in appreciation of the set – which presented a smart dressmaking establishment: not just its showroom but its office and its staff canteen. All this was especially ambitious, I thought, considering how regularly it must have needed to be adapted to different-sized venues. (And to have had this pointed out in advance greatly increased my admiration: the Wren on the train had been knowledgeable about ENSA, having a sister touring in some production in the Middle East.)

Yet for roughly the next forty minutes – until almost the end of the first act – I felt perplexed by the play itself. Not by its content; more by its supposed appeal to an audience composed mainly of troops. Admittedly there were several glimpses of young women in their underclothes. But apart from that? Surely members of the armed services didn't by and large take any great interest in the intricacies of women's fashion? It seemed to me that these opening scenes were filled chiefly with comings and goings, which – despite their undoubted air of busyness – didn't add up to very much. Along with the venting of petty grievances and the pointing out of rivalries amongst the staff there appeared to be a good deal of unnecessary chatter.

Just before the first-act curtain, however, the stock-keeper stole a dress; and at last you felt the drama might be getting under way.

During the interval many people stayed in their seats (some had trays of tea and biscuits brought to them) but at least half the audience headed for the bar. I did so myself.

And at the bar – to my surprise – I deduced from several animated conversations that the play was being enjoyed. Yet most of what I overheard had little to do with its intrinsic dramatic appeal: female voices were raised in appreciation of the costumes and the hats; male voices – equally expectedly – in appreciation of the women who were modelling them.

All the same, when in the second act several more dresses went missing, the acceleration of interest was maintained. And, by the third, the play had turned into an eloquent diatribe against social injustice, and it had grown to be affecting.

The stock-keeper was the person you mainly cared about. The thief. And I knew I didn't feel this way only because the role was being played by Sybella...Sybella Standish, so the programme had informed me. Naturally I'd felt impatient for her to come on, and naturally I had been conscious of her, all through that first act, not as Freda the stock-keeper but as Sybella the fiancée of Bill Martin. But long before the final curtain I had almost forgotten the true purpose of my being there and had become thoroughly caught up in her actual performance and with the character she was portraying... If it hadn't been for the cast list I wasn't sure I should have recognized the woman *giving* the performance. She was pale, downtrodden and defeated. Gone was all the vivacity of that snapshot.

Of course, such vivacity wouldn't be present in real life, either – not for the time being.

But at first even her voice had come as a shock – despite my rapidly perceiving how stupid this was. What had I expected? A replica of her mother speaking down the telephone from the Manor House?

After that initial jolt, however, I felt very much impressed: not only was her accent flawlessly consistent; it conveyed – without any trace of comic condescension – all those grinding years of poverty and hopelessness that had finally reduced her to this moment of sobbing self-abasement in front of her employer.

"Yes, all right, I stole them because I thought you were getting everything and me nothing. I thought I had a right to them – a right to have pretty things to wear so I could look decent on my holiday and perhaps get off with someone that had money enough to give me a good time."

That was the climax to the play. When the curtain came down a few minutes later, the audience appeared dazed. As at the end of any compelling drama (and this one contained in its last line the just-learned revelation of a loved one's death) the silence that descended on the theatre was disconcerting. You thought that nobody was going to clap.

Yet, bit by bit, the clapping did break out.

And eventually became tumultuous.

By this time, though, the curtain had risen again and the whole cast stood in a row, smiling its acknowledgment. Mrs Pembroke, the kindly proprietress, was positioned in the centre, with her daughter Clare to her left and Freda to her right. In fact, because of the even number in the line-up, you could certainly attest Freda stood as fully in the centre as her boss. But it was an ensemble piece – there were no 'stars' – the young woman at either end (each of whom had played a junior) seemed to receive as much recognition as those who had been given the more demanding roles.

The curtain came down and went up a further three or four times. On the last occasion there were wolf whistles mixed in with the applause – and at least one ebullient invitation. "Want to get off with me tonight, darlin'? Here's someone that can give you a good time all right!"

The soldier's wording suggested precisely whom he had in mind but it was Mrs Pembroke, probably in her late fifties, who then stepped forward.

"Yes, I'd love to!" she said. "Where shall we meet?"

Whereupon, there was a good deal of laughter and a fresh wave of applause. I noticed that Sybella herself was laughing – a very different person from the one she'd just been playing. More the woman in the photograph again.

And then it suddenly occurred to me.

Oh, my God! Supposing that their secret engagement had been kept secret even from the War Office? Supposing the War Office hadn't been aware of her existence?

Supposing she doesn't *know*?

It was too awful to consider. Wouldn't *anybody* have informed her? Mr Martin, in spite of his depression? Or, at the very least, Mr Gwatkin?

Yes, they must have, I decided. Must have! I felt a great surge of relief. Even if they hadn't realized the news itself still needed to be broken, a message of sympathy would surely have been sent.

Oh, sweet heaven. Only imagine – if Sybella hadn't known that anything had happened! Had continued to think of him as being alive and well!

The lights went up.

A scratchy record of the National Anthem was then played.

The first few bars produced instant calm and brought the audience to its feet. The sixteen members of the cast now led the singing. But as the last notes died away there was again a moment of deep silence. It seemed that people were actually thinking about the meaning of the Anthem and didn't like to resume chatting too soon afterwards. Or even to start putting on their coats.

The curtain descended for the final time.

Outside the theatre I went and stood on the opposite pavement. As the crowd moved off, my view of the stage door became less restricted.

I was feeling nervous again. I'd decided that I wasn't going to mention to Sybella (or to Miss Standish, as she'd now perforce become) either of my recent telephone conversations – on the grounds that, even if she had spoken to her mother in the interim or to her flatmate, there still wouldn't, *inevitably*, be anything to connect me with that unknown caller. I should have to change the name, of course.

My wait on the pavement was a short one.

A dark blue charabanc drew up close to the stage door. This was in Birchett Road, not Gordon – the theatre stood on a corner. The driver didn't get down. He lengthily sounded his horn. Then he rolled a cigarette and leaned back in satisfaction, from time to time exhaling the smoke through his partly lowered window.

And it wasn't long before the stage door sprang open and all the ENSA women emerged – well, I didn't do any counting but it seemed it must be all of them; Sybella was certainly amongst them, carrying the flowers presented to her following the performance. There was laughter as the women climbed onto the coach.

Through the windows I could make out nothing except for a jumble of moving shadows but when everybody was aboard I distinctly heard the driver say:

"One of you girls must have a suitor! That bloke was standing over there even before *I* ruddy well arrived. Lucky thing you've got yours truly here to protect you!"

"And to deliver us up to the soldiers!" cried out one of his charges, seconds before somebody else called, "Well, then, why not let him on, for Gawd's sake?"

Both sallies were greeted with guffaws.

I watched as the coach drove into the darkness and rounded a further corner. The streets became still again.

Slowly I too moved off into the night; turned back towards the quiet guesthouse where I had booked myself a room.

15

The following day I should have gone to church; but church for the present seemed a luxury. Instead, at roughly half past nine, I arrived outside the barracks. I gave the guard at the gatehouse an envelope bearing Sybella's name and did my best, without causing him irritation, to stress its urgency. He only nodded and looked poker-faced.

Then I retreated to the edges of a park I had passed on the way. I had a book with me: a detective story I had bought in Mold and had read two-thirds of whilst travelling comfortably to London. I now sat on the bench closest to the park entrance and wondered how long it might be before Sybella received my letter.

Well, actually it wasn't a letter. The envelope had held merely a postcard.

I wondered if she were awake yet and whether things appeared more bearable when she first awoke – or whether it was like receiving the news afresh every time that memory resurfaced?

A postcard had struck me as being preferable, since this meant I could withhold my address. In the first place the B and B wasn't that impressive but, more important, I didn't want her making do with just a phone call in return, or a quick line dropped through the letterbox, suggesting our meeting at some future date. I needed to see her now. Today. Already my allotted week was half over.

After much thought I had written:

"Dear Miss Standish,

"I saw *Nine Till Six* last night and thought your performance incredible. I represent the London office of an American film company and currently we're looking for an unknown face for a new movie. I was wondering if maybe we could meet for lunch today? I shall be in The Tap and Tankard from opening time until one-thirty but in case that's not convenient I shall also be at Daphne's – likewise in the High Street and just opposite the pub – from half-past-ten.

"I very much hope to see you, then, at one or other of these places.

"Yours sincerely,
"Oliver Redgrave."

I regretted having to be so corny – and still more regretted having to fill her with such extravagant expectations. But I couldn't think of any other way. And, after all, this was war, wasn't it? Maybe huge decisions would depend on the strength of the bribe I offered.

And, indeed, I had tried my hardest to devise some alternative. But what? I could hardly have hoped to pass myself off as a friend of Bill Martin's – not to Sybella – not knowing so pitifully little about him. I'd have been asked questions; would naturally have been expected to reminisce. Reminisce about schooldays or something. The pitfalls along this route were innumerable.

Anyway, of course, it was *she* who needed to reminisce. That was the whole point of it.

Even as it was, I felt far from confident that my cheap little dodge would succeed. (Whether it *deserved* to succeed was a different thing altogether.) Her friends would say, "Oh, Syb, just listen to us, please. Use your common sense. This is the oldest trick in the book. The man could be a rapist – killer – anything!"

"No," she might say, "he's arranged to meet me in a very public place. There can't be any danger."

Her friends would not be reassured.

"Oh, doubtless he'll appear quite normal at first. Then he'll draw you off to some dark place and pull out his penis or his bloodstained carving knife. Or both. Well, at least if you do go you'd better take a chaperone."

Yet I didn't believe that she would even tell her friends. My belief wasn't rational. Was based simply upon instinct.

Perhaps I was banking on her curiosity – that, coupled with her ambition and possibly a sense of adventure. *If I pass this up, shall I always think my future, my whole life, might have been different? Might have been better?*

Curiosity? Ambition? A sense of adventure?

Oh, for Pete's sake!

Had I forgotten? Here was a woman in mourning. Did I truly expect her, *already*, to be thinking about new beginnings?

Only connect, E.M. Forster had insisted. Only connect.

Well, at any rate, she didn't come.

Not to Daphne's.

But in fact I had scarcely thought she would. Even if my card had been delivered without delay – and at breakneck speed – I still hadn't given her much time.

Nevertheless, when I eventually moved across to the pub, I felt anxious. I went into the lounge bar, bought a pint of ale and took it over to a small polished table that had a chair facing the door. If she didn't turn up this time, what lure could I possibly cast out on a second occasion; and why should I fare any better with that one? It would be easy enough to discover where the troupe had gone; easy enough to pursue it and then find my way backstage during one of the two intervals. But inevitably she'd be sharing a crowded dressing room and that – obviously – would render her difficult to get at. I hadn't realized she was going to be so thickly…and so constantly…surrounded.

I tipped back in my chair, hoping to feel more relaxed. But I stiffened, automatically, every time the door opened.

A couple…composed of a RAF officer and a Wren…

Three elderly women, all wearing civvies…

An old man, carrying his Jack Russell…

A group of five (sixteen-, seventeen-year-olds, you might have said, but each of them in uniform), its arrival giving rise to a collective cry of welcome from beside the bar.

Door-swing after door-swing… Two-way traffic, of course, but more customers coming in than were going out.

At twelve forty-two I glanced at my watch for possibly the fifteenth time. I believed I had never known any period of waiting to pass so slowly; had probably forgotten what it felt like to be a child impatient for Christmas.

I suddenly remembered the opera house in Berlin: how I had once stood outside it in the cold for more than ninety minutes. Frieda had been a girl I'd met at a party (Frieda – huh!), an attractive and apparently soft-hearted girl whom I had liked a lot. Even without that pair of tickets in my pocket – that pair of ruinously expensive tickets – my feelings of disillusion and hurt would still have been pretty much the same.

By one o'clock I had more or less persuaded myself that this second Freda wasn't going to show up either. (Although, really, there was no legitimate comparison.) Another thirty minutes remained until the expiration of my deadline – yes, I realized that – but equally it was now about three and a half hours since I had delivered the envelope. In three and a half hours she could have crossed between the camp and the High Street ten or twelve times. If she had truly meant to come, she could have been with me at least two hours earlier. Easily.

An entirely forlorn hope, therefore. I wasn't so surprised. I had been patently over-optimistic.

Perhaps I should have said on my postcard: "I need to speak to you about your dead fiancé."

Confronted the issue head-on. Seen where that might lead me.

Into jail, most like.

She came at seventeen minutes past one.

16

She was wearing an elegant green dress, woollen, with narrow lapels and short sleeves; it had self-coloured buttons down the bodice and a self-coloured belt emphasizing the trimness of her waist. On her head she wore a light brown pillbox, the same shade as her gloves and shoes and handbag: a shade that harmonized not only with her hazel eyes and bobbed hair, but even with her legs, which were bare and carefully made up. The lipstick whose absence I had mourned from the fifth row of the stalls, along with the impression of any colour in her face, was today discreetly present. She looked good. Extremely good.

And scarcely was she through the door than I was on my feet and walking towards her.

"Mr Redgrave?"

"I'd almost given you up," I said.

And since this was true I now felt considerably more at my ease. If she'd arrived ten minutes earlier, I shouldn't have been able to greet her with at all the same composure. I was reminded of my telephone call to Lucy – and of Reggie's most opportune assistance.

"But why?" she asked. "Oh, I'm not late, am I? Didn't you say you'd be here until half-past?"

"Yes, I did. Definitely." I found it hard not to stare. She was prettier than her picture.

Then, as we shook hands, she added: "And I only received your note about an hour ago – shamefully, whilst I was still in bed! On Sunday mornings, you see, we're inclined to pamper ourselves."

At the time, I didn't question this, but afterwards…? Only an hour in which to get ready, then walk the near-mile between the barracks and the pub? I doubted it. Her pencilled stocking seams appeared too straight; her nails too newly polished; her make-up too perfectly applied. And also – despite my first impression of her appearance – I now thought she seemed no more rested than she had looked the night before, while playing Freda.

Yet should it come as a surprise that she wasn't managing to sleep?

"What will you have to drink, Miss Standish?"

"A dry sherry, please…if they have one."

They had. She sat across the table from me and as she twined her fingers round her glass and made over-lively conversation she reminded me of Mr Martin – or, rather, of Mr Gwatkin *telling* me of Mr Martin…the connection was probably the sherry. She had taken off her gloves, and it was at this point I could have felt tempted to challenge her on her duplicity: on her defamation of the camp's delivery service. I decided against it, though. I also banished the reminder of Mr Gwatkin. She helped me there – simply by talking.

"My goodness, only imagine if I *had* been late? Or if your note had got even more delayed? Or – heaven forbid – if it had been *lost*? Goodbye to my whole big Hollywood career!"

Her remark had been satiric. In case I hadn't realized this she ended on a laugh.

"Not that at the moment I'm positively relying on that – my whole big Hollywood career!"

She was an actress...an actress still very much playing a role. Her laughter wasn't natural. Her gaiety was forced. I wanted to say to her: Please don't.

I wanted to say to her: I promise you I understand. Don't feel you have to sparkle.

But my reply came out only in kind.

"I'm afraid it's terribly clear that you regard me as a sham."

"No," she protested. "No! How could you possibly think such a thing? All I meant was...can I quite believe in fairy tales?"

"Oh, well, as to that," I said, "I'm sure you can't. Who can? Especially in the midst of a world war? A fairy tale is Lana Turner sitting at a soda fountain in Schwab's in LA, drinking a milk shake and filling out a sweater! Your performance last night was built on years of solid hard work and frustration and disappointment. Blood, toil, tears and sweat. Not the sort of thing to find its way into the fairy tales!"

"Oh, but I disagree," she said. "Look at *Cinderella*!"

I looked at *Cinderella*. I had never envisaged it as being any part of a secret agent's brief to look at *Cinderella*.

"Yes, you're right. So, from now on, please don't believe anything I say. All you should believe is what I wrote on my postcard. You're a fine actress."

"Thank you. That's kind. And it makes me feel so fortunate, too."

"Deserving. Not fortunate."

"No – you misunderstand me. Beginning from this morning, I'm taking a few days off. So if some lucky star hadn't brought you here to Aldershot just in the nick of time...!"

"Really?" I said. "Well, then, I'm the one who's fortunate."

"I'm curious, though. What lucky star *did* bring you here to Aldershot just in the nick of time?"

"Oh." I took a long pull at my beer and then had to pause to wipe my mouth. "Oh, simply some silly little mix-up. Absurd but providential."

I added quickly: "Both me and RKO."

"I'm sorry?"

"We're the *two* who are fortunate. And please don't tell me you haven't heard of RKO." I looked at her severely. "RKO Radio Pictures? RKO Radio Pictures, *Inc*?"

"Well, yes, naturally I have. Although you're probably right: could I have felt completely certain if I hadn't caught that *Inc*?"

"Exactly. But I expect you're growing impatient to be told about the film?"

"Very much so."

"Hold onto your seat, then. We've just acquired the rights to a novel called *Laura*. And it's a project which has got us all tremendously excited."

"That's very good to hear."

"As a matter of fact I have a copy of it right here beside me."

I retrieved the book from where it lay on the chair next to my own, most of it covered by my trilby. It was the novel I had bought in Mold. Its plot concerned a detective investigating the murder of a young woman. He was supposedly hard-boiled but during the course of his enquiries had begun to fall in love with the dead girl – partly because of her portrait over the mantel but partly, too, because of everything he was finding out about her. As it turned out, though, Laura wasn't the girl who'd been killed. The real victim, her face rendered unrecognizable by the shots fired into it at the front door, had actually been a friend – a friend who had not only borrowed Laura's apartment for the weekend (with its fatefully soft lighting in the hallway) but also her housecoat. The book was a love story as well as a murder mystery.

Sybella looked at its dust jacket and blurb; read the novel's opening paragraph.

"And what part would I be playing?" she asked. "If the screen tests and everything proved okay?"

"Oh, didn't I make that clear? You, Miss Standish, would be given the leading role. Laura."

"No!" she said. "No! I don't believe it!"

"Well, how can I convince you?"

"Only with unparalleled difficulty, I should imagine."

"Clearly, then, from now on I'll have to concentrate on being Herculean…superhuman…"

"Yes, that might help."

She flipped through the book with an awe-filled and distracted air.

"But do you really think they'd accept an English girl in the role of an American?"

"It *has* happened before," I murmured, drily. "And not so very long ago, either."

Her expression still betrayed mistrust.

"And just look at what you did with Freda," I went on. "With *her* accent. And, basically, how much difference can there be? If Vivien Leigh could do it so can you."

She answered in the same light tone.

"Indeed, in terms of accent, New York could be even *easier* than Atlanta. Wouldn't you agree?"

"And furthermore – who knows? – they might put it in the script that Laura had been raised in England."

She briefly returned my smile. But almost immediately shook her head.

She said: "Things like this don't happen." She had reverted to *Cinderella*.

I nodded, understandingly.

And guiltily.

Reminded myself that I probably couldn't have got her here in any other way. Reminded myself that there was no secondary role in the novel that she could possibly have played; the doomed girlfriend had featured only as a corpse.

"No," I said, "you're right to be sceptical. In this life you do need to protect yourself. 'There's many a slip 'twixt the cup and the lip.' Who was it who wrote that?"

"Some aspiring actress in Hollywood?"

"Bull's eye!"

And now her laughter seemed more natural. She gave the impression of someone obliged to attend some especially

87

daunting party, who, against all the odds, had suddenly realized that she was having a good time.

"Tell me," she said. "In this life do you protect yourself?"

"I don't know. I think I like to shift that onus onto God, give *him* the responsibility." But I instantly remembered my having questioned Mannheim's *carte blanche* in an attempt to establish a possible defence against failure. "Or let's just say, I trust the two of us are working on it together."

"What – you and God?"

"I know it sounds presumptuous. Since the beginning of time there must be countless millions who – apparently – haven't received a lot of protection from him. Even since the beginning of this war…"

Then I quickly changed the subject; that aspect of it, anyway.

"But talking of self-protection, Miss Standish, did you tell your friends about all this?"

"About all what? Hollywood…and Lana Turner at the soda fountain in LA?"

"Yes, but slightly more to the point: about some stranger in the pub a little closer to home."

"No."

"*No*? Why ever not?"

"I'm afraid it's very clear that *you*, Mr Redgrave, have never lived at close quarters with upwards of a dozen forthright women! I'm very fond of most of them. But, oh, the hoo-ha there'd have been if in fact I had told them!"

"Maybe so. But at the risk of sounding boring I still feel you should have. You'd never heard of me until today. For all you knew, I could have been a white-slave trafficker. White-slave traffickers don't *always* come clean about their particular line of business – or, at any rate, not on the backs of postcards. You may be a little too trusting?"

The strange thing was: that although I'd guessed she wouldn't mention it, part of me had still hoped I was wrong. Why? *I* knew I wasn't a white-slave trafficker.

"Oh, I don't know," she said. "It's not like being a child and accepting sweets from a stranger."

"Isn't it? Why not?"

She pulled a face. "And, apart from which, the girls will all be getting onto the coach at any minute now. Off on their way to Blackpool. So there'd be nobody left to worry about me by the time I got back. Or didn't get back, as the case may be. Does that make sense?"

"I'm not sure. Let's have another drink, to help us decide."

I returned with our replacements.

"Something I was wondering about just now: how is it that you're getting time off? It hadn't occurred to me you'd all have understudies."

"Oh, no. We don't. Not in the regular way. What we do have is a stage manager who stands in for us whenever anyone gets ill or goes on leave."

"Good grief! She must have the most incredible memory! I mean, thinking of the length of some of those parts..."

"She has. But she'd rather be Mrs Pembroke – even if she *does* have to grey up and remember twenty times as many lines – than stand about in her bra and panties doubling as one of the mannequins."

"Not to mention doubling as *two* of the mannequins?"

Sybella smiled. She explained how in the event of more than one of the cast being sick at the same time – and if the women couldn't juggle things amongst themselves, "because none of the parts is really *that* large!" – then ENSA had what they called a Lease-Lend department: a pool of unattached artistes who could be sent anywhere as substitutes, either at home or abroad, generally very willing and able substitutes.

"So, you see, I really don't have to worry," she said. "Nor do you, Mr Redgrave. There is often chaos at headquarters, but somehow – finally – we always manage to pull through."

"Well, Miss Standish, you'll never guess how immensely reassuring I find that small piece of information!" I allowed a little time to go by. "So – if you don't mind my asking – how do you plan to be spending your few days off?"

89

"Oh, I shall be heading back to London. I share a flat there."

"You aren't going home, then?"

It was out before I realized. Not so important this time, but even so. I should really have to watch it.

"Home?"

"Sorry. I just assume that everyone has parents. Everyone, that is, of more or less *our* ages."

"Yes, well, that's true, I suppose. I do have parents and I love them dearly. All the same, this time it suits me better to return to London. Do you have parents, Mr Redgrave?"

"No, unhappily. They're dead. Both of them." And I apologized to my father even as I said it.

But before she had time to express any sympathy I hurried on. "I do have grandparents, however. They live near Shrewsbury. And at least you couldn't find a nicer pair of proxies...not if you were to go searching for a hundred years or more."

"That's wonderful," she said. Then – after a pause – "I've never been to Shrewsbury."

"It's a nice place. I'm always happy there. Where does your own family live?"

I knew, of course; and I supposed she must have had some pretty special reason for choosing London over Marlborough – and all the more so during this present spell of fine weather – since Marlborough itself wasn't actually that far from Aldershot.

My comment, however, was only indirect.

"Have your parents come to see the play yet?"

"My parents? Oh, not simply my parents! My sister. My granny. A multitude of uncles, aunts and cousins." She laughed. "In fact, my mother's seen it so many times *she* could be employed as my understudy – I think I must suggest it to Lease-Lend. Mr Redgrave? May I ask you something personal?"

"Like why aren't I in uniform?"

"Mmm."

"Two reasons. Asthma and a perforated eardrum. Neither of which is very serious. I'm hoping that the medical board will shortly change its mind; decide to take me in."

"Ah."

"But since we're talking about taking people in..."

I paused. We looked at one another. Her look was understandably expectant.

I grinned.

"Only, Miss Standish, I think it's now the moment to take you into the dining room. I hope you're feeling hungry? Remember – you had no time for any breakfast."

17

Indeed, we were both feeling hungry.

Yet our appetites in no way interfered with our conversation.

To begin with, we talked mainly about *Laura*. Then we discussed films in general, and what experience she had so far picked up in the theatre. She asked me to use her first name; I naturally did the same. We spoke of our families. She hesitantly enquired how my parents had died. I dispatched my father in a car crash – back in 1938, before our falling out over *Kristallnacht* – but, outside of anything to do with place-names or the film world, this was the only time I actually needed to lie. She very gently pursued the question...and my mother? I told her that my mother, who had been a VAD when she'd nursed my father back to health in England during the last war (and who had married him quietly at the beginning of 1919, also in England, with a boy of some thirteen months wriggling in her arms), that my mother had then, so ironically, had to struggle for more than eight years in order to become pregnant again – whereupon, to compound the irony, she had finally died in childbirth...leaving her nearly ten-year-old son desperately stupefied and missing her forever.

The single thing I omitted was any emphasis on setting; Sybella would have taken the setting of my early life for granted. I didn't believe I was being disloyal in speaking candidly about my parents' first union (and certainly I didn't feel in any way embarrassed or ashamed) but evidently I couldn't have sounded quite so matter-of-fact as I'd intended; I saw the tears well up in her eyes. We were by then drinking our ersatz black coffee, after what had otherwise been a remarkably good meal, and I had to look around the pub's emptying dining room with an air of immense diligence. Instinctively, it seemed, she laid her hand on mine, in mute commiseration, but an instant later appeared to realize what she'd done, and awkwardly drew back. I, too, felt awkward.

"So what would you say if I settled up now and we went out in the sun for a bit?" I was aware that my question had sounded stilted and abrupt.

For the most part we got our sunshine in the park. A mum and her two sons were flying a garishly-coloured kite. We watched for a while: the way that the kite strained, the expressions of excitement on the boys' faces. The older one was probably about seven; you could see his pride and his absorption in the whole of the shared experience. I remarked unthinkingly, "It must be marvellous having a brother," then hoped that I hadn't sounded pathetic – I had mentioned earlier that my mother's stillborn child had been a male. Luckily, she didn't reply.

We wandered on. There were several dogs being exercised, and a couple of makeshift games of football; but a key element to a normal family Sunday in the park was missing: the participation of fathers. This made things look surprisingly unbalanced despite the fact that with Aldershot being a garrison town we frequently saw pairs of soldiers, or else small groups of them – obviously perspiring on account of their uniforms. But I still felt obtrusive…me in my grey flannel suit. Even if I didn't see them (and I assuredly wasn't on the watch) I imagined I might be getting many of what my grandmother used to refer to as speaking glances; and particularly getting them from women of about my grandmother's own age.

"At any minute," I told Sybella, "I feel that someone's going to thrust a white feather into my hand!"

She had been strolling beside me in a reverie.

"Just let them try!"

But then she rather spoilt that fine spontaneous cry of indignation by mumbling lamely that in any case it could easily be herself to whom the feather would be given. "Do you remember all that fuss about Faith Brook?" she asked.

"No, I don't think so. Remind me."

"It was while she was playing at Bristol in *Aren't Men Beasts?* There were headlines like, 'Why hasn't she joined up? This woman ought to be fighting for her country!'"

Suddenly, she sounded angry.

"And, believe it or not, the matter was even raised in Parliament! Although, as it turned out, she had already applied to ENSA. Aren't *people* beasts?"

"Yes, I remember now. I'm not sure what happened."

Almost, her anger seemed to transfer itself to me. It very nearly sounded, I thought, as if she had recognized my lie.

"What happened? I'll tell you what happened. Before you could say Jack Robinson – or in this case Robertson Hare – she was bundled into the ATS! I hope you haven't *also* forgotten who Robertson Hare is?"

"No, of course not."

I felt sure that it was in her mind to call my bluff. But at the last moment she restrained herself, presumably took pity on me. Shame. I would undoubtedly have followed my hunch and said he was an actor – was it possible I could ever have heard my grandparents discussing him? – and even that he had been Miss Brook's co-star in Bristol. (Naturally I found it extremely galling when later enquiries revealed I'd have been right!)

"But at least the story has a happy ending," Sybella observed. "She was afterwards transferred to Stars in Battledress, which is pretty similar to ENSA." Her tone had softened a little.

"Anyway. Thank you for offering to spring to my defence if some old biddy *should* come bobbing and weaving at me, wielding a white feather."

"I spoke without thinking," she said. Her tone hadn't softened *that* much.

But she added after a few seconds, "I mean, I consider you fully large enough to deal with such a thing on your own."

"You recommend I sock 'em on the jaw?"

Yet it was puzzling. No smile – not even a glimmer. I wondered if I might have said or done something to offend her.

But then I remembered. What *was* the matter with me? Why did I keep on forgetting how recently she had lost the man she had become engaged to? Her anger at life clearly had to be channelled somewhere. And for the moment it was I who was handy.

"All the same, Sybella, it was instinctive and I still value it, even if you've now decided to retract."

"Why did you come to Aldershot?" she asked, sharply.

Just like that. Without preamble.

Admittedly, I got the feeling that as soon as she had spoken she might have wished she hadn't.

"Oh, well," I said. "It was on account of a cousin being transferred to the barracks here. He wasn't looking forward to it and I thought that if I turned up unexpectedly it might give him a bit of a lift. But I got the dates wrong; it's next week he arrives!"

Even if it were justified I should never have been happy to award myself such credit. I hoped she wouldn't comment.

And she didn't. She didn't say anything. Not for a while. But shortly she appeared to rally. I admired her for this; admired her enormously. If I myself had lost somebody I was in love with, I believed it might have taken me weeks to recover, weeks, even months. To recover just the ability to cope; just the ability to get dully through the days. And yet here was she, maybe up and down a little, yes, but really doing her utmost to be brave – to be brave and to be buoyant. I found it very humbling.

We left the park and visited the Prince Consort's Army Library. This contained a large assortment of military books and maps and models. We also looked in at the Royal Army Dental Corps Museum. But after seeing the tooth-key allegedly used to extract the molars of Napoleon we decided that perhaps we felt a mite too squeamish to remain. A mustachioed attendant – almost certainly a retired military man himself – told us that soldiers had once required exceptionally strong teeth in order to make ready their muskets.

"Having to bite right through *them*, don't you see?" He was pointing out the paper cartridges and tapping insistently against the glass case.

"Pretty bad luck," I said, "for those whose gums weren't up to it?"

"Quite right, young man. Quite right. Which of course illustrates one of the many links still existing between dentistry and the Army."

"*Still?*" I exclaimed.

Outside again – I didn't know how it happened, it shouldn't have happened, either in Sybella's situation or my own – we succumbed to a fit of the giggles. Not because of anything truly funny: only because of the attendant's Lord Kitchener moustache and military bearing and the parade-ground satisfaction with which he had articulated, "Quite right, young man. Quite right."

I thought my own impersonation passed muster but he'd have been an easy man for anyone to imitate. We both added increasingly unlikely scraps of dialogue, plus an adoring wife and goggle-eyed daughter (Happy Families: Colonel and Mrs and Miss Honoria Musket), and by the time we stumbled out of Evelyn Woods Road our giggles were recurrent. Our only possible hope, we reiterated firmly, lay in a pot of really good strong tea.

Or even in just the thought of one – for by the time we eventually arrived at Daphne's (or arrived *back*, in my own case) we were behaving a little more like adults.

The manageress welcomed me as if I were a favourite customer; and as this morning I had drunk not merely one, not merely two, but *three* cups of her definitely odd-tasting coffee, perhaps I was.

"No, please don't try to be amusing," cautioned Sybella, when I quietly mentioned this. "To be amused right now is not what I require."

To me there was an ambiguity here which I found instantly sobering, although I was well aware it hadn't been intended. While we waited to be served I asked at what time her train left.

"Or aren't you going by train? Or aren't you going tonight?"

"Oh, yes, by train," she said. "But I was thinking I mightn't travel now until the morning. Stay on at the barracks. Nobody minds."

"In other words – because of me – you've lost a full day of your leave?"

"That isn't quite how *I'd* have put it. I'd have said that – because of you – my leave began a little earlier than anticipated."

"That's kind," I said.

"Not at all."

I had to steel myself.

"Nevertheless, I feel I ought to try to make it up to you. You see, I have a troublesome conscience. And – perhaps what matters more – I also have two theatre tickets for tomorrow night."

I barely paused.

I tried to keep my tone as casual as I could.

"It's for something called *Strike A New Note*. George Black's *Strike A New Note*. It's playing at the Prince of Wales."

18

She hesitated.

I knew, of course, why she hesitated.

Should she say she had already seen it – or should she lie, in order not to spoil my pleasure?

"I'd love to go with you," she said.

"You hesitated."

She laughed. "A girl should never sound too eager."

I answered rather slowly.

"I thought you might have seen it?"

She sighed. There was a pause.

"I have. You're remarkably astute. Or else I'm just a rotten actress. But perhaps I shouldn't be saying that – not to you, of all people?" She nodded towards her handbag. *Laura* was in her handbag.

God, I felt so tempted to scotch that silly story – right here and now – and simply see what came of it. Obviously I couldn't.

Yet I told myself I would. Somehow. Before I left England.

Giving me just three days! *Less* than three whole days!

"I'd truly be as happy to settle for something else, Sybella. Please. Tell me the name of whatever you'd like to see."

"*Strike A New Note*," she answered, firmly.

Now it was I who hesitated. "Are you sure?"

"Positive. I really like Sid Field."

"Me, too."

I went on quickly – fearing she'd ask what I had seen him in. "Whom did you go with?" I said.

"A friend."

But her tone made it clear she didn't wish to add to this.

"I'm sorry. Why should I even assume you went with anyone?"

"Fairly natural. Not many women go to the theatre alone these days. Or maybe ever did."

"Was it long ago you saw it?"

"No."

"I suppose your stage manager had to double up on *that* occasion, too?" My smile was meant to suggest jokiness.

"Our ASM," she corrected me. "*Assistant* stage manager."

At least I had the common sense to let it drop. A moment afterwards, in any case, the waitress brought our tea.

"Look," Sybella said, when the woman had departed with her tray, "maybe this isn't such a very good idea."

"What isn't?"

"The theatre. Our meeting when we get to town."

I had to be careful to conceal my disappointment. "All right. If that's the way you feel. I do understand."

"Do you?"

For about ten seconds she appeared to concentrate on stirring the contents of the pot.

"Exactly what, Oliver, do you understand?"

"Well – naturally – that you feel your boyfriend wouldn't like it."

"Boyfriend?"

"Yes, don't you have one? I'm sure you must have."

She poured our tea. I cut my toasted bun in half. Waited for her to start on hers.

"No, actually," she said, "I don't have any boyfriend." There was a further pause, while she replenished the teapot with hot water. "Not any more," she said.

"But this fellow who took you to the Prince of Wales?" I sensed it was all right now to help her out, so long as I was gentle.

"Or again," I added, "perhaps I'm only jumping to conclusions?"

She shook her head.

"No. The thing is, however…"

I heard the tremor in her voice. I waited, feeling uncomfortable – uncomfortable for myself, *unhappy* for her. I stared down at the tablecloth, at the Shippam's paste jar with its little bunch of daisies.

"The thing is…," she repeated.

And then she managed to say it. "That fellow you talk about is dead."

I had been dreading this moment: doubting my ability to appear natural. But when I looked up again, just the stricken quality of her expression dispelled my self-consciousness.

"Oh God, I am sorry." And this time it was my hand that reached out to touch hers. "I am so *very* sorry."

She said, "Please don't. I'd rather not. Let's talk about something else."

"Yes, of course."

I withdrew my hand. I wanted to respect her wishes, I truly did. And the present atmosphere of chattering activity and cheerfulness, with people all about us tucking into their toasted buns or scones or thinly iced fairy cakes, only served to confirm my inclination. Very clearly, that atmosphere stated, these were not the right surroundings in which to be speaking of bereavement.

Yet – against this – if she really thought it better not to see me in London, I decided that I absolutely had to remain focused. There was simply nothing else for it. Being too scrupulous over the niceties was a luxury that no one in my position could afford. I said: "You must have loved him very much."

And immediately despised myself for having said it – partly because it was such a cliché, a line I must have heard in upwards of a dozen movies, and partly because, at such a moment as this, I should actually be thinking about its being a cliché.

But it had come to mind before anything else; no – almost shockingly – in *place* of anything else. *You must have loved him very much.*

"Yes," she said. "Yes, I did."

Silence.

She added: "And he was going to be my husband."

Maybe only a minor amplification. But definitely a major sign of hope.

"I'm sorry, Oliver. I honestly didn't mean to spring it on you like that. About his being dead. About his being my fiancé."

"You didn't spring anything."

"Because I'm not normally the type who discloses things which… Things which…"

"Hurt?"

"Yes. I'm not normally the type who discloses things which…hurt. I think that somehow you must bring it out in me."

"Good," I said.

"Good?"

"Yes – nowadays, the psychologists lay great stress on the dangers of our bottling up emotions."

"Do they?"

"You must know that they do." I briefly touched her hand again. "So what was his name?"

"Why?" she asked.

"No particular reason. I'm only aiming to help out the psychologists."

"Bill Martin," she said. "*Major* Bill Martin. Of the Royal Marines. They tell me he died a fortnight ago yesterday. Dear God! Only two days after we had been to see *Strike A New Note*!"

I said: "I can't imagine how you carry on. To get up in the morning – brush your teeth – walk out on stage. Make conversation. You've got more courage than *I* would ever have." It was merely a repetition of what I'd been thinking in the park.

"Huh!" she exclaimed. "Courage, you call it? Only look at me now!"

Her eyes had begun to water again. Inevitably, mine did, as well.

"I *am* looking. Tremendous courage."

"Don't," she repeated. "Please don't. We *must* talk of something else! It's only because… Well, of all the things on the London stage at the moment, you just happened to pick out the very show which…"

"I know," I said. "I know. It was cruel."

I wondered whether – if I'd kept my mouth shut – this might have rendered me less of a hypocrite.

Yet, on the other hand, fate *was* cruel. Even without my own connivance.

Was it really such hypocrisy?

I said, "I remember how my father was, after my mother died. Dear Lord, I don't need to remember how *he* was. I remember how *I* was."

She gazed at me, momentarily, with all the compassion I'd been directing towards her.

"One slight difference, though. You were just a boy."

"Sometimes boys are more resilient."

We had started on our teacakes. But Sybella was doing scarcely more than play with hers.

"In any case," she said, "*I* wouldn't call it courage. Carrying on with your job is possibly the best way – the *only* way – that someone can survive. When I'm on stage, you see, I actually a*lmost* forget."

She had now cut her bun into quarters. She seemed to be thinking of making still further divisions.

"Except, of course, it all comes back. And then I sometimes wish it hadn't gone away – well, partly gone away. But that's ungrateful. In the end I'm sure it will prove beneficial. And everyone's been wonderful; wonderful. Even a total stranger like yourself…"

I looked down at my plate; stabbed a few crumbs with my forefinger. I would have liked to say, I don't feel like a total stranger, please don't see me as such, but then it appeared she even felt some need to underline her assertion – as if actually meaning to remind herself of something. "A total stranger," she repeated.

She had said it very quietly, whilst gazing at the chequered blue tablecloth. And it then occurred to me she could possibly have guessed my thoughts; was wanting to emphasize, as kindly as she could, the utter foolishness which lay behind them.

The foolishness of feeling wistful about any future that could possibly connect the two of us.

Any future, that was, beyond Wednesday.

She looked up.

"And talking of forgetting," she said – and this was now in her more normal tone, one pitched again at conversation – "I can hardly believe that it was me who was giggling so imbecilically when we left the museum… "

"Oh, but – good heavens – you weren't alone in that!"

" …even if I do think now it may have been a little closer to hysteria than to genuine amusement. Which isn't to say," she added tactfully, "that your take-off wasn't amusing. It just wasn't all *that* amusing. Was it?"

I said: "What nonsense! Of course it was all that amusing."

She may have been caught slightly by surprise. At any rate, she laughed. Not simply out of politeness; her laughter was spontaneous.

"And please don't tell me that *that* was closer to hysteria, also?"

.   "No, I won't," she said. "You're right. I suppose that, little by little, the darkness really may be lifting."

She still seemed puzzled, though.

"But – do you know – in a way I don't even want it to. I don't want to start forgetting him…not if that's what it would mean to have the darkness disappear."

"No, you're not going to forget him – of course not – not ever! Yet there are bound to be some days easier to get through than others. And I'm only glad if today may have proved to be one of the easier ones."

Yet I had a reservation…and she quickly realized it.

"Something's struck you! What is it?"

I thought she sounded anxious but even so I paused.

Afterwards, I was aware, I might regret saying this. But at the same time it was a concern I felt I had to express.

"You've told me how it helps to be on stage. Therefore I'm worried that if you take a few days off – "

She had relaxed. Relaxed to the extent that inadvertently she now broke in on what I was saying.

"Do you know – you're very nice. You really are very nice!"

"Am I?"

"Yes!"

"Thank you. So are you."

"I'm sorry if I sounded surprised."

I laughed. "Even vaguely defiant?"

"Oh dear, did I sound defiant? The truth is: I may have felt slightly prejudiced. I suppose I thought anyone who worked in the film industry – on the business side of it, I mean – might turn out to be a bit of a hotshot."

"If that means successful or important – oh, I've never been one of those!"

She may have thought I was angling for compliments. I went on hurriedly, "Believe me, I don't care how surprised or defiant you sounded."

"If it helps at all, I knew right from the start you *weren't* some Hollywood hotshot."

"Nor even an Elstree one? Well, I'll happily give up all thoughts of being a hotshot anywhere – if that still means you think I'm nice."

Suddenly, however, I felt unsure of how to continue. Therefore, as if running back to it for refuge, I returned to the question she had so gratifyingly interrupted – whether or not, at present, she should be going on leave.

She considered it for a moment. "I believe I really do need to take time off," she said at last.

"Yet nevertheless…"

But this was no longer a case of my being wayward. I had realized by now that she would surely have thought about these things – probably been given lots of counsel on them.

"I mean, will your flatmates be able to spend much time with you – presumably they both work? Will they have the chance to be quite so supportive? Diverting? Just two women as opposed to…" I shrugged. "Well, upwards of a dozen."

"I'm not too sure at the moment I even want to have diversion… Does that sound ungrateful?"

"No. I can appreciate that, too."

"You see, perhaps what I really need to do is to look back. To look back and relive."

"To mourn Bill properly?"

"Yes."

"All right," I agreed.

We were silent for a short while.

"And I truly don't mean to put pressure on you. But don't you believe, in that case, that coming to the Prince of Wales might actually start to fulfil those functions?"

"It might."

And it was now with a feeling of suspense that I waited for her fully to make up her mind.

"If you thought that you could stand it?" she said.

Having answered that I *thought* I probably could, I dabbed my finger once more amongst the crumbs – the crumbs, this time, of what the menu described as Daphne's Iced Dainties. Sybella emptied our tealeaves into the slop basin, whilst complaining, not very forcibly, about the uselessness of the strainer; then poured us each a second cup.

As I watched this very ordinary, domesticated, almost intimate activity, I wondered if anyone had noticed us at all, noticed in the sense of speculated upon us in any way (oh, the arrogance of that, when up to now I hadn't even particularly noticed the people at the next table!) and, if so, whether they might actually have seen us as a couple. Not as a husband and wife, of course, she hadn't any ring on, but certainly as more than just a brother and a sister.

I felt absurdly proud to think that we might, in fact, all unwittingly be looking like a couple.

Well, perhaps all unwittingly wasn't – I mean, not in my own case…

Oh, God!

How could it have escaped my attention?

She hadn't any ring on.

19

"Dearest Bill, I'm so thrilled with my ring – scandalously extravagant – you know how I adore diamonds – I simply can't stop looking at it…"

And I hadn't even thought about it! That was what mattered. In itself, maybe, it wasn't too important: the absence of a ring which she had no doubt stopped wearing as soon as she'd heard about Bill Martin's death. I guessed that in Sybella's position some women kept on their engagement ring, some didn't. It could be as simple as that. But all the same, it seemed unforgivable that I hadn't even thought about it.

Yet this was now the least of it.

This was now the *very* least of it. Since – almost immediately – the discovery of one oddity had drawn attention to another.

"I'm so thrilled…scandalously extravagant…you know how I adore diamonds…"

Oh, for Pete's sake! It didn't even sound like Sybella.

"Your letter made me feel slightly better (you do write such heavenly ones) but I shall get horribly conceited if you go on saying things like that about me – they're utterly unlike ME, as I'm afraid you'll soon find out. Here I am for the weekend in this divine place with Mummy & Jane both being too sweet & understanding the whole time, bored beyond words & panting for Monday so that I can get back to my crowd of silly females, not always *that* sweet & not always *that* understanding. What an idiotic waste!…"

I remembered it word for word – although admittedly I had mentally interpolated a sentence from her second letter. She handed me my teacup and I could hardly take my eyes off her.

"Why are you staring? Have I a smudge on my face? Has my lipstick smeared?"

"No, of course not. Was I staring?"

She nodded.

105

"Well, then – I don't know – perhaps I *could* have been thinking about its being a nice face, an honest face. A poet might even call it pretty."

"If the poet were in his cups, you mean, and getting impossibly carried away?"

"Something like that."

Heavenly? Divine?

And not simply the phraseology now appeared false; even her actual sentiments. That crowd of silly females who weren't always *that* sweet or *that* understanding was presumably the same crowd about whom she had said before lunch, "I'm very fond of most of them," and also, more recently, "And everyone's been wonderful; wonderful."

Plus, she didn't even strike me as the sort of woman who would care a great deal about diamonds. Although how on earth could I be any judge of that, merely because the frock she was wearing this afternoon happened to be a simple one and seemed so very much her style?

But then, of course, a woman could have more than just one style. What about in the evenings, say, when she might be dressed in a floor-length gown and have her hair piled high to show off pretty earrings and have on a sparkly necklace, or a bracelet, or a brooch? What about in London, say, rather than in Hampshire or in Wiltshire? (And it suddenly occurred to me – not that it mattered, probably – *where* exactly would that 'rather dreary dance with Jock & Hazel' have taken place?)

Yet anyway, irrespective of location, would a dancing Sybella have metamorphosed into the kind of person who 'adored' diamonds? How could I possibly tell?

However, if Bill Martin had bought her a diamond engagement ring, it could only have been because he knew her taste, had taken pains to find out what type of stone was really going to please her. "You *know* how I adore diamonds…" Even in the unlikely event that he had got it wrong – indeed, had chosen the ring which best pleased himself, not her – she would still have wanted to convey her gratitude convincingly. And, okay, maybe in the process she *had* come across as sounding a little precious; but in view of the specialness of the occasion wasn't that allowable? She might have thought she was sounding appreciative rather than affected.

Or was there another possibility? Did a woman happy and in love perhaps express herself differently from one who had recently suffered an enormous loss? When you were grieving, did *heavenly* and *divine* and *beastly* – yes, even *beastly* – virtually disappear?

Alternatively... Did people sometimes use a separate set of words on paper to the ones they used in conversation? Whether they were happy or not? Whether they were in love or not?

Unanswerable questions – for the moment – that also had to be filed.

And besides, now that I was thinking along such lines, such deeply distrustful lines (admittedly a bit late in the day, but at least not *too* late in the day, thank God), there was still another point to be considered. Again, how could I have missed it?

Lease-Lend.

ENSA's Lease-Lend department must have been kept extraordinarily busy on Sybella's behalf.

"A train going out can leave a howling great gap in ones life & one has to try madly – & quite in vain – to fill it with all the things one used to enjoy a whole five weeks ago..."

Which suggested – surely? – that she and Bill Martin had spent a period of five full weeks together; and that she at least had been away from work throughout it.

More than suggested. Practically stated.

So the question then emerged: would Lease-Lend have been likely to show itself so accommodating even for the sake of Major Bill Martin? Who, publicly, was not a figure of importance. He was certainly somebody who had been one of Mountbatten's officers; who had enjoyed his chief's 'entire confidence' and who had 'really known his stuff'; somebody possessing a brilliant future, yes; but not somebody as yet eligible to pull strings – in this case ENSA's strings – solely to make life easier and more pleasant for himself and his fiancée.

Though come to that, of course, she *wasn't* his fiancée. Hadn't become such, I still maintained, until the 14th of April. So would Sybella at that stage even have notified ENSA about the existence of Major William Martin? Remembering how cagey she had been about him generally.

Which led me to a further thought – tangential, maybe, but soon to regain prominence. How long until Sybella next saw her flatmate? I tried to remember what I had actually said to Lucy; I hadn't as clear a recall for the spoken word as for the written. I wanted to reassure myself there wasn't any real link between that man on the telephone and this talent scout for RKO. Wouldn't Sybella simply ascribe it to coincidence: the eruption into her life of two wholly unknown males: one on the Friday, one on the Saturday-stroke-Sunday? Of course she wouldn't ever hear again from the earlier of the two, the chap who had known, or had known of, Bill Martin; who had passed on the news of her engagement.

But anyway. Erich Anders would have left London well before she began to ponder the true strangeness of it. Both the man who knew too much and the man who apparently knew nothing would have quit the scene for good. Leaving the one thing that did of course betray a link. *Aldershot*, Lucy had said. She's going to be in Aldershot.

However… Figuratively, I gave a shrug. Even if Sybella did eventually put two and two together, what would it matter? By then I'd already have told her – so long as I honoured my vow, as I intended – that *Laura* was a scam; that I had seen the play on Saturday night, become captivated by her, could think of no other way in which to engineer a meeting. In other words, I should have left her to infer I was unprincipled, only one step removed, perhaps, from that white-slave trafficker of whom I'd spoken. (But simultaneously I should have persuaded her she had nothing whatever to fear from me: persuaded her I was about to vanish out of her life forever.) And if afterwards she started to suspect that things hadn't been quite as above board as even *that* sleazy confession had sought to make them sound…well, yes, again…so what? By that time, I should not

108

only have left London; I should have arrived back in Berlin and have made out my report – a report, of course, counselling nothing but the greatest caution.

And by that time, too, the German High Command would have ratified my implicit recommendation. Word would have gone out ordering the immediate consolidation of all defences on Sicily. The bulk of our manpower in the western Mediterranean would *not* have been lured off to faraway Sardinia.

For how could anyone deny the obvious? It made *sense* – far better sense – that the Allies should attempt to get into Italy via Sicily. (And surely no element of surprise, sir, could ever compensate for that.) Sardinia had been a bluff; it had to be. Sir Archibald Nye had been misleading us. Lord Louis Mountbatten had been misleading us. And sadly – but incontestably – Miss Sybella Standish was simply the latest in a long line of deceivers.

An actress – and not only on the stage. An actress at The Tap and Tankard and in Manor Park and at the museum and right here, as well, at Daphne's. An accomplished actress, and putting her training to sound practical use.

But to what end? To what conceivable end?

And if all of this was just a performance, why was it being put on for *my* benefit? What in God's name had I done to alert anyone to the fact that I needed to be duped?

Although whatever it was I had done…this was almost irrelevant. 'Duped' itself was what counted. If for any reason, any reason at all, I was needing to be duped – why, then, I could return to Germany tonight (or, at least, as soon as such could be arranged), secure in the knowledge that my mission was complete: Sardinia was most definitely a bluff.

But…return to Germany and say what?

That Lease-Lend had been too kind to her? That her letters had not been written by herself? That she hadn't been wearing her diamond ring?

And furthermore: that her flatmate hadn't previously heard of Major William Martin? That William's father had never stayed at the Black Lion in Mold? But that he'd apparently been working on a settlement for his son's marriage (following some negative feedback from Sybella's own family) about a week before the major had even got round to popping the question?

For me, all of this would have been more than enough to destroy our credence in those letters from the sea. Destroy it totally. But, of course, the evidence was purely circumstantial. Could I be certain that others would regard it in the same light?

Added to which, few of my colleagues understood the nuances of English as well as I did. I might say: "She just wasn't the type to use 'madly' or 'divine' or 'too sweet'." Yet how much weight was this going to carry when thousands of lives and millions of Deutschmarks and the whole future of The Third Reich might actually depend on it? Even to my own ears it didn't sound convincing. (Assuredly not so, in fact, when I tried to imagine myself having to say it aloud. And Mannheim – although he might be scared of English prepositions betraying a *German* – would inevitably require more than English adverbs and adjectives to betray a native-born Englishwoman.) So what then? It was clearly my job and my duty to provide ballast.

And also my resolve. It had become essential to show that I was someone who could indeed shovel ballast. To show that I was now someone to be taken seriously; those words of Heinrich Buchholz had been difficult to shake off. "Which is maybe why they sent an agent so relatively young and inexperienced." And what was perhaps even harder to cope with: I was suddenly realizing that during the past few hours my approach to things had not been…well, let us just say…*unreservedly* professional.

Might even have been – well, let us just say again – slightly dilettantish.

Yet hell's bells! My superiors had certainly had enough time in which to study me. I couldn't still be that much of an unknown quantity. Over the years, they must surely have studied my weaknesses as well as my strengths.

110

So could it honestly have been the case – as Buchholz had basically been intimating – that almost from the start they had viewed the documents as genuine; had looked upon the dispatch of an agent into Britain merely in the light of a formality, an exercise? *Therefore why should we send of our best? Isn't the outcome practically guaranteed? And isn't it about time, too, that we made some little use of Erich Anders?*

Dear Lord! Was that the way it might have been? Was that what 'hand-picked by the Admiral' had finally come to stand for?

Then sod them! Sod them all! If the choice of myself had been little more than just a sympathy vote I would damn well prove I wasn't a man they could afford to patronize. I would damn well make them wake up in cold sweats in the middle of the night…only to think of what might have happened if they had sent somebody else. Or if they had not sent anyone at all.

Yes, all right. I could acknowledge it. Ever since meeting this woman I might have been behaving in a vaguely adolescent way. I might indeed have been allowing my personal feelings to get the better of my judgment. All afternoon perhaps (and why even try to hide it?) I might have been half-consciously aware of something being – what? – not *altogether* right.

And in that case might have been – yes, half-consciously – suppressing my unease? I really didn't know.

But what came to me suddenly and mercifully and with the full force of unexpected absolution…I really didn't need to know! It was *now* that mattered. And *now* – although this was paradoxically so hard to admit, more than hard, since it filled me with a feeling that was close to desolation – *now* the all-but-inadmissible truth was this: Sybella Standish was leading me up the garden path.

She was flagrantly deceiving me.

*

111

Your responsibility, Mannheim had said. I couldn't forget that. I now felt practically certain this whole thing was a hoax. But was that quite enough – 'practically'?

'*Your* responsibility' was what he had implied.

20

"Anyway… Now that I've finished staring…?"

She didn't answer. But she looked encouraging.

"I've begun to wonder about your attitude to dress rehearsals," I went on.

"Well, *naturally* you have."

"Are they essential?"

"Yes. I'd have said so. Definitely."

"Then taking that into consideration (for, of course, I trust you *implicitly*) – and as a dress rehearsal for the live theatre in London tomorrow – will you come with me to a *picture* theatre in Aldershot tonight?"

I eventually carried the day. Therefore, after I had paid my bill at the counter, I asked the manageress for information. She found me a copy of the previous Friday's *Aldershot News*.

Or, not to sell it short, the previous Friday's *Aldershot News and Military Gazette, Farnborough Chronicle and Fleet Times*.

"My word!" exclaimed Sybella, when – back at the table – I had proclaimed this to her in its full majesty. "You really get all that for just threepence?"

I turned directly to the entertainments page.

"At the Empire we can see Humphrey Bogart as *King of the Underworld* and Cesar Romero as *The Gay Caballero*."

"Right."

"At the Alexandra, *The Doctor Takes a Wife*, with Loretta Young. And *Jungle Man*, starring good old Buster Crabbe."

"Why good old Buster Crabbe but not good old Loretta Young?"

"I don't think *she* ever played Tarzan or Flash Gordon. Not to mention Buck Rogers."

"And as soon as she does, things will automatically even out? Fair enough. But are those the only two cinemas open on a Sunday?"

"No, not at all. No, at the Ritz – oh, yes, let's settle for the Ritz – Greer Garson! As Mrs Chips she absolutely stole my heart! And apparently *this* film happens to be The Most Memorable Of All Motion Picture Love Stories, Ever. Which must be true because it says so here. Therefore it seems we just can't afford to miss it."

Yet then I was suddenly mindful of dashed futures and drowned fiancés and wondered if I hadn't been appallingly tactless. I added hurriedly, "Oh, but no second feature. That's a bind."

"I should have thought it was a definite advantage, if our choice is only between jungle men and gay caballeros. But what's the picture at the Ritz? Whatever you do, please don't say it's *Random Harvest*!"

"Why, yes! How did you guess?"

She gave a groan.

"Oh, it isn't fair," she said. "First, you invite me to the last West End show I went to with Bill; and then – as if God feels the joke has to get funnier with repetition – you pick out the last film we saw together, too!"

But she quickly held up her hand, pre-empting my reaction.

"Don't worry, though. I think you'll find that during the past hour or so I have managed to gird up my loins, wonderfully."

"Oh God," I said, "the film as well! I had absolutely no idea."

"Not like you had before, of course, when bringing up the subject of the show?"

We both smiled a little.

"So," she said, "it will indeed be like a dress rehearsal. More than you imagined!"

"Oh, no, it won't," I said. "Not to that extent. We'll see *The Doctor Takes a Wife*. Or – here now – how about *The Perfect*

Crime…which they're showing at the Pavilion? We didn't get so far as that."

"We didn't get so far as that," she reminded me, "for one very good reason. We were stopped by Greer Garson. Greer Garson stole your heart. We must go to see Greer Garson."

"Oh, bugger Greer Garson," I exclaimed. "Let's both learn about the perfect crime! At some stage, that's something which might… "

I had been going to say come in handy. But now I suddenly heard the echo of my recent words. Previously, I hadn't blushed in years.

"Oh, forgive me! Please forgive me. I didn't mean that!"

She was smiling. It might have been the broadest smile I had seen from her all afternoon, apart from the hysteria. "I think Dr Freud might say you did – or, anyway, that you meant something very much like it. And it's rather sweet: you've gone all red. Although I know it isn't nice of me to point that out!"

"No, I deserve it."

"In that case I must take full advantage of your penitence. I should like to see *Random Harvest*, please. I should really like to see it."

She paused.

"And if I do start snivelling I promise you that it will be at nothing but the film. I tell you I've girt up my loins and this will be the perfect test."

We said goodbye to the manageress (in fact, the owner – she admitted to us shyly that she happened to be Daphne) and, after an unplanned but timely hour spent at evensong, sat in another café, in the café of the cinema itself, whilst awaiting the conclusion of the afternoon performance.

Over a glass of ginger beer Sybella showed herself still resolute; still keen to rise to the occasion.

"I'll tell you where we saw it," she said. "At the Empire Cinema in Leicester Square. If you've never been there, it boasts one of the most barnlike auditoriums you can possibly imagine. *Bill* hadn't been there and he bought tickets for the rear stalls. We had to move forward twice. He said that if people ever stayed at the back he hoped they'd be given binoculars for gazing at the stars."

I decided I could risk it. "Sounds as though *his* jokes weren't any better than mine."

"Perhaps that's why I feel so much at home with you. Before the cinema we had dinner at *l'Ecu de France* in Jermyn Street and it was all very jolly because we started off with double champagne cocktails."

Her compliment hadn't gone unnoticed. Nor had her phrase, 'all very jolly'. Was that, perhaps, coming just a degree closer to the style of those letters?

"It really surprises me," I said, "that you can still get champagne cocktails."

"On that particular evening we could."

"So I'll tell you what strikes me now: is it any wonder you should need to see this film again? If champagne is what you started off with, you probably found the whole storyline more than a little confusing. Boy meets girl you could possibly have coped with. Boy loses girl was beginning to get tricky. Boy finds girl again... Well, I don't know, I imagine by then you were both getting desperately out of your depth. Might have done better just to stay at the back and rest your legs. Are you honestly sure you want to do this?"

"Do what?"

"Go through it all again."

"You're meant to be helping me, you know. You volunteered."

"Okay," I said. "Merely checking."

"Very well, then." Her manner was bright but might have seemed a shade relentless. "Like I say, it was all very jolly – or should have been very jolly – except that the next day he was going off to Scotland and I didn't know how long he'd be away; *he* didn't know how long he'd be away; and I was already beginning to miss him and feel homesick. Well, obviously I was."

"Homesick?"

115

"Yes. That's the form my missing him always took. I was reduced to being a baby."

Now her voice did falter.

"Of course, at the time, I didn't know even the first thing about missing him!"

She unclasped her bag and fumbled through it for a hankie. I had seen her fumbling for one last night – although, admittedly, *that* had been in an overall pocket and not in a handbag. But something about her expression must have reminded me. So now it was I who might have seemed a shade relentless: annoyed that I could have forgotten, for so much as a single minute, that this was a performance, a charade: the catch in her voice, the handkerchief, the whole damned lot… And she had asked me emphatically – asked me more than once, hadn't she? – to put her to the test.

"So when was this, then? Your double champagne cocktails? His going up to Scotland?"

But by this time she was dabbing at her eyes – doing so with a rueful, even a half-humorous air of apology. And I found myself thinking that I must be wrong. This could *not* be a performance. This could *not* be a charade. What kind of a hardened brute was I, to allow myself to go on doubting her love for him?

And abruptly – trying to make out that I hadn't even noticed her distress – I glanced at my watch and stood up.

"I think you should be finishing your drink. The programme's about to end at any moment."

I walked across and gazed through the glass porthole in one of the dividing doors – myself being gazed at by the adenoidal waitress whose starched white circle sat precariously on a mass of woolly chestnut hair and whose expression seemed gently protective.

"You'll know when it's over," she explained kindly, "when they all start coming out."

I thanked her with a smile and only five seconds later – as if her statement had been the trigger – the shuffling exodus began. As the last of the audience leisurely emerged we went in and took our seats…far earlier than we should have done, as it turned out, since no one had yet arrived to let us through. An usherette was waving around a flit gun – wafting misty clouds of disinfectant onto the fuggy, tobacco-laden air – but simultaneously carrying on a desultory conversation with her male counterpart downstairs who was performing the same service for the one-and-ninepennies and whom she twice addressed as Grandpa. Her spraying done, however, she went to take up her position in the doorway; but not before she'd made a reluctant detour to tear in half our own wickedly pristine tickets and to tell us off.

We had something of a wait until 7.50…the advertised start of the performance; *much* later – as Sybella now pointed out in mild mystification – than the beginning of tomorrow night's show in London. At first we had thought we were going to be the sole occupants of the dress circle and we boasted to each other of how grand we were. But during the last few minutes the place filled up surprisingly fast; and we actually had to admit to feeling pleased about this.

21

The programme started with a Pathé newsreel.

This showed us the calling-off of the coal strike in Washington, just minutes before Roosevelt would have signed an order to seize the mines. Next, we saw General Sikorski broadcasting from London to his people at home, warning them that they must remain friendly to the USSR. Then – appropriately – we had some footage of Stalin himself, in Moscow, stating his desire for a strong free Poland after the war.

Although I'd been fearing that I might have to watch the Allies entering Tunis and have to witness the rapturous acclaim of the Tunisians – watch the Allies, too, going into Bizerte – I now experienced a twinge of disappointment on realizing that all of this was obviously too recent for the ABC in Aldershot.

Likewise, of course, the Germans declaring martial law amongst the Dutch in anticipation of an Allied invasion. Yet at the necessary exclusion of *that* I felt nothing but a frankly recognized – if slightly disturbing – sense of relief.

The news ended with something more lightweight. Its final segment showed fresh batches of US troops arriving in Suffolk and dispensing chewing gum and toothy smiles. It contained an interview with a group of countrywomen who declared that the Americans would all be made warmly welcome and that, no, they had never yet seen any coloured men – other than at the pictures – but, yes, they would now be looking forward to meeting some.

However, it still wasn't time for the feature. First came a Fitzpatrick Traveltalk – "and now as the sun goes down and we reluctantly take our leave of beautiful Buenos Aires…"; and then a trailer for the following Sunday's seven-day offering, *Casablanca*, which, like every other English or American movie since the outbreak of war, I naturally hadn't been able to see. *Gone with the Wind* was also coming back. It occurred to me that this cinema must have a policy of reintroducing 'by popular demand' all of the biggest romantic money-makers of the previous few years.

Then the lights came up once more and the massive theatre organ arose out of the depths in stately style and provided brief selections from *Showboat* and *Me and My Girl*; the entire audience sang the lyric to 'The Lambeth Walk'. Afterwards, the startlingly raven-haired organist took his bow to both stalls and circle: "That was worrying," I whispered, but his sleek toupee, with its neat central parting, remained spiderlike in place. He and his sturdy spaceship then sank smoothly out of sight and the lights finally dimmed. The curtains swished apart (but not before the censor's certificate was already waveringly on screen) and at last it was time for Leo to roar and for *Random Harvest* to begin.

Well…!

What can one possibly say?

Random Harvest tells the story of an amnesiac army officer who – during the Armistice celebrations of 1918 – escapes from an asylum in the English Midlands, marries a music hall singer and is idyllically happy for about a year, living in a cottage with roses round the door. Then he writes an article and goes off to Liverpool to meet the newspaper man who has agreed to publish it. But, whilst there, he is knocked down by a motorcar. The shock of this rejigs his amnesia. He now recalls that he's the head of a noble family; yet he doesn't know his wife any longer, nor have the least remembrance of their marriage…not even when she re-enters his life to become his selfless secretary.

Years later, though, his parliamentary duties – for he is now a well-respected MP – take him back into that same area of the Midlands and he begins to recollect things subsequent to the Armistice…while, most fortunately, not again forgetting things *prior* to the Armistice. So he now rushes back to the cottage with roses round the door, which is happily still vacant and exactly as he and his secretary-wife had left it.

Even more happily, on a sudden sentimental whim, *she* has turned up at the cottage at the same time. So they meet by the garden gate (its hinges still squeaking) under branches still heavy with blossom.

There quickly follows instant recognition – reawakened love – re-impassioned clinch…and final fade.

All this, of course, was preposterous; and not simply that, it was shameless. Why didn't Miss Garson accompany Ronald Colman to Liverpool? Because the script provided her with a baby. What happened to the baby? That obliging little scrap, having served his purpose, then dutifully died, so that his mum could dedicate herself uniquely to the welfare of his dad. He must have got his notions of self-sacrifice from her.

However – for all its faults – the film was in its way quite splendid and you couldn't help but be drawn in; not even on a second viewing, to judge from the state of apparent absorption at my side. We left the cinema feeling uplifted. Uplifted and light-footed. I suddenly realized something: that from the moment we had walked unauthorized into that spray-swept auditorium, neither Sybella nor I had once mentioned the name of Bill Martin.

Nor had we mentioned *Laura*. I hadn't been forced either to intrude or to lie.

Added to which, the sky was a profusion of stars. On nights like this you could feel positively thankful for the blackout.

"God's in His heaven," I said, "all's right with the world!"

She nodded.

"And yet," I added, "Robert Browning never went to the movies. So how would he have known?"

"Beats me," she said.

We held hands and sauntered. I escorted her to the camp gates and there took back the jacket I had placed around her shoulders.

And somehow – as I did so – we found ourselves in an embrace.

22

I didn't get to sleep till after three. Therefore when I received my wake-up call at seven-thirty I felt as heavy – both physically and mentally – as I had felt lithe and weightless just eight hours previously. But the bathwater into which I lowered myself was practically stone-cold (on purpose) and, even though adhering to the regulatory couple of inches, efficiently supplied the shock a sluggish system required. By the time I had eaten breakfast, settled my account and walked to the station, I felt fine again and was looking forward to seeing Sybella. Yet it was now a different kind of anticipation from the one I had experienced earlier: quieter and less heady, more questioning and less accepting. I was back at work. I still felt happy to be spending time with her but I had stopped believing in roses round the door and had become re-infected by

120

suspicion. The very fact that at the camp gates she had responded to me in the way she had: even this now troubled me – shamingly unfair though I realized it to be.

Thankfully, today's journey resembled Friday's rather than Saturday's: no more perching on my suitcase whilst the military squeezed by. Today, seats in a third-class compartment: a compartment shared by only three others, excluding Sybella. She and I sat close and I revelled in our closeness…yet at the same time felt divorced from it. It was almost as though I were having an out-of-body experience, my spirit up in the luggage rack, lying on its stomach maybe, with its head propped on its hand, a dispassionate observer. Dispassionate? More like sardonic. Sitting – or, rather, lying – in judgment.

Even my voice sounded distant: a sensation similar once more to that at the solicitor's.

"Last night, you know, before I fell asleep, I was thinking about Bill."

"Me, too," she said.

"Sort of wondering how he might have felt if he'd been watching."

"Happy – I hope."

"But a difficult situation. Even in heaven, when you've only recently arrived, wouldn't it be hard not to feel a little jealous? Resentful? *She didn't exactly wait for very long, did she? And I used to think she loved me.*"

"He knew I loved him. And he was always extremely understanding. About everything."

"Perhaps it's easier to be understanding about everything, than about one thing in particular."

"He'd have understood how lost I felt. How lonely. And he'd have understood how – when suddenly someone came along who was just so sympathetic and so very easy to talk to…"

Don't let yourself feel flattered, I told myself.

"That's kind and I appreciate it," I said (feeling flattered), "but all the same – "

"Quite apart from being so easy on the eye," she added.

121

She could hardly have known it, I supposed (or, yes, probably she did), but this was *not* going to help me in my attempt to stay objective. My tone became brusque.

"Despite his tendency to blush?" I asked. She looked at me.

"Yes, you do rather have this tendency to blush."

"No, actually I don't. I think it's merely you who has this tendency to bring it out in me."

"Me and Greer Garson both?" She stopped. "Oh, I'm sorry. That was brazen! I can't believe I said it."

"Nor me. And I trust – I really do trust – that *you're* now going a little red?"

"Not in the least. If I am brazen I shall have to brazen it out. When I set off in quest of Miss Garson – shortly after my arrival in California – then she and I can have an interesting little powwow about a young man's propensity to blush. I think I shall look forward to that."

"Yes, it should be fun."

But I was thinking: she does realize, doesn't she? About me and the movie business. Surely she does? At this point who precisely is taking in whom?

I was immediately struck by something quite nonsensical – that, in a way, I didn't know which would be worse: whether she did realize or whether she didn't.

Presumably it was the thought of this enlightening Hollywood encounter which now made her laugh and which now made, too, each of our three fellow passengers look up, agreeably. One was a clergyman, sucking on his brier; the other two, middle-aged women, also smoking, who somehow had the air of civil servants – possibly high-ranking ones. They both wore tweed suits, lisle stockings, sensible shoes; but they sported different types of headgear: a porkpie hat with a pretty feather, and a cheerful silk scarf depicting flower girls in Piccadilly.

After a moment, though, they all returned to their newspapers. Then it dawned on me, guiltily, that I had not only approved of their approval of Sybella, I had even taken a stupid sense of pride in it. I tried to be a good deal firmer with myself.

122

And also with her.

"So, then?" I invited. (Although, in fact, I moved an inch or two away.) "Tell me about him. Tell me about Bill."

"What sort of thing?"

"Anything…it's not important. For instance, I think you mentioned he went up to Scotland? What was that to do with?"

"Oh. Something or other for the government. Naturally, he'd never speak to me about matters of that sort. And I knew better than to ask." (*OF COURSE I won't say a word to anyone – I never do when you tell me things...*) "What makes you think it wasn't just a spot of leave?"

"Well, if it had been, wouldn't he have taken you with him?" I paused. "Oh, no, I suppose he couldn't have."

"Why not?"

"Thinking of the play, I mean."

She frowned a little.

"What's the play got to do with it? We've only been doing the play for the past couple of weeks."

"Really?" I said. "The past couple of weeks?"

"Yes. Didn't you realize?" She raised an amused eyebrow. "I've only been with ENSA for the past *three*! And Bill went up to Scotland in…oh, in early March. Though he wasn't there for long; merely a few days. Even if it did feel like a lot longer..." She said this with a grimace.

But in any case I wasn't thinking about Scotland. Not any more. For the second time in a matter of seconds I found myself simply repeating what she had said.

"You've only been with ENSA for the past three weeks?"

"You look surprised. But the thing is: I was absurdly late in applying – don't ask me why – up till then I'd had nothing but a deadly boring job in a bakery!" She smiled. "But at least with regard to *Nine Till Six* I got the timing right. They were just on the point of casting and beginning their week's rehearsal."

And at least too, I thought, with regard to the double champagne cocktails on the night before Bill Martin left for Scotland – as well as to that worrying matter of the five weeks' absence from work – she had likewise got the timing right. Lease-Lend no longer entered into it.

So was I mistaken? *Was* I? Just too clever for my own good?

But what about that other question: the discrepancy in style?

Well, suddenly a solution to even that suggested itself. It was like when you had finally overcome some critical impasse in a crossword puzzle; probably you hadn't thought about it for a while before going back to it afresh. Several other clues at once fell into place.

So how about this? The letters had *not* been written in Sybella's style; there was no gainsaying that. Yet, all the same, the solution didn't – inevitably – need to be a sinister one. They had been written in Bill Martin's style.

And this was the reason.

Bill Martin had not merely liked his women beautiful; he had liked them well-born. At least upper-middle-class. And perceptibly so. Using all the speech patterns of the upper-middle-class. Wasn't that possible?

And I surmised he had also liked them to be just a fraction scatterbrained. By no means dumb but simply not quite so intelligent as himself. Sybella would have been everything he had wanted…except scatterbrained. But Sybella was an actress and because she had loved him she had been prepared to play along. Galatea to his Pygmalion. Privately, she might even have enjoyed the notion of creating a part and of secretly – but affectionately – being able to smile at his fallibility.

An innocent enough deception…and one, of course, which took us right back into ampersand territory.

Yet if Bill Martin had really not wanted a fiancée who matched him in intelligence I had to concede I was a little disappointed in him.

On the other hand, if this meant that – while his own image tarnished – Sybella's reverted to what it had been…well, here was something that could easily outweigh my disappointment. *Any* disappointment.

And it might even explain why she had reacted to myself as unreservedly as she had. She possibly hadn't realized that it had been something of a strain living up to the expectations of the major. No matter how enjoyable. She had certainly loved her fiancé – no question as to that – but she had also needed to remain in character. Yesterday, for the first time in a long while, she might have experienced the relief of once more being herself in the company of an unattached male who…who had clearly considered her attractive.

Despite his attempts not to make this too apparent.

So – now that I finally understood – I could even, without saying anything, move in closer again, reach out for her hand; start savouring both her nearness and the moment itself with renewed pleasure. Renewed wonder. My spirit hopped down from the luggage rack and rejoined me in my seat. I felt ashamed of my suspicions, yet mightily glad, naturally, that I hadn't communicated them. (So far as I could tell.) I should have liked to talk exclusively about ourselves but I thought that for her own sake, while she seemed able to speak of him composedly, she ought to be encouraged to get Bill Martin out of her system; insomuch as such a thing would be either possible or right.

"When did you meet?" I asked.

"Last Christmas. At a party. In Wales."

"In Wales? Good gracious. Long way from home!"

"Yes, maybe – but Bill had a large number of Welsh friends with whom he'd always kept in touch."

I laughed. "I meant from *your* home."

"Oh, I see. Well, I had an old nanny, you know, and sometimes around Christmas I'd go and stay with her for a few days. After she left us, she retired to Cardiff. Which is where Bill was born and spent the first fifteen years of his life."

"With a coalminer for a dad?"

"No. With a pharmacist for a dad."

"Ah."

"I only met him the once. In some ways a bit of a dry old stick. But with a droll sense of humour and… "

"And?"

"And I think I might have grown to be quite fond of him, that's all."

"What about his mum, then – Bill's mum? A little easier?"

"Not really. No. His mother had been dead for years. And we couldn't find a Ouija board."

Oh, praise the Lord! Hallelujah! She was making jokes. She was actually making jokes! Not about Bill himself, of course, but about things very closely connected. I sent up a quick and silent thank you.

"How long was it before you got engaged?"

"On April 14th," she said. (Why had I even asked?) "Or on March 31st; I'll let you take your pick!"

"What!"

I had spoken too fast. My tone had sounded sharp. But she didn't seem to notice.

"In some ways, you see, Bill was fairly old-fashioned. March 31st was the day on which he asked me to marry him. But before we could become *officially* engaged, he said he would like to do the thing properly…and that meant asking my father for his permission. But when I first dropped a hint to Daddy – such a hint that he guessed at once why Bill was wanting to meet him – he proved unexpectedly stubborn. No getting married until the end of the war! And aren't appearances deceptive: Bill's father wasn't stubborn in the least! Was all for getting in touch with his solicitor immediately, to draw up a marriage settlement!"

As Sybella finished, she was smiling very faintly. Nostalgically.

"A marriage settlement?" I said. "Aren't marriage settlements a bit old-fashioned, too?"

"Oh, yes." She gave a nod. "And I know just what you're thinking. *Like father, like son.* A chip off the old block!"

"I'm not sure that I was thinking anything."

"But, anyhow. Bill wasn't *that* old-fashioned. As soon as we realized my father wasn't going to budge he said, 'Oh, to hell with it! No one's going to stop *us* getting married, just because there's a war on!' And so the very next day he went right out

126

and bought a ring and we counted that as the date of our engagement. I'm sorry, I seem to have turned what should have been a simple answer into a full-scale novel!"

"All the same, a very interesting one," I said.

Indeed, a lot *more* than merely interesting! Without knowing it – and either intuitively or else through sheer, amazing providence – she had taken care of practically every uncertainty I'd still been feeling, concerning the major and the letters he had carried.

"But I rather wish he'd had that earlier date inscribed," she told me. "Because as far as the world knows we were only engaged for ten short days before he died – just *ten* days – and I'd have liked the world to know that it was longer. Which is silly, isn't it? What difference does it make?"

"Sybella?"

She looked at me enquiringly.

"Yesterday I didn't feel that I could ask. But today perhaps I can. How *did* Bill die?"

"He was drowned," she said.

"*Drowned?*"

"Yes. Somewhere off the coast of Spain. His plane came down in the Atlantic."

"His plane? You mean – he was a pilot?"

"No! Good heavens, no! Bill wasn't piloting the plane. He was a major in the Royal Marines."

"Oh, yes, you said. I'm sorry. I forgot. Then I suppose he was on his way to North Africa?" It seemed a reasonable assumption.

She nodded. "Apparently, there were certain things which had to be delivered to General Alexander in Tunis. Hugely urgent. Hugely confidential."

Her tone changed.

"That's why they sent Bill! According to Bill, Mountbatten had picked him. Picked him out especially! It appears they could have sent any number of others, but they just wanted the best, he said." (*Who* had said, I wondered. Mountbatten or Bill?)

She turned her head and looked through the window which gave onto the corridor and, for the moment, onto the patchwork of fields beyond.

"*Damn them*!" she said. "Damn them, damn them, damn them! Damn them for only wanting the best!"

I quickly took her head onto my shoulder; put my arm around her.

"Hey, it's all right," I said. "Hush, now – hush! Poor thing, you've *really* been through it, haven't you? You've *really* had enough!"

There was a sudden sharp cough. The two women sitting across from one another on the other side of the carriage had both lowered their papers, both taken the cigarettes out of their mouths, and were both staring at Sybella – but with something less than their earlier seal of approval.

Yet – oh, for the love of Mike! – they should have seen that she was overwrought. They should have seen that I was trying to comfort her!

The one in the porkpie hat, however, began to shake her head; she, the more likely perpetrator of that cough.

"Careless talk, my dear…you must at least *try* to be discreet! Careless talk costs lives and even walls have ears."

She looked about her as if meaning to illustrate this, yet didn't look so much at the walls, which might have been the most accurate form of illustration, nor so much at me, which would *undoubtedly* have been the most accurate form of illustration – her gaze finally came to rest on the clergyman. Presumably, she was only seeking his agreement, but one could easily have thought that here was the villain she was hoping to unmask.

However, as befitted a man of the cloth, particularly one who was so pre-eminently Chaucerian, being both rotund and round-faced and having a suitably jolly demeanour, he didn't appear too dismayed at having been found out.

"Ah." Even his voice was plummy and his manner of speech consistent with his image; so consistent, indeed, that perhaps he *was* a fifth columnist. "How right you are, dear lady.

'Switched-on switches and turned-on taps…make happy Huns and joyful Japs!'"

This seemed to have nothing whatever to do with the present situation, but surely he must have supposed that in some way it had; for having delivered the couplet with all the authority of an old actor manager who was now gloriously embarked upon his definitive rendering of Lear, he smiled gently, and improvingly, upon the four of us and then retired, contented, behind his week-old copy of the *Church Times*.

We others all looked at one another in a state of some confusion; and no further reference was made by anyone to the subject of careless talk.

Nor to the undoubted wisdom of trying to save energy – wherever and in whatever fashion any of us could possibly contrive.

Nor even to the birth, engagement or death of Major William Martin of the Royal Marines. Sybella had recovered her equilibrium. Her head now rested on my shoulder once more and I had put my arm back round her. We both closed our eyes and actually succeeded in dozing a little during the next twenty minutes or so. Then the ticket inspector slid open the door and, with his arrival, I awoke to rediscover Sybella's and my own newfound, entirely natural-seeming, intimacy. I had never smiled at any ticket inspector quite so benevolently.

23

I felt good again.

At Waterloo I saw Sybella into a taxi, having arranged that we should meet at half past four. She had given me her telephone number in case of hitches – jotted it down, along with her address, on a paper serviette; apparently she always carried two or three in her handbag. There was only one drawback. She went off with my pen. This wouldn't have mattered, except that it was German. But at least the brand name was unobtrusive and made it sound more Greek than German. *Orthos*. It had been careless of me to bring it over here – careless but not catastrophic.

At any rate, nothing like that could spoil my mood. After I'd waved Sybella off in her taxi I caught one myself. I was driven to Coventry Street. There, without the slightest problem, I booked two seats. If the performance had been sold out, I would have bought tickets for another show and suggested to Sybella that she should now try to put some distance between herself and what had happened; would simply have told her I had given away those earlier reservations. I felt tempted to do this, anyway. It would have been much more fun to go to a different revue and hear her laugh spontaneously at sketches that were unfamiliar. But unfortunately – since I had the option – I knew that I was honour bound to stick to my word: present her with a further chance to grieve.

So I turned away from the box office hoping very much that I had made the right decision. I looked at the photographs outside the theatre; Sid Field – I assumed it was Sid Field – gave me a cocky, reassuring grin. Therefore, as I covered the negligible distance between Coventry Street and Leicester Square, I was thinking less about the rightness of having booked the tickets than I was about the name I should now have to invent: the name of the girl I had originally meant to accompany me to the theatre. Indirectly or otherwise, Sybella was sure to ask – and, going on recent past experience, I thought it might easily be *otherwise*. I laughed. Even the minor aggravation of my unwieldy suitcase – although it was amazing how people's shins still seemed irresistibly drawn towards it – couldn't cause any dent in my exhilaration. I wondered if this part of London was always so busy on a Monday morning: a Monday morning in the middle of a war. Actually, there were remarkably few civilians. It was mainly a kaleidoscope of uniforms, both men's and women's, both overseas and British. Most of the men had girls upon their arms, many of whom were laughing and vivacious. (But not one of whom, naturally, could ever have measured up to Sybella!) The chance meeting of eyes

130

– of strangers' eyes – elicited, almost automatically, a warm and friendly smile. Yesterday, in Manor Park, the relative absence of men had seemed surprising; today, in Leicester Square, it was the absence of children that one noticed. As I slowly made my way down the left-hand side, I said a little prayer that everybody's leave would be a happy one.

Especially, I meant, Sybella's.

Yet wasn't it a fraction odd, perhaps, that ENSA was already allowing her some? After only three weeks?

No, for heaven's sake – why? Had I never heard of a little thing known commonly as *compassionate* leave? Of course I had. Even in Germany that phrase existed.

(Why had I thought *even* in Germany?)

But, anyway, the point was – it added up! The whole thing added up! "Panting for Monday so that I can get back to my crowd of silly females." A description, I now saw, possibly penned with some forethought and bearing in mind the preferences of the major.

Yes. 19th April. Three weeks ago exactly.

And then: "Here comes our 'Lady Producer' who feels by rights she should be directing Thorndike & Evans & Ashcroft rather than the likes of little old us." Again – insidiously appealing.

That had been written on the Wednesday. Two days into rehearsal. And the play had been scheduled to open on the following Monday.

A fortnight. I frowned. Her family had certainly been fairly quick off the mark, hadn't it? I tried to imagine my own family responding with a similar alacrity. Not only her parents but her sister – her aunts and her uncles – her cousins and her granny too. Already, it appeared, they had all rushed off, helter-skelter, to see *Nine Till Six*. Descended on it in stampeding droves.

Well – and why not? How far, for instance, was Wolverhampton? (I meant, of course, from Marlborough...or, at least, from the general locality thereof.) Wouldn't a journey to Wolverhampton have been reasonably straightforward? And over the past couple of weeks there could easily have been closer or more convenient venues. Why did I even have to think about it?

("Oh, my darling, how you do so like to split hairs!" I could recall my mother saying this when I was five or six years old. Later my father would rephrase it a little differently. "Why will you never accept *anything* you're told?")

Clearly, it was not a very lovable characteristic: a person's being so mistrustful; my satisfaction grew tinged with regret. But also with resolution. (*Renewed* resolution; I remembered the previous Thursday evening.) Now I didn't grip the handle of my mother's suitcase so much in mild impatience. Now I gripped it for connection. For communication.

So, *yes*, I thought. Why couldn't they all have gone together to the same performance, not only a convivial and supportive family outing but a commendably practical one too, pooling the petrol coupons? And, okay, Sybella's mother *might* have seen the play so often that she could apply to be her daughter's understudy; but obviously on occasion you just had to make allowances for a touch of poetic licence. She might have been twice? Three times? My parents were right. Why did I always have to be so literal-minded – to interpret and analyse and doubt?

Good. I was at peace once more, and although it was perfectly true (I grinned shamefacedly) that I was now all set to check on something else, something else that simply didn't require it, this was only through sheer force of habit – and because I was right there on the spot – and because I still needed to prove myself a professional.

Yet, in the fullness of time, habit could and *would* be broken.

Just not today, however.

I reached my destination some five minutes after I had left the Prince of Wales. From one box office to another.

The Empire was showing *Mademoiselle France*, the Joan Crawford picture I had read about in the *Express*. ('Miss Crawford isn't making all the sacrifices implied in the script… Dressing like a refugee is certainly not in her contract.')

132

I consulted my watch. The first performance of the day was probably half over – many of its patrons, no doubt, already beginning on their lunchtime sandwiches.

I asked if I might see the manager.

The female clerk, bespectacled, mousy-haired, none too busy while the actual film was showing, glanced pointedly at my suitcase.

"May I enquire what it's about?"

I smiled. "Don't worry, I haven't come to sell him anything. I just wanted to know when a particular picture would have been playing here."

"Oh… Possibly I could help?"

"*Random Harvest.*"

She was disappointed. "Ah, yes – for that, I'm afraid, you will need to see the manager. And unluckily he's just stepped out for a minute or two."

She explained how she herself had been working there only since last November. She neither looked nor sounded anything like the receptionist at the Black Lion, but there must have been something in her manner, or in her conversation, to transport me back to Thursday.

"Last November?" It took me three seconds, maybe five, to assimilate this detail. "Does that mean, then…?" And it cost a real effort even to say four words.

I tried again but it seemed I couldn't get any further. "Does that mean, then…?"

She regarded me sympathetically.

"Well, sir," she said, "all I know is I saw the film myself – when was it, now? – I think it may have been in August or September-time. Summer, anyhow. Me and my better half; we saw it at the Queen's in Bayswater. Or it may have been the Regal, Harrow Road. So I reckon it would have finished here in June. Maybe July."

At least she had given me a moment to recover.

(To *recover*?)

"And no revival of it since then?" I asked. "No revival at all? None, say, in early March this year?"

"Not at the Empire, sir. Nor at the Ritz next door, which is our sister cinema, although of course it's a good deal smaller..."

And she proudly informed me that she hadn't missed a single day's work in her full six months.

"So a revival couldn't just have slipped me by, as it were. Besides, sir, it isn't any part of our policy to hold revivals."

I had the impression she might now have been willing to forestall the manager by leading me step by step through all the intricacies of the MGM release and distribution system. But I thanked her as courteously as I could and – feeling as though I might actually need to vomit – turned away and headed for the pavement.

Where, after a while, beneath a blown-up and violently tinted picture of airman John Wayne, I took out the serviette which Sybella had given me. She had written her address in longhand rather than in block capitals. I took out her letters, too.

Allegedly her letters.

But the writing wasn't hers. (As if I'd really believed any more that it could be!) Enough said.

Absolutely enough! It furnished undeniable proof of deception. What did it matter that the film hadn't been showing at the Empire when she'd said it had? – Sam Spade could have saved himself *that* little effort of investigation. Not to downgrade it, however – purely on its own, it would also have furnished ample evidence of deception.

Not quite so comprehensive, maybe, but still pretty damning.

I wiped my lips on the serviette. If this was meant to be vengeance, though, it didn't work. King Pyrrhus would surely have sympathized.

Besides all of which, my glance was now drawn to a single fragment of sentence in the second letter. (That crossword puzzle syndrome: one delayed solution sparking off another.) The words might have been illuminated.

I read again: "Wolverhampton – Wolverhampton for one night only…"

Ostensibly written during her first week with ENSA: the time, supposedly, of the play being cast and of everyone's lines being learnt and of frenetically intensive rehearsal.

And no more than just two days into that chaotic first week...already a preview in Wolverhampton? Really? No! *What* an achievement for our long-suffering Lady Producer!

Another fragment of a sentence – this time from the earlier letter. I read again: "Panting for Monday so that I can get back to my crowd of silly females."

Sweet Jesus!

Was it possible?

How in the name of God could I have seen it so many times and yet still never have noticed?

That one little adverb.

Back, she had said. (Had allegedly said.) B*ack*.

*

No, I didn't like loose ends. And – who knew? – perhaps I even felt that strange compulsion to punish myself still further. I telephoned ENSA and this time, on my first shot, found the number unengaged. The *Nine Till Six* contingent had been performing in the play since January.

And yes – right from the start – Miss Sybella Standish had certainly been a member of the cast.

"Oh, and a most *valuable* member of the cast!" gushed the tactful and obviously well-intentioned woman to whom my call had been transferred. "I hear that she always gives a remarkable performance – yes, a truly remarkable performance!"

24

First I sat absent-mindedly in some snack bar, over an untasted cup of tea, until the soldier who was sharing my table felt driven to exclaim, "Sorry, mate, but don't you think you've stirred that long enough? You're giving me indigestion!", and I put down my spoon with a start of apology, wondering how anyone could ever kill a man in close combat…when simply the idea of ruining his pleasure in a poached egg was sufficient to induce strong guilt.

(By 'anyone', of course, I meant myself. And yet I had joined the Abwehr! And yet I had become a spy!)

Then I caught a taxi back to Abbey Road, but in the taxi the same dull ache continued…the same agonizing refrain.

The former involved Sybella.

The latter involved her, too.

But more obliquely.

Explicitly, all it asked was: Why *me*? Repeatedly – why *me*?

Yet at least I could acquit myself. It wasn't a phrase prompted by self-pity. Rather, it arose out of mystification; out of the basic need to know.

Where had I gone wrong? In what totally unwitting way – in what desperately stupid, shamefully amateur way – had I managed to announce my presence over here as an enemy agent?

During our progress up Regent Street, I made myself try to review everything I had done since my arrival at Holyhead – not even excluding the few words I had exchanged with other passengers on board the boat before my conversation with the neighbourly woman who had informed me about Mold being her birthplace.

Review *everything*? In fact I didn't feel as though I had actually done much.

And what little I had done…at the moment it required a fierce effort of will simply to keep my mind on it.

Surely nothing had happened in Wales which could have implicated me without my knowing?

No.

No – definitely not.

Basically, I had just put up at an attractive small hotel and looked through its register. Not even stealthily but with the help of a kindly receptionist. (Who certainly – certainly? – wouldn't have recognized my fountain pen as being German. And even if she had…well, what of it? More than likely 'Orthos' had been purchasable over here in the thirties. Failing which, there had never been any law forbidding holidaymakers from bringing back souvenirs…)

Nor, upon leaving Wales, had there been anything underhand about my interview with Mr Gwatkin. Again, at Waterloo Place, I had been greeted by a kindly receptionist who…

I stopped.

Yes.

Who had changed in her attitude towards me.

Who had most *assuredly* changed in her attitude towards me.

But it was only now that I began to pay this proper attention. At the time I had naturally been aware of it, yet it just hadn't seemed important. She had started off by being friendly; by greeting me with a pleasantry to which I had responded, and a jokey remark about the other Mr Gwatkin being absent. But then she had altered – I had vaguely supposed she must have received a ticking off.

Yet try to think, I told myself. Did you *hear* her being ticked off? No, you did not. You merely assumed it.

But why did you assume it? Try to think. Isn't this what occurred?

I had given her my name, of course. Earnestly requested to see Mr Gwatkin. Told her that I needed to get in touch with a client of his – a Mr J.G. Martin.

Nothing wrong so far.

137

The woman had passed on this information. The connection had been poor. She had needed to repeat several points. It was as though she were talking to someone a little hard of hearing.

But Mr Gwatkin wasn't hard of hearing. And the woman had grown flustered. "Yes, very well. Yes, of course, Mr Gwatkin. Yes, I will."

I had asked whether I myself had been responsible for her discomfiture. But no, she had assured me, oh no, the trouble had been to do with something else entirely. Yet she still found it difficult to look at me. Before the call she'd been relaxed; now she appeared harassed. Was it even fanciful to say she suddenly seemed fearful?

"Yes, of course, Mr Gwatkin. Yes, I will."

Will what?

Will nothing…apparently. Other than confirm I would be able to see the solicitor after his present client had departed.

She had also offered me a cup of tea – which I had declined. However, she had then gone off with the declared intention of making one for herself. It had admittedly struck me as a little odd that this should be considered a good enough reason for leaving the switchboard unattended.

Odd, too, that when she came back she had forgotten her cup of tea. But I hadn't really thought about it. Why should I? I had vaguely supposed she might have gone to the lavatory – whilst there, had remembered something important which required her immediate attention.

I hadn't *at all* supposed that on leaving reception she had hurried straight into the office of Mr Gwatkin. I hadn't *at all* supposed that her suggestion of tea could have been merely a subterfuge. To indicate normality. To cover up confusion.

But what if the solicitor had said something like this on the telephone? "For Pete's sake, woman, stall! Say I have someone with me, then get in here fast! But calmly…we can't afford to make him suspicious. Why not offer him some tea? And if he says yes – well, he'll just have to wait for it, that's all."

Or was I simply imagining things again? After all, what had I done?

Nothing. Nothing but mention the name of J.G. Martin.

And wasn't it more likely that Mr Gwatkin was indeed with a client but hadn't been able to locate some crucial piece of correspondence? "Oh, yes, you may *claim* it hasn't been misfiled, but would you please come in to show us – right away!" He could at first have been overriding almost everything she had been trying to tell him; which was why she had needed to repeat herself.

Yet – in that case – why the cup of tea?

No. I couldn't make sense of it. It didn't hold up.

But anyway. What next?

Well, the poor woman had returned to her position at the switchboard, that patient, undemanding switchboard. Currently, the office didn't – not in any way – give off the air of busyness that her appointments book had promised.

And probably just as well. Even during a lull as pronounced as this one her agitation appeared unabated.

If not positively enhanced.

But then?

She had put through an outside call.

And, unexpectedly, this had soothed her. Not because of any actual conversation but because the individual she had wanted had proved accessible – she obviously hadn't supposed her task was going to be an easy one. Transferring the call to Mr Gwatkin she had shown her relief not only in her face but in every detail of her posture. The metaphorical deep breath – the evident sense of relaxation – these had provided me with a gentle amusement. I'd scarcely given a thought to the indirect cause.

The individual she had wanted…?

No, previously this person hadn't held much interest for me. But now, during the course of my present taxi ride, every aspect of my visit to the solicitor's had suddenly become of interest. Overwhelming interest. And now I endeavoured to concentrate on one specific moment passed in the reception area of Messrs McKenna & Co. I tried to rid my mind of every last hovering thought of Sybella and of the attendant mire of depression she had cast me into. I remembered – in connection with that name the receptionist had asked for – some chance association flitting into my head.

And just as swiftly out of it – tarnation! But I thought that in some way it might have related to clothing.

To tailoring? To outfitting? The image of a dog-eared receipt flashed upon me. Gieves was the shop in Piccadilly where the major had bought his handkerchiefs and shirts. But that lost association had nothing to do with Gieves.

My attempt at recollection faltered when I became aware (and did so for no reason at all which I knew of) that we were passing Lord's cricket ground.

I had come here once with my granddad. That must have been nine years ago but I recognized instantly the slab of white stone commemorating the world of sport…with at its centre, amongst the golfers and the footballers and the cricketers, a near-naked athlete clearly symbolizing the link with Graeco-Roman times. It was strange to reflect that, on the last occasion I had viewed this, my life had been so vastly – almost, I would have said, poignantly – different. I could even recall the feel of Gramps's arm lying companionably across my shoulders as we had stood there looking up with interest at the detail on the slab. *Play up, play up and play the game.* The sculpture had been extremely new then, and evidently in those days that slogan, so quintessentially British, had not appeared in the slightest bit risible. Only 1934?

But now the taxi had pulled away from the traffic lights.

So, all right, then. Not Gieves.

And not Austin Reed.

Nor Aquascutum.

Nor Montague Burton. Nor –

But – *yes*!

Yes! That was it!

Montague Burton. The fifty-shilling tailors.

That name she had asked for on the telephone…

Montague!

Montague! Montague! Montague!

And appended to some rank or other in the navy. Admiral, vice-admiral, rear-admiral? Captain, commander, lieutenant commander?

Oh, yes – again, yes! "I'm phoning on behalf of McKenna & Company, Solicitors. I should like to speak to Lieutenant Commander Montague, please." *That* was what I had heard her say. There had been some other word attached, a word sounding remarkably like 'mincemeat' and I remembered wondering what she could actually have said?

In retrospect, I supposed that what I *should* have wondered was whether I myself could in any fashion be involved, instead of merely continuing to sit there and idly leaf through *Punch*. But service titles were everywhere at present. Why should this Lieutenant Commander Montague, whoever he might be, have stood out as being anything other than some perfectly ordinary client? What legitimate reason would I have had to feel alarm? I hadn't been acting conspicuously: nothing remotely cloak-and-daggerish. All I had done was to ask for Mr Gwatkin and to mention knowing Mr Martin. How on just the strength of those two things could I possibly have thought myself involved? *That* would have been over-imaginative. Fanciful beyond question.

Very well, then. She had transferred the call. And looked relieved.

After which, she had instantly reverted from the switchboard to her typewriter. Had started pounding away on it as though she were the very model of efficiency. Had hardly lifted her eyes from her supposedly indecipherable shorthand.

And then at last I had been summoned. I hadn't seen any departing client but had presumed there must be a back entrance…which conceivably there was, although I myself hadn't been shown out by it. Apparently the solicitor hadn't heard my suggestion, despite its being made a moment before the office boy might well have drowned it out beneath the rattling of his teacups.

Therefore Mr Gwatkin *might* have been a little deaf, even if in his own room he hadn't appeared to have any difficulty about hearing. Where he *had* appeared to have difficulty was in making himself sound natural or at ease. Particularly at the onset. Gradually, of course, he had overcome this diffidence; managed to overcome it to such an extent that eventually he had launched into that scathing little speech concerning wills and irony and income tax…and from then on had given the impression of being a wholly different person – a person grown drunk at the spring of his own creativity.

Now, did *that* little circumstance happen to put you in mind of anyone? Anybody else at all?

Yet, unlike certain others, Mr Gwatkin was not a professional actor; so his initial fit of stage fright might have seemed slightly more noticeable than that of certain others.

No. He was not a professional actor. In any context of stagecraft or stage management he would have appeared – unquestionably – a fish out of water.

But a fish out of water with friends in high places?

Maybe.

High places such as the Admiralty? Such as the Naval Intelligence Division at the Admiralty?

Maybe.

Not necessarily a friend, of course; possibly a relative or a fellow club member or – yes, sure – why *not* a client? Someone, in any case, who would have known him well enough to be able to request a favour?

Maybe.

Someone who would never have revealed *why* he was requesting that favour. But someone who, in answer to a frenzied SOS by telephone, might just have spent a full quarter of an hour in priming his panic-stricken friend – or relative or fellow club member or family solicitor – on how to handle a crisis that had not been envisaged as being likely?

Maybe.

In which case…'mincemeat'?

A codeword meaning *Emergency*?

Emergency, I need help!

If so, how remarkably fortunate for our friend on the switchboard, not to mention her panic-stricken employer, that

142

those telephone lines that day should have been working so very smoothly. There could have been many a time when they wouldn't have been. No wonder she'd looked anxious.

Yet, anyhow, to return to the point where all that liberating invective had begun to flow along a different channel; to swirl about the feet of somebody depraved enough to steal from a person in uniform. Obviously a Kraut – "the only kind you could ever believe capable of doing it! But you'd think you'd be able to smell him, wouldn't you, like rotten eggs or sewage?"

Oh, yes. Gwatkin had *known* all right.

Had not merely known but had found it blatantly hard to conceal the fact. "I'm only surprised Mr Martin didn't mention it when he met us so soon afterwards! Oh, and by the way, why were you wanting a solicitor?"

But at least he hadn't grown quite so intoxicated that he had lost all self-control and started to invent unashamedly – again, not like *some* whom you might want to mention – unable to resist the clever, self-regarding thrill. The piling up of detail upon detail. The Empire on the Prince of Wales.

No, he had simply shaken my hand and shown me out. What a hero – when my hand was offered he had actually managed to bring himself to shake it! (Had he rushed off immediately afterwards, screaming for the hot water and soap?)

And he had shown me out the way I had come in, taking me past the receptionist. (With my receiving no more than a hard-faced nod from a woman who fifty minutes earlier had greeted me so pleasantly.) I had descended those impressive stairs and returned into Waterloo Place. There I had noticed the man who was chatting to the newspaper seller: the man in the battered felt hat and grubby raincoat. Had paid him scant attention, though, until I had seen him sometime later in the Strand. Had naturally lost interest again when he had turned off towards the bridge.

Yet what about that other man? The one lolling against the barber's shop in Paradise Street, with a copy of the *Evening News* concealing the lower part of his face?

In London, then, I was being followed.

Had they also set a tail on me in Aldershot?

No. In Aldershot, unnecessary. In Aldershot there had always been Sybella Standish to keep her beady little eye in focus.

But how in God's name had they guessed? At what point would they have told themselves I needed to be watched?

Yes, that was the abiding puzzle. What had I done but go to a solicitor and speak of my desire to contact Mr Martin?

And, anyway, there was nothing new in that. I had already been trying to seek him out in Wales – and without (well, apparently without) attracting to myself any undue attention.

Therefore where – last Friday afternoon – where had lain the crucial difference? Martin was a fairly common name. What had been the signal that had triggered the alarm? Had triggered it inside the Admiralty, let's say? Inside its Naval Intelligence Division, let's say? What had been the signal that had unerringly declared: *Here is a German spy*?

And following on from that, of course, why if the authorities had known, or even just faintly suspected, why hadn't they apprehended me?

Well, who was it who had once said that – in the solving of any mystery – all you had to do was ask yourself the right question?

We were now in Abbey Road. Its absence of battle scars made a welcome change from the West End; a *very* welcome change, or so I had been hearing, from the East End. Abbey Road was a thoroughfare with a nearly rural aspect. Tree-lined and sunlit. When I finally awoke to an awareness of where we were, my taxi must have been driving along it for roughly a couple of minutes, because already we were pulling into the left-hand kerb, outside the home of Mrs Hilling.

But I was still practically oblivious. I went on sitting in the taxi until the driver turned round and gazed at me enquiringly – until she slid back the partition and actually spoke to me.

"Mister, isn't this the number you were wanting? Or have you now had second thoughts?"

Second thoughts? *Second* thoughts? I smiled – almost laughed. But it clearly required far less exertion to move my facial muscles than it did to move my limbs. I stepped down from the taxi and dragged my suitcase after me; closed the door, pulled out the money for the fare, gave the driver a ridiculously large tip. (But it was one which she deserved, for being the woman who had driven me in such a way as to encourage, or at any rate not impede, enlightenment.) I stepped down from the taxi and went through each of these small acts in a state of virtual automation.

Yes, well. Who *had* said it, in fact – that the only thing needed was to ask yourself the right question? The piece of the puzzle that was going to form the keystone, locking all the other pieces into place.

Because... I had just been shown the keystone.

And like St Paul (in this one respect) – St Paul set down on the road to the abbey at the end of a lengthy and despairing taxi ride – I had finally been floored; floored by the awful power of revelation. And now felt shaky. As indeed he must have.

For even the revelation granted to *him* could scarcely have seemed more God-sent or less logical: the kind of breathless leap dismissed by sceptics the world over, whether on the outskirts of Damascus or in the purlieus of St John's Wood – the kind of breathless leap which would have failed you automatically in a geometry exam, despite that instant click of recognition from within. What had I done but mention the name of Mr J.G.Martin?

The right question! (I had realized it at last.) It had pointed me to a solution that was clean and astonishing in its simplicity. And more than that – still in time to be of service to us.

So once again, as when previously it had seemed my assignment over here had been complete, I should really have been feeling cock-a-hoop.

But I wasn't.

In fact, I was feeling almost anything but cock-a-hoop.

The taxi driver was rejoicing, though. Clearly delighted by the size of her tip, she gave me a broad smile, touched her cap in mock salute and waved to me twice as she drove away. By then, Mrs Hilling had come to the front door and even she appeared elated. Elated by the simple fact I had returned. She asked if I'd had a good weekend and conveyed the idea she'd have been more than pleased to hear about it in some detail. A pretty woman in a flowered overall, she offered me a glass of beer and a corned beef sandwich and mentioned, quite wistfully, that it was ever so comfy in the kitchen – quiet, as well, with her two young monsters back at school and her oldest one just recently called up.

Yet, whereas at any other time I might have responded more graciously, I now made the excuse that I'd already eaten and in addition had a headache; told her that what I really needed was to lie down.

"Ah, yes," she said, "I didn't like to say anything, it wasn't my place, but I felt quite worried you might be overdoing it! Coming up to London for a change of air is one thing. But gallivanting all around the country with that heavy old suitcase of yours…!" She wagged a gentle finger in reproof. "Your regiment isn't going to take you back, you know, not until you're properly in the pink again; and you can't hope to pull the wool over *their* eyes, any more than you can over *mine*!"

(In the meanwhile she was under the impression that for the most part I was spending my convalescence tranquilly in Mold, carrying on with my architectural studies and living with my sister who had lately become a Land Girl. My sister, Priscilla.)

But for the present, she explained, she hoped I wouldn't mind that she had to put me in a different room. Not knowing for sure if I'd be coming back, she had given the larger one, only about an hour ago, to a nice young couple who had spotted her advertisement on the newsagent's board at the corner of Belgrave Gardens.

"So let me show you your new room – and on our way up I'll get you some aspirin; they're kept in the medicine chest in the bathroom. Oh…and, Mr Andrews…you've had an urgent message from your friend Mr Smee. I think he'll be so relieved to know that you've got back to us safe and sound."

She paused on the staircase, to reassure herself that I could manage with my suitcase.

"Still, I only wish I hadn't forgotten to enquire after the health of that nice mother of his. Such a cultured woman, you know. She used to be an actress."

Right at this minute, however, I could have told her I had precious little time for cultured women who used to be, or still were, actresses.

But it was definitely perverse how, also right at this minute, everything conspired to remind me of them. *Everything.* Even something so unlikely you'd almost have sworn it couldn't happen.

A small framed notice hung over the washbasin in the room I'd now been given. This was a card written in red Gothic lettering but otherwise unadorned. I dully wondered who had judged it worthy of the piece of glass – of the passe-partout, the backing, even the length of wire.

> "Switched-on switches and turned-on taps
> Make happy Huns and joyful Japs."

And what was especially painful about that – to have felt such a very happy Hun myself at the moment I had first encountered it! To have felt happier, indeed, than for several years I'd even have considered possible.

No, stop it, I said, stop it this instant, just think about the task at hand!

In spite of which I vividly recalled the expression in her eyes. *Oh, please! Not again! You can't – you cannot – have forgotten yesterday! Colonel and Mrs Musket, of the Royal Army Dental Corps?*

Was that only three hours ago, that silent but renewed and desperate plea for restraint?

A fleeting voyage through a fool's paradise. And 'fool' was truly the appropriate word. Even if that paradise had proved solid, I could scarcely have felt sadder for having lost it. I remembered her comment about missing someone. Like homesickness, she had said.

But, no doubt, a comment just as sham as all the rest.

Anyway, if for nothing else, I ought to feel thankful that there'd been this telephone message from Buchholz. Which meant that I didn't merely have to stay up in my new room and think. Or do my best *not* to think.

Which meant that I didn't merely have to stay up in my new room and wonder. Or do my best *not* to wonder.

(Wonder if I really had to see Sybella Standish tonight. Really had to sit beside her at the Prince of Wales. Really had to sit beside her and simulate enjoyment.)

But that would have been pure self-indulgence – my even wondering about it. I had no option. Under no circumstances must she be allowed to realize I had cottoned on.

Or was I wrong? Perhaps there did remain one further option.

To throw myself out of this top-floor window. The small yard beneath was paved in concrete.

However… I smiled wanly and I shook my head.

It might hurt a little.

25

I went into the post office on the corner of Marylebone High Street and Weymouth Street. If I *was* being tailed (as I felt sure I was) I still didn't believe that anyone would actually follow me in – the space was too confined, as well as being too public. But even so I remained facing the doorway; I stood in a quiet corner and filled in the lettercard I had just bought.

I used the pencil attached to a holder on the counter.

"Received message via Mrs H. Discovered I'm being watched, have been since Friday – regrettably, before coming to see yourselves. Enormously sorry. Maybe correspond by letter? Or phone after ten? Alternatively, meet at Ridgeway in fifteen, twenty minutes? Will try to shake off tail."

The Ridgeway was a restaurant up the road, where Devonshire Street met the High Street. Buchholz might prefer some other place – which would obviously be perfectly all right with me.

I licked the edges of the card. Addressed it. Looked around me for a likely messenger.

And saw one straightaway. A middle-aged woman had recently joined the lengthy queue. A lad of ten or eleven, presumably her son, stood next to her. He wore a school cap, blazer, grey-flannel shirt and grey-flannel short trousers. He was reading a story in the *Wizard*.

"Excuse me, madam?"

Although addressing the woman, I was plainly including the boy.

"I was wondering if your son would like to earn himself five shillings. I need someone to deliver a letter to the newsagent's in Paradise Street. It wouldn't take long."

In one hand I was holding my hat; in the other I had two half-crowns, conspicuous beside the lettercard.

The woman turned towards her son.

"Ronnie?" she asked.

"Yes, please!" replied the boy. "I could be there and back in probably under a minute!"

"I would think more like three," I said. "You see, Mr Smee will want to send an answer; a short one. But if it takes you longer than *five* we'll increase the rate of pay to seven-and-sixpence. What do you say?"

Actually, I felt it was likely to take ten minutes rather than three, but didn't aim to be discouraging.

His mother said, "Well, as long as he isn't late for his appointment!" (But there wasn't any fear of that: she informed me of its time and place.) He crammed the comic into her shopping basket, took the letter and rushed off with an air of great importance – Robin being dispatched by Batman, on a

149

tricky mission to help save the world. His mother had tried to straighten his cap before he left. "Careful as you cross the road!" she called.

I made sure that when he pushed through the inner swing door it would look to anyone standing on the pavement as if I was simply waiting there in line. Silently. Self-sufficiently.

He was soon back. It could even have been under the specified five minutes – I hadn't been timing him and his mother was only just at that moment getting served. In any case, I held out the third half-crown.

"No, thank you, sir. The job was easy. And the old woman in the shop gave me an aniseed ball as well, while the man wrote out his answer."

"A business deal is a business deal," I told him. "It was nice of you to say no, but I'm adamant you've got to take it."

I added: "And I hope everything goes okay at the dentist's! Thank you for helping me out."

Then I touched the woman's elbow and thanked her, too. I returned to my corner and tore open the envelope her son had brought back. The contents read:

"Come anyway. If they were watching you on Friday the damage is done. But they may have assumed that you were visiting friends."

Which was ridiculous – as Buchholz must have known. I wondered if he were trying to assuage my guilt; to atone for that jibe he had made about my lack of experience.

No, not a jibe, of course.

A justified comment.

26

So – a little sooner than expected – my return to Paradise Street.

We were again in the bedroom. As before, Buchholz wore slippers on his inordinately small feet, and was once more lying on the bed, his back supported by the various bright cushions piled against the wall.

But there were differences this afternoon. Firstly, he hadn't offered me a whisky and, secondly, there was a lot of custom in the shop below…with many who came in to buy their evening paper smelling pungently of BO. "In England people *do*," had said Frau Buchholz, after she had greeted me dourly from behind her counter and made some reference to the grandfather and toddler who had just left – Frau Buchholz, Mrs Smee, who despite her veneer of grime and her filthy-looking scarf, was certainly not afflicted with BO.

A third difference was maybe more important. The man outside the barber's shop had disappeared; a young woman wearing pigtails and dressed in the tunic of a schoolgirl had taken his place. She was playing with a puzzle: I guessed, from her careful tilting of the flat glass-fronted box and from her tapping of its sides, that it might be one of those containing the hard outline of a map, jaggedly indented, along which you had to coax a piece of grooved Bakelite. Up from the Bay of Biscay all the way to the Baltic Sea. It was a game, as I could easily recall, that demanded total concentration. (If while you were playing it, that was, you cared for absolutely nothing but the game.) I sat in the same chair by the window and watched with wry amusement. At least I no longer had to wonder why they should be bothering to have me followed.

You could say that this was something.

Buchholz had asserted – the same as he'd done before – that he had no wish to know the reason for my being in Britain.

"But would you say your task has been successful?"

"Yes," I replied.

It sounded curt: an accurate reflection of the way I happened to be feeling – despite his having pardoned me for the situation into which I had thrown both him and his clearly adored mother.

I couldn't keep it up, though. I added less abruptly: "Yes. I'd say I've now done everything I had to."

A statement not intended as a boast…my mood could hardly have encompassed that. All the same, he congratulated me.

But I paid no attention to his irony. If that was what it was.

I said: "I was sent over here to check on the veracity of something. It turns out there's no veracity attached to it whatever."

"Which – I take it – is exactly as our superiors in Berlin expected?"

"Which – you may take it – is exactly as our superiors in Berlin did not expect at all."

He hesitated.

"Are you certain of that?"

"Completely."

"There's no faint chance that you might be mistaken?"

"About what? The nature of their expectations?"

"No. The truth of your own findings."

"Not the faintest chance in the world." I shook my head, decisively.

"I see," he murmured. "Tell me: what are you finding so very fascinating down there in the street? MI5?"

I sighed and turned away from the window. He came and stood beside me and, without lifting the net curtain, stared for several seconds at the pavement opposite.

"You mustn't blame yourself for that."

"As you keep on reassuring me. Not everyone, I think, would be so kind. I appreciate it."

"But your tone still sounds remarkably flat."

"Maybe that's because my tone actually *is* remarkably flat, and for the moment I can't be bothered to do anything about it."

"You seem a little different from the way you were last Friday."

I didn't answer.

"Even a great deal different," he remarked.

Had he known, I reflected, he could have added with similar accuracy that I seemed a great deal different from how I had been in the post office a mere ten minutes ago. That, too, made me uncomfortable. Was it only because in the post office I had been in need of a favour? Or was it also because in the heat of the moment certain memories had receded, and because a silly unfortunate thought hadn't yet occurred to me – as it had when I was scarcely six feet away from the paper shop. *The last time I was here I felt happy.* My present state of depression ignored the fact that such, in any case, was not the full unvarnished truth.

"Look, Heinrich, Mrs Hilling told me this was urgent."

"Yes, you're right. I stand corrected. We shall proceed."

I thought that, if he had been dressed for it, he might have clicked his heels, sprung smartly to attention, and solemnly saluted.

But his slippers were far too soft and – besides that – he was now back on the bed.

"The thing is, Erich, you say you're taking back to Germany some information substantially at odds with what is generally expected? To Germany and also, of course, to Willy Canaris?"

"Of course to Admiral Canaris."

He began to gnaw at a patch of dried skin beside one thumbnail.

"Do you remember that on Friday you spoke of a newspaper article aiming to give us the lowdown on our valiant employer? A highly irritating article suggesting that possibly his days in power are well and truly numbered."

"Heinrich. Why are you even wasting your time – or indeed *my* time – by referring to that?"

Buchholz tore away the piece of dead skin, removed it fastidiously from between his teeth, then investigated his thumb and seemed satisfied. From below we heard a sudden chortle, almost a cackle, but even the son was unable to identify it as belonging – or not belonging – to his own mother.

153

"Often down there," he said, "there's this neighbourly foregathering of the local crones and witches. Voices indistinguishable! I'm still so enormously impressed by the way she can blend in!" The shred of dry skin was relegated from fingertip to bedspread.

I wanted to say: *Oh, for God's sake! Can't you get to the point?* Wanted to shout it, more like.

"How well do you know him?" he asked.

"Know the admiral? Well, how well do you think I know him? He's the chief; I'm a nobody. Why don't you ask me how well I know the Führer? Or will that be your next question?"

Buchholz disregarded my outburst, and studied his thumb again.

"You see, I felt it was absolutely crucial I should speak to you before you went back," he said. "I've received disquieting news about him – and from sources far more reliable than those of the *Sunday Express*."

"What sources?"

"That really doesn't matter. But as I say – practically unimpeachable."

"Okay, then. So of what do all these sources that are practically unimpeachable now take great pleasure in informing us?"

Buchholz also disregarded my heavy-handedness. He disregarded the actual question, too.

"Erich, what makes you so protective of him? Especially when you tell me that you don't even know him? It seems quite evident you like him."

"Oh, for heaven's sake! How could I be qualified to say I know him? For such presumption you'd be the first to shoot me down."

"Would I, indeed? How extraordinarily harsh of me!" He even looked repentant. "But, you see, I myself have met him on only two occasions. Both times briefly. Eight years ago? No, nearer ten. So talk to me about him, if you would."

Abstractedly, I glanced out of the window again. Then wearily returned my eyes to the bed.

154

"Why?" I asked.

"Just humour me," he said. "I'd appreciate it."

"Well, what do you want me to tell you? First conjure up the popular image of your typical storm-trooper." And it actually made me smile: the expression on his face. "Now picture the exact opposite. Small…frail…nervy. Even almost timid. In short, just about the least military-looking man you could ever hope to find in Germany today. I mean, amongst the top brass."

"*Hope* to find?" queried Buchholz, amiably.

"Oh, all right, Heinrich. *Expect* to find. What's in a word?"

"Precisely."

"He's witty, urbane, astute. Well-read: often quotes from the Greek philosophers. Observant, too: I get the feeling there's nothing that he ever misses. I also think – "

"Does he quote from Nietzsche and Hegel, Schopenhauer and Spengler? Those a little closer to home?"

"Oh, yes, more than likely. As I say, he's well-read."

"Like you yourself are; no wonder you admire him!" He smiled. "You seem to know him rather intimately – despite your strange reluctance to admit it."

"Nonsense. I've learned all this at second-hand. Studied his writings and heard what people say about him. And naturally I see him around from time to time; can form my own opinions. On occasion, he even drops me a friendly word."

"Really? How interesting. But I am sorry; I didn't mean to interrupt."

"What?"

"You were talking about his powers of observation: how there's nothing he appears to miss. And then you said, 'I also think…'"

"I also think he has a stealthy love of adventure."

"*Adventure*?"

"Yes, that's pretty much my impression. Even if I don't have a lot to back it up."

"What *do* you have to back it up?"

"At interview, I remember, he spoke about the importance of the calculated gamble; of being prepared to risk everything for what you consider right; of never closing your eyes to the possibility of change…or, at least, the possibility of improvement…"

In view of my despondency, it was odd how swiftly I was warming to my subject. Like Gwatkin on Friday; like Sybella, both yesterday and this morning. There was one big difference, though. *I* believed what I was saying.

"He strikes me as being sympathetic," I ended hurriedly. I recognized the bathos. "I feel comfortable in his presence."

"Notwithstanding his nervousness? His timidity?"

I had to reflect on this. I would have agreed that the question pointed to a contradiction in the admiral's character. (Or, at least, in his character so far as *I* was capable of understanding it.) But possibly such a contradiction made him yet more sympathetic to somebody like myself…somebody increasingly aware of the divided nature of his own feelings.

A sudden thought occurred to me. In spite of his numerous idiosyncrasies…had I gradually come to see him as a father figure?

Canaris was older than my actual father. But he seemed younger…more open to life…more curious about it. Warmer. Whether I would have felt this way prior to *Kristallnacht* I wasn't quite sure – yet at the same time I couldn't forget how one big difference of opinion had done nothing whatever to alter the love I felt for my grandparents. And, something I sensed unreservedly about Canaris, *he* would never have excused anyone at all for their pleasurable participation upon that grim November night. If only off the record, he would have declared – unequivocally – that such barbarity was not, was absolutely *not*, excusable. Whereas my father had repeatedly condoned it.

"My friend, that question wasn't rhetorical, you know. All nervousness and timidity notwithstanding?"

"I'm sorry. My mind wandered." I quickly had to rein it in. "Yes, I agree that it's surprising. But, Heinrich, who knows? It's common knowledge he's religious. And maybe that's what

156

comes across so strongly and what makes people feel comfortable in his presence."

"Makes *you* feel comfortable in his presence."

"I realize that being a Christian doesn't altogether square with his being timid. But I was probably wrong to say timid. At heart, perhaps, he's confident and fearless."

But for the moment, obviously, it was neither the admiral's timidity, nor lack of it, which interested my host.

"A Christian?" he repeated, slowly. He looked thoughtful.

"Again, like myself."

"Evidently. But as you're naturally aware – for, even as we speak, I can see that you're regarding me with something of the martyr's glare – a religious outlook isn't called for any more in Germany. The Führer is our God. We don't need deputies."

He said this straight-faced…it was difficult to gauge his true opinion. For a while, we stayed silent. Buchholz drew himself up on the bed. He rearranged his cushions.

"So then," he said at last. "All very fascinating. But who can tell what bearing it will have? For the minute let's just go back to that article in the *Express*. As we agreed – an arrant example of the British press plumbing new depths, yes? Complete rubbish from start to finish. Yes?"

Again, like on Friday, Buchholz appeared to be waiting for an answer. Obediently I supplied it.

"Yes!"

"Well, no," he said. "In fact, not."

"Not?" For a foolish second or two, I thought he was merely retaliating for my joke about the storm-troopers.

"Oh, don't misunderstand me. That article…I wouldn't present it as being worthy of the Pulitzer. But at least it may have contained one single, lonely grain of truth. And I suppose we should have realized, yes? Seldom any smoke…"

Once more I felt assailed by apathy.

"What single grain of truth?"

"Well, now – would you credit it? – of late, we hear, there's been a rash of key German spies defecting to the Allies? Most particularly, it seems, in Turkey. And, rightly or wrongly,

Adolf was blaming our own dear boss for this. The consequence, you're all agog to know? Summary dismissal, no less!"

Buchholz laughed but I couldn't see why; the sound conveyed no element of humour.

"Though you'll now be pleased to discover," he went on, "that in the end it was nothing but a storm in a teacup. Full of sound and fury, signifying naught. Our Führer is a little subject to these sudden whims. Your friend was reinstated."

"Thank God for that," I answered. Albeit listlessly.

"But just don't thank him in public, that's all – not if you know what's good for you – not around Berchtesgaden, at any rate."

27

"Now then," he continued. "That interesting little titbit about his dismissal and reinstatement was fact...solid fact. Not rumour. Yet I have to acknowledge that there *are* rumours... which, in certain quarters, are as rife as rats' fleas – let's not attempt to minimize!"

"Oh...rumours! Well, I for one don't want to hear them."

"And I for one consider that you should."

At which point I myself nearly became subject to those same sudden whims of the Führer. Felt strongly tempted just to push back my chair and flounce out. Gwatkin had aroused a similar response when speaking about Krauts. I was damned if a Kraut should do the same when speaking of the admiral.

But, as before, my temper luckily cooled and then I contented myself merely with adopting a bored tone and enquiring why such rumours should be circulating *now* of all times.

I said: "It couldn't have anything to do with simple jealousy and malice, could it? With kicking a man while he's down? And the better the man the harder the kicks?"

"Yes, of course it could, my dear! Of course it could! It could have *everything* to do with that."

I felt marginally appeased. Even if in such a context I couldn't exactly warm to the manner of address.

"Especially so," he said, "in view of the kind of thing they're now raking up. Some of it tends to hark back, you know."

"Hark back?"

"It's said, for instance, that halfway through the thirties he even advised Franco not to side with Hitler. I think one could fairly term that as harking back."

I made no reply. I looked across the narrow road at the supposed schoolgirl still trying perhaps for the Baltic.

"And the reason he gave?" went on Buchholz. "I'm sure you would wish to know this. That when the war came we were definitely going to lose."

Surprisingly, I didn't feel incensed by what I heard. Not even indignant. Was this because there was probably nothing for the time being that appeared sufficiently important? Or was it more because I could actually accept the feasibility of it? Certainly Canaris – who spoke Spanish fluently – had always liked General Franco and the two of them had always enjoyed a good working relationship. So the thought of casual advice given by one friend to another ("If I were you, old boy, I shouldn't side with *us*!") was hardly very shocking. The admiral's lack of faith in the victory of the Fatherland ought perhaps to have been more worrying; but the fact that I myself didn't feel particularly upset by it...? Well again, I wondered, had this solely to do with the timing. I turned back from the window.

"Is that it?"

"Oh, by no means. It's also claimed that Canaris was heavily implicated in the coup attempts of 1938 and 1939..."

"So once more, as you say, not precisely of the here and now! And I fondly imagined that if you coughed in Paradise Street at three, Hitler would know about it by five-past."

He affably conceded the point. "So I think," he said, "we can now skip across to the present."

"You sound as though you're granting me a boon."

"To the time when – as recently as just two months ago – Canaris flew to Smolensk to meet conspirators on the staff of the Army Group Centre. *Allegedly*," he added, rather fast.

"Allegedly!" I repeated. "Huh!" Sadly, this seemed the best riposte I could come up with.

"But evidently," went on Buchholz, "our Führer has the luck of the devil! As a result of that meeting, a miniature bomb was concealed inside a bottle of Cointreau and travelled beside him the very next time that he flew. For better for worse, however, it failed to detonate."

He smiled.

"Though, naturally, I mean for better. But while we happen to be speaking of liqueurs and suchlike…" He spread his hands toward the Johnny Walker.

I nodded my acceptance and he moved off the bed again with some agility. Became bartender beside the chest of drawers.

And whilst raising my glass I actually managed to laugh – a laugh that sounded far more genuine than his own last pitiful attempt. "Down with the scandalmongers, then! Seedy, small-minded, pathetic!"

I suspected that Buchholz – one side of him, anyway – had wanted to see me rendered furious by his tale about Smolensk. Yet he appeared to take my toast in good part. He sipped at his whisky and seemed quite as relaxed and appreciative as ever.

"Though on the other hand," he observed, cordially, "didn't we just say – seldom any smoke without fire?"

"No, Heinrich. You did."

"*Touché!*" He smiled and shrugged and gave a fair-minded nod.

I said: "But what I still don't follow – *one* of the things I still don't follow – is why you're so keen that I should listen to all this."

"Ah, well," he said. "I'm simply trying to sketch in a dab or two of background."

"Background to what?"

At first I couldn't be sure whether Buchholz was answering this question. I soon realized he wasn't.

"You know, there are even those," he remarked, "who assert that the admiral sees our leader as being – what? – as being very mildly (only *very* mildly, of course) unhinged; who assert that although at the start Canaris simply hoped to steer him away from some of his...well, again, what shall we call them?...slightly more ambitious excesses, or desires, he fairly soon gave up on that endeavour and instead..." Buchholz became deflected by his drink.

"Instead?"

"Decided to oppose a little more drastically what he has allegedly spoken of" – he hesitated again – "as being nothing less than criminal folly, 'the criminal folly of our Führer...'"

'Allegedly' might rapidly be growing into a favourite word around here but I certainly didn't mean to let him hide behind it forever.

"No, Heinrich!" I exclaimed. "Now you've really gone too far! Admit it! He would never have said that! Never!"

"Perhaps not on the parade ground, nor over the wireless. But, as I say, there are those who would attest to it – who maintain that in private – "

"Those, no doubt, who would have numbered themselves among his very dearest friends!"

"Ah," smiled Buchholz. "Withering, withering! Though I think – oh, Lord! – you're going to like even less the thing I'm now about to mention. Apparently Smolensk wasn't just an isolated incident."

"No?" I enquired, icily.

"For it's said, you see, that he continually uses his position at the Abwehr to aid and abet the army conspirators. To abet them..."

There came another burst of laughter from downstairs. Our whole conversation had been punctuated by such sounds but

161

this one was yet more full-throated than the first of them I'd heard.

"Precisely!" I approved. "The single really suitable response! I only hope I would have thought of it myself!"

"...to abet them in their numerous overthrow attempts. Or else assassination bids. And furthermore..."

But Buchholz must at last have taken heed of my expression and decided that 'furthermore' could wait.

"My dear boy. I'm purely trying to show you that – just possibly – your beloved Admiral Canaris doesn't always see our interests, our *official* interests, as being his absolutely top priority."

He went on quickly and without giving me the chance to comment.

"Though here's one rumour which I'm sure you won't have so much trouble in believing. To wit...that recently he's prevented the killing of dozens of captured French officers in Tunisia."

"Well, at last! There you are, then! That sounds a bit more like it!"

Buchholz regarded me with amusement.

"So – finally – something which you find you're able to accomodate?"

Did he suppose he was being funny? My stony demeanour didn't change. Nor did the harshness of my tone.

"Like I've told you," I said. "Canaris is a Christian. Christians don't plan assassinations. They do step in – if it's at all within their powers to do so – to put an end to senseless slaughter."

"I don't think that, in the main, anyone could contradict that."

"Besides," I added, "why would you even speak of this as rumour? There must be literally hundreds who can either confirm it or deny it. Right?"

"Right," said Buchholz. He stood up. As before, he poured a generous double for us both, with only the smallest splash of soda. "And it certainly sounds a bit more like the man who –

reputedly – wouldn't spare himself in trying to stop Reinhard Heydrich's brutality in Russia. Not *every* rumour needs to be malicious, you perceive."

"Oh, Heydrich!" I said, in deep disgust. "Reinhard Heydrich and his *Einsatzgruppen* forces!"

"Yes. Even I would have no wish to whitewash Heydrich."

This actually surprised a laugh out of me which was genuine.

"You mean – as you've been trying your hardest to whitewash the admiral?"

Buchholz himself laughed. "No, no…how can you compare them? With Heydrich we're talking war crimes. Genocide. No one has ever accused the admiral of genocide. Nor even of war crimes. Not that kind of war crime, anyway. Against the Führer, maybe, but not against the peasants or the unprotected. I have never said – no one I know has ever said – that Canaris isn't essentially a very decent human being… "

I muttered slowly: "I thought you were having trouble in remembering him."

It was now his turn to sigh. "Oh, my good friend, do you really have to be *so* argumentative? Hasn't it occurred to you that for the moment we seem to be in perfect harmony?"

"No, I'm not certain that it has. You've allowed him to be a very decent human being – I give you that – but only after you've appeared to be suggesting, non-stop, that he's some kind of a liability to us, some kind of a… My God, yes. When all is said and done, you've been suggesting that he's a… That he's a…" I couldn't even bring myself to use the word.

"But, Erich, I stress – only maybe. *Maybe.* There isn't any actual proof. Merely a mass of circumstantial evidence. Yet the weight of that evidence is coming increasingly to alarm a number of very highly placed and influential people."

"A number which clearly doesn't include the Führer."

"No, not so far. But how long can it be before it does?"

I raised my previous point. "Well, if the admiral was really implicated in the coup attempt of 1938 and the Führer hasn't even tumbled to that yet…?"

But Buchholz responded neither to the sweet forbearance of my tone nor to the validity of my implication. Instead he suggested:

"Shall I tell you the nickname already being conferred on him by some of those who say these things?"

"No, I'd much rather you didn't. Please don't. I'm just not very interested."

"Young prig!" he said – but amiably and with indulgence. "You know you'd now find it quite tantalizing *not* to hear. He's being spoken of as the *Hidden Hand of the Wehrmacht Resistance*."

"What!"

For the second time in about two minutes – and again whilst least expecting it – I was obliged to laugh. The *Hidden Hand of the Wehrmacht Resistance*! It sounded like a title splashed across the cover of some penny-dreadful boys' adventure. Or like next week's cliffhanging instalment at the Saturday morning picture show. It was absurd; it was ludicrous. It was very nearly appealing.

Shades of Buster Crabbe?

No, it was *not* appealing – and, damn it, the instant stab which that stupid, ridiculous name could now deliver! (Only twenty-four hours ago…! Had we yet arrived at Daphne's twenty-four hours ago, or were we still having hysterics in Evelyn Woods Road? Either way, I didn't want to think about it.) Suddenly I felt confused.

Confused – or maybe just plain tipsy? I'd had nothing but a cup of tea since breakfast-time.

Or quarter of a cup of tea. If that.

Simply, it was all beginning to be too much. On top of everything else that had happened to me today…dear God, it was all beginning to be too much.

And what did I mean – beginning?

Not that, in fact, I *was* tipsy. And not that, in fact, the whisky wasn't helping. I thought that the gnawing ache, the emptiness, the sense of desolation…by this time they'd all have been unbearable without it. (You could only stave things off for

164

a limited period.) Now I knew it was bedtime I really had to fear. Continually, I had to push away the thought of that: the long, long night: the theft of further chance to drive away your misery. The sleeplessness, the silence.

The silence…

"Heinrich? *The Hidden Hand of the Wehrmacht Resistance*! Surely you don't subscribe to any of that rubbish?"

"No, my young friend. I have no business subscribing to it. Or, indeed, not subscribing to it. I'm only here to put the case."

"Why?"

"That, you will find out in a moment. One last thing you need to know and then you're in full possession of the facts. Or else in full possession of the rumours. Could you ever have wished for someone more impartial than myself?"

I remained quiet. *One last thing*? I knew I wasn't going to like it.

"Although, actually," he said, "this 'one last thing' has to be divided into two parts. The first part of the allegation is this: that over the years our friend has allowed certain secrets concerning Hitler's war strategy – going back as far as his offensives against the Low Countries and France and even including his plan to invade Great Britain itself – has allowed these, as if by accident, to filter through to Whitehall. And the second…that he's several times misled Hitler into believing that the Allies either *will* or will not do something which – "

But he got no further. I had hurled my tumbler to the floor. Indeed, had only just prevented myself from hurling it at him.

The glass shattered.

There then followed the sort of stillness that little else might ever have produced. I became aware of the astonishing hush downstairs. I imagined everyone with faces turned upwards, totally rigid and aghast, as if Medusa herself had come crashing through the ceiling.

It was a silence ended by a drawl. (That was, the silence pertaining upstairs.)

"My dear fellow, if I wasn't so damnably lazy, I'd jump to my feet and sponge that up. What a waste of good whisky –

lamentable! But when I'm sure you can be trusted I may even offer you another."

The sheer ferocity of my act had siphoned off all aggression. I left my chair and squatted to retrieve the fragments of glass from the lino and the rug. Carried them to the wastepaper basket; wrapped them in several sheets of an old *News Chronicle*, conveniently discarded.

"I'm sorry. I must pay you for the damage."

"Nonsense!"

"Where can I find a floorcloth?"

"My dear good man, it's simply not important. Now please sit down; you're blocking out the view."

I looked quickly at my watch but – still in chastened mood – ceased fussing and did as he bade me.

"I mustn't stay long. I have an appointment to keep."

"What time and where?"

"At half past four. Corner House in the Strand."

"Business or pleasure?"

"Oh, business! Most definitely business!"

But I was uncomfortably aware I hadn't yet made any bid to explain myself – far less receive absolution. (Afterwards, it occurred to me Heinrich would surely have understood; but, there in his bedroom, I only knew I had behaved abominably and couldn't merely walk away.)

I said again: "I'm sorry. What I did was childish. It's just that you were passing on lies which made out the admiral was a traitor; not simply a double agent but an out-and-out traitor." (Was this a form of progress? I now found I could say it.) "And you've told me yourself he's a very decent human being. Why would he want Germany to lose the war?"

Buchholz gave me a slow and unexpected smile.

"Tell me something," he said, softly.

"Yes?"

"Why wouldn't he?"

"Why wouldn't he what?"

"Want Germany to lose the war."

166

28

What a question!

And yet suddenly...suddenly it seemed almost sensible. I had naturally heard gossip before – well, as thousands must have heard it – about Hitler's being subject to fits, or at any rate to tantrums. And if this were indeed even partly true (and what had Buchholz now twice suggested: no smoke without fire?) then we Germans were being led by – at best – a man who was unstable, a man who had plunged us into war, war with roughly half the world, whilst reiterating over and over his intention of making us the most superior beings in the universe (no, we already were that, he said...his standard, laughing reassurance), of making us, then, the *rulers* of the universe, with himself, of course, remaining our dearly beloved and godlike inspiration. Therefore, at best, unstable. At worst, delusional?

So – in view of such a question – this was the worst possible moment to remember *Kristallnacht*.

But *Kristallnacht* was what it unfailingly came back to. Every time. Every single time.

Every single time that I allowed myself to doubt.

Unfailingly? There were certainly those who'd add 'simplistically'. All I knew was this. It had almost literally evolved into a nightmare; a constantly recurring nightmare.

My English grandparents had compiled a folder of newspaper cuttings (or, rather, my grandmother had) which they had wanted me to read in 1939, the last time I had stayed with them. I had read only the first of these cuttings – yes, yes, the one to do with *Kristallnacht*. I had obviously known it would unearth all the emotions buried several months before, and afterwards I couldn't think why I had ever allowed it to occur – this painful exhumation. Probably it had been a mixture of my hoping to appear reasonable before my grandparents and of my subconsciously wanting, and needing, to put myself to the test. Bravado, cussedness and a genuine desire to work out how the thing had happened, really to come to grips with its

167

underlying logic – all these must assuredly have played their part.

The account had covered two entire pages of newsprint: reporting that – in marked contrast to past anti-Jewish outbreaks – on *Kristallnacht* Hitler's storm-troopers were no longer the most prominent demonstrators. Throughout Germany the militia had now been joined not only by the proletariat but by thousands of the middle classes. In Berlin itself, fashionably dressed women had clapped, screamed with laughter, and even held aloft their babies to watch the Jews being beaten senseless by youths who used lead piping. The paper had stated that this night of brutality and arson bore all the hallmarks of an officially organized pogrom. Over seven thousand Jewish shops had been looted. Hundreds of synagogues were burned down. An unknown number of Jews had died. The report said insurance companies were being authorized not to indemnify the victims; and that all these grimly unparalleled hours of mayhem – without precedent in modern times in any civilized country – were already being grotesquely prettified as Crystal Night, since the broken windows alone accounted for millions of marks-worth of damage. Supposedly Goering was enraged when he heard that most of the replacement glass would have to be imported and paid for in scarce foreign currency.

"They should have killed more Jews and broken less glass," he had fumed…according to the paper.

The lengthiness of the account owed much to repetition.

However, spurred on by a nearly hypnotic fascination, I had read the full report: the whole centre spread of the *Express*. Some of the details, whether or not they were authentic, had been new to me. During that previous November – or during the relevant part of it – I had been with my father and stepmother in Innsbruck celebrating the golden wedding of my other set of grandparents, and on our return it seemed that no one had wanted to talk about the atrocity – only about the most probable cause of it: the assassination in Paris, immediately beforehand, of a German diplomat.

168

People had even implied (in an apologetic sort of way) that the reaction could be understandable – not forgivable, of course, but almost understandable – since the assassin himself had been a Jew. And, however regrettably (they had suggested), there was always one small section of the community all too easy to inflame.

Which was, in fact, the exact line of reasoning supported by my father...starting at suppertime on the day following our return. By no means all the evidence on the streets had so far been obliterated and I had found myself incapable of letting the subject drop. But up until then I hadn't even *begun* to realize how anti-Semitic he was (for when news of the barbarity had broken in Austria its truth had been so massively soft-pedalled that it had scarcely affected us). Yet back in Berlin, over the dinner table and much to the growing consternation of my stepmother, growing but ineffectual, our discussion had rapidly disintegrated. My father had become impatient, lost his temper, accused the Jews of crimes he couldn't substantiate...things which afterwards he may have wished he hadn't said but which I simply couldn't forget he *had* said. If he'd climbed down and apologized – or even climbed down and omitted the apology – it might have made a difference. But, as it was, I couldn't refrain from repeatedly mulling over the main points of our argument. Indeed from mulling them over for the next few days, or even week, practically without cease.

And undoubtedly because of this I had been cast into a dangerous mood on reading that first horrific clipping of my grandmother's; had nearly left for home that very afternoon, truncating my holiday by more than half. Yet somehow – and this had struck me later as being something close to a miracle – both I and my grandmother had eventually managed to calm down; thanks in no small measure to the gentle patience of my grandfather, who was invariably the peacemaker.

But afterwards they had clearly given up any hope of persuading me to stay at home with them – well, if not actually at home with them, at least in some internment camp, in whose

169

locality, for the Duration, they would willingly have taken up residence.

Our parting, too, had been more than usually upsetting; the letters which we wrote – until inevitably there came a suspension to the postal services between Germany and Britain – more than usually affecting.

In Berlin, of course, I had re-investigated the whole issue of *Kristallnacht* as thoroughly as circumstances would by then permit me to.

So perhaps the question that had now been put to me by Buchholz – "Why wouldn't he want Germany to lose the war?" – was not, in some ways, such a wholly unreasonable one.

29

"Because plainly," he went on, "no patriotic German would ever wish to see the Fatherland defeated. But, on the other hand, thousands might sympathize with a decent human being who was cracking up under pressure and who saw only the scum and the sadists rising to the top; who saw none of the good men: the heroes and the idealists. How many of us, do you think, would *truly* applaud the likes of Reinhard Heydrich?"

He was still speaking softly, although the noise downstairs now appeared to have returned almost to full strength. But I had no trouble in catching what he said.

"And one thing's undeniable, my friend. That after we've won this hateful war, the first step we must take is to clip the wings of all the overly ambitious. Even – and obviously I only whisper this – the wings of the great Führer himself! Not necessarily Adolf; I mean *any* Führer. For as some blessed Englishman once put it, all power tends to corrupt. And *absolute* power, of course…"

He broke off and gave me a grin bordering on the impish.

"But it doesn't follow – just because the English sometimes get things right – that they still don't thoroughly deserve to lose. I trust I have your full agreement *there*?"

"Well, naturally you have."

"Your own heart being unreservedly committed to the Fatherland?"

"Heinrich, for heaven's sake! I resent such a question! I'm sure that you would as well. Why do you find it necessary even to ask?"

He gave a shrug.

"But just don't break another glass, there's a good fellow. They're Waterford. Not easily replaceable right now."

This had the humbling effect he had obviously hoped to renew. Buchholz got up, left the room, returned with a second tumbler. At my own request the amount he poured into it was smaller than before.

"And anyway," he said, "you'll have to dispose of it fairly fast, if you mean to be at Charing Cross by half past four."

He replenished his own glass.

"Therefore – to sum up what I've said. It all comes down to only one thing."

For a moment he fixed me with his hard blue eyes, in the evident hope of adding emphasis.

"Erich, disclose your findings to as many people as you can, not simply to the admiral. He'll doubtless try to swear you to secrecy, but remember that no pledge given unwillingly need ever be binding. So tell your section head; tell every high-ranking officer with whom you come into contact. Fuck it, my dear, put it in writing and send it off to the Führer himself. Put it in writing *again*, that is, if you can't walk out of Willy's office bearing a copy of your own report. I think that by now you probably get my drift?"

"I think that by now I probably do. I'm still not happy with its basic premise."

"You don't have to be happy with it...only aware of it! Canaris may be quite the sweetest fellow on earth – present company excepted – yet all you need remember is the crucial

171

importance of whatever you've been checking on and whether you want to see its substance treacherously perverted. You may worship old Willy like your own dad," (it was odd that he should say that) "but is he really a friend to you?"

He smiled and tapped his bedside clock.

"Is Willy a friend or is he a foe? It's after four – so off you go!"

A cheery couplet to send me on my way. Cheery and, again, coincidental. The ampersand experience: *cherchons, cherchons*. (Though had it, after all, really been such a coincidence: the curious case of those ubiquitous ampersands?)

Anyway, I made my farewells fast and without fuss, both to Heinrich and his mother; and the impression I carried away of the son, maybe partly on account of that concluding couplet and of the consideration he'd shown in remaining mindful of the time – these, I mean, on top of his generally forgiving attitude – this impression was more agreeable, by far, than previously I would ever have thought likely.

He told me that he'd be in touch with me as soon as he'd relayed the successful completion of my assignment and been informed of my departure details.

"God willing!" I said, under my breath.

But then it occurred to me, as soon as I'd left, that Buchholz and his mother would certainly be safe for as long as I chose to remain in Britain. The authorities wouldn't want to give me any reason to panic. It was only after my return to Germany that they'd finally feel free to move in, because then there wouldn't seem to be a link between myself and their beating down a door at dawn – enemy agents were being flushed out all the time. More than one thing could have led to the apprehension of the Smees, inside their tiny spyhole in Paradise Street.

An idea blossomed.

As I passed the young woman in the gymslip, I gave her a cursory nod.

"Sorry I've been so long. But I also kept your friend waiting here on Friday – and, from the looks of it, I doubt his *Evening News* was half as entertaining as that puzzle of yours!"

My reasoning had been as follows. If I could make out I had realized from the start I was being watched, then the British wouldn't believe I had knowingly compromised my compatriots.

Therefore the Smees must be innocent. They weren't conspirators; they were simply friends of mine – and British ones at that! (Heinrich could have been more correct in his note than I had realized.)

Even if suspicion lingered, it would no longer be a matter of priority to pull them in. Buchholz and his mother would have more time to effect their escape.

Indeed, I imagined that as soon as the shop closed tonight – or, at any rate, as soon as Frau Buchholz had had sufficient chance to step properly out of character – they might be discussing this very eventuality. I should have let them know that for the present they were safe.

I thought about hurrying back, but I was already running late. I would return after the theatre.

So much for my reasoning, then. I saw the confusion on the girl's face, yet didn't wait for her reaction.

It followed me, however.

"Mister, I dunno what you're on about! You a bit cuckoo or summat? On leave from the loony bin?"

Briefly, I paused to look back.

Then, although I was by now several feet away, she held up the puzzle as if to ward off the blows of a maniac.

"I warn you, mister, jus' you try an' touch me an' I'll be screamin' for me mum! An' she won't 'alf give you a proper seeing-to!"

Before I rounded the corner into Marylebone High Street, I glanced behind me a second time. She hadn't moved – was looking understandably irresolute. For a moment I thought I had behaved badly. *Unsportingly.* Had it really been so necessary to let her know she'd goofed?

But then I recollected myself.

Of course it had.

I hailed a passing taxi.

My third taxi of the day... The first, carrying me from Waterloo to the Prince of Wales, had provided me with a really happy journey; my second, from Leicester Square along to Abbey Road, with an outstandingly profitable one. This present ride, taking me to Charing Cross, saw me filled with self-disgust.

Oh, God!

What a fool I had just been!

30

And I had believed myself so clever! I had truly thought that I had discovered a way to save my friends. But why – *why* – hadn't I realized? That instead of saving my friends I had only sabotaged my own future. Made MI5 aware I could no longer be of service to them. That there was now nothing left but to move in and arrest me.

And how long was *that* going to take? How long before my latest inept tracker could make contact with HQ? (She was hardly any distance from the post office, admittedly, or even from the phone box I myself had used on Friday; but it was more than possible she'd find a queue in both places.) Perhaps I should rush back now, while there might still be time, to knife her in the back or garrotte her with one of her girlish pigtails?

Oh, yes. Sure! Perhaps I should cut it off and use it to garrotte myself? Carry my self-destructive tendencies to their logical conclusion.

For to have spoken to that woman in the first place...hadn't that been inexpressibly self-destructive? And I was convinced that – if he'd seen it – Johnny Walker would have given me a very understanding nod.

But while I'd been sipping at those three good measures – no, more like two really; I'd drunk only a small amount from the refill in the broken tumbler – I had thought that absolutely nothing mattered any more...that all I had to do was somehow get through this awful evening that approached, without letting Sybella Standish tumble to the fact she'd been unmasked. And how clear-headed would I need to be for that? – she was far too pleased with herself ever to suspect discovery, unless you actually announced it. As regards anything else, I simply hadn't *cared*. Most definitely I hadn't envisaged having a brainwave during that brief journey between the newsagent's shop and the High Street.

Now, ironically, the shock of what I'd done seemed to have left me utterly and non-self-destructively clear-headed…when this was obviously too late to be of any consequence.

*

I got to the Corner House four minutes late. She was there. This afternoon she was wearing pale blue with white polka dots, a white jacket and a small jaunty hat that had a wisp of veiling. I paid off the taxi and strode across the pavement. On reaching her I uttered an exclamation. I looked back towards the kerb.

"Oh, damn! That was silly!"

I had naturally raised my hat, but appeared not to have noticed that I hadn't kissed her, nor made any comment on the way she looked.

"What was silly?"

"I should have kept the taxi."

"Why – aren't we stopping here for tea?"

"Yes, but there's something I should see to first. You don't mind?"

"Of course not."

"Only five or ten minutes along the Strand. We can easily walk it."

I may not have kissed her but despite all good intentions I couldn't push her hand away when it brushed against my own. Although I knew she was a fraud – that her professed liking of me was probably no more than purely that: *professed* – and although in addition she was wearing gloves, white cotton gloves, still, the physical contact continued to supply a charge.

175

But now the situation was about to change. And when it did, she would be free to suppose that my own behaviour had been every bit as calculated as hers. This thought brought satisfaction.

Well no, to be honest, it *didn't* – not as yet – but I was hopeful that it soon would…certainly by the time I was back in Berlin and being hailed as a hero, a shrewd manipulator; a thorn in the flesh of MI5.

Even the admiral would approve – and all the more so for having realized that I wasn't just a yes-man.

(But, of course, this presupposed that I wasn't going to be arrested…which I felt quite positive I was.)

She began to swing my hand. But when she stopped doing so, even then she didn't release it and, despite myself, I felt powerless to draw it away. "What lies along the Strand?" she asked. "Only five or ten minutes along the Strand?"

"Oh," I said, "any number of fine things."

"Yes, but don't be annoying. What in particular?"

I spoke the words lightly. "Did no one ever tell you that when you grew up you'd need to learn a little patience?"

A shrewd manipulator, they would say – oh yes, assuredly. But how about a Pagliacci? No, they would never say that. Yet as an epithet I thought I might have valued it more highly. Even as an epitaph. *He could appear light-hearted, no matter how he hurt.*

"Well, that will be all well and good for when I do grow up," she said. "But in the meanwhile I feel it's actually the here and now that matters."

Earlier, I might have replied: Then in that case you must *never* grow up!

But since this would have implied a future in which I hoped to be involved, I now confined myself to something a great deal more relevant.

"Anyway, you'll soon find out what lies along the Strand."

"Oh, all right. I can see I'll have to give in. Naturally I shall attempt to do so with rare dignity and grace."

"And as it's somewhere I've never been into myself – but possibly somewhere you have – I'm hoping you may be able to advise me. At any rate, I shall be interested to note your reaction."

Mean, I thought. Mean and nasty and below the belt. *No matter how he hurt.* More than a shade ambiguous, perhaps.

"Somewhere I may have been into? Well, now, let me see. I've been into Simpson's. If only on the very rare occasion. Or – not to put too fine a point on it – just once. Their roast beef was excellent."

"It isn't Simpson's," I told her.

"I've been to the Tivoli many times. Oh, *many* times. Anything up to four or even five."

"Nor the Tivoli," I said.

"I saw *Jezebel* there…and *The Adventures of Robin Hood*…oh, and something else…and possibly something else."

I myself had seen both of those films, but held back from saying so.

"No, it isn't the Tivoli."

"Oh dear, now I'm running out of inspiration. Of course, I've been to the Civil Service Stores, but that's well in the other direction. I *haven't* been to the Savoy or the Savoy Grill, which I can see we're fast coming up to." She sounded apologetic. "So, apart from lots of oohs and ahs, I'm not sure if my reaction *there* could ever be precisely helpful."

I shook my head. "Never mind. It won't be necessary."

"Oh, but that's sad!" I received a sideways glance from beneath demurely lowered lashes. "Because the fact I haven't been there, not even to the Grill, doesn't mean I've never wanted to. You mustn't think that."

"Really? Well, in that case, I can only express my surprise."

"Surprise?" She laughed. "Surprise at what?"

"At the notion that you haven't yet managed it."

It was some three or four seconds before she replied to this.

"Mmm. I may have to reflect on that one for a bit. But I was only speaking foolishly, you understand. Who gives a fig about

177

the Savoy Grill? And I hope you realize I'm the modern type of woman: one who always likes to pay her own way!"

"Oh, bravo," I said. "Yes. Bully for you!"

With her free hand she lightly punched my upper arm, her handbag knocking against my sleeve, but I could tell her playfulness was now becoming strained.

"That is, I mean, when RKO isn't picking up the bill. Or *aren't* picking up the bill? It gets a bit confusing, regardless of the *Inc*."

I didn't reply.

She persevered. Oh, what a plucky little find, I thought, for the Intelligence Brigade! They should have put her on a poster. No doubt one day they would.

"Ah, yes, I've got it!" she exclaimed. "At last! Simpson's, the Tivoli, the Savoy – you must think me very stupid!" She smote her forehead in exasperation. "No, we're heading for a shop of some kind, aren't we? It's all so depressingly simple! There's a girl you want to buy a present for; a girl whom so far you've been keeping ever so quiet about! Therefore a girl you've clearly got designs on – perhaps are even secretly engaged to – "

"No," I said. "It isn't anything like that."

I took a deep breath; half hoping she might step in to fill the gap.

"Because, after all," I went on, when it became clear that this wasn't going to happen, "I don't think we can both have fiancés. Can we?"

I even allowed myself a further short pause.

"Secret *or* otherwise."

She didn't say anything. Nevertheless I'd felt the shock that ran through her. Illogically, it made me wince.

Yet on the other hand... Yes, on the other hand! Why should I even care – why in the name of heaven should I even care? It was no more than she'd have done to me, had our positions been reversed.

She still kept pace with me – although she wasn't, like myself, just staring straight ahead: I remained conscious of her

178

scrutiny. Well, at any rate, that obviously reduced the need for any schoolgirl with her puzzle and pigtails. *She* in fact had almost certainly been given the rest of the evening off. Bad luck, of course, if Sybella and I parted company much earlier than envisaged. Bad luck for all of those shifty secret service types, the Lieutenant Commander Montagues of this world, together with anyone else who was wanting to keep tabs on me. Wanting to know, presumably, how long I meant to stay.

So all right. They'd just have to resume their surveillance later on, when I got back to Mrs Hilling's.

It was galling to have to admit that up till now I hadn't been aware of them in Abbey Road.

Though, damn it, I kept on forgetting, didn't I? Kept on forgetting that their little game was up. *Their* little game? My own little game, equally. That at any second now a car could come skidding to a halt beside us and a couple of plain-clothes men leap out of it…one of them brandishing handcuffs.

Stupidly, from force of habit, as we crossed Lancaster Place I put my currently *un*cuffed hand beneath her elbow. She pulled her arm away sharply. I carried on as if I hadn't noticed.

"I hope you're going to agree that it wasn't a bad estimate."

"Estimate?"

"I said five or ten minutes along the Strand. In fact it's taken twelve."

She looked about her. "Well, surely you can't be meaning *here*?"

"Somerset House? Well, why not? Why ever not? You seem surprised. But people do come to Somerset House, don't they? People who want to trace their family trees or find out who inherited from Uncle Max; and just how much the old man had to leave. Or whether So-and-So was really born in wedlock – and where – and what on earth was the name of that rapacious widow whom he upped and married? Hundreds of good reasons for *everyone* to flock to Somerset House. Don't tell me you yourself have never been?"

"No, I have never been to Somerset House."

She declared this emphatically, as though she were speaking to someone of severely limited intelligence.

"Oh dear. Then, after all, you won't be able to tell me where I ought to go. What a shame! I'm sure they have a special section."

"A special section for what?" she asked, dully. "What are you after?"

"Nothing fancy. Merely a birth certificate."

"Why do you want your birth certificate?"

"I don't. Not mine."

We had reached the main door. I didn't push it open immediately. Perhaps I felt some need to prolong this moment of heady victory.

"Whose, then?"

"Well, what makes you think it would be either mine *or* my father's?"

"Your father's? Who ever brought your father into this?"

I didn't answer. Produced an enigmatic smile. Enigmatic – and also, I guessed, immensely irritating.

"And anyway," she said, "why should you want to have the birth certificate of somebody who's dead? Even supposing it were going to be here, which I – "

She broke off.

"Oliver, why in God's name are you behaving like this?"

"Actually, if it helps at all, I don't believe it's going to be here, either. We're wholly at one on that."

"Oh, what *is* the matter? I really don't understand. I don't understand *anything* any longer."

"Oh, on the contrary," I said, "I think you do! And, by the way, my name isn't Oliver. It's Eric. Or Erich – depending on who happens to be speaking it at the time. Shall we go in?"

Yet if this were truly the prologue to my moment of vindication…well, to be honest again, it didn't feel like any of it would provide a lot to write home about. I had been so much happier this morning.

So *very* much happier.

There was an official who stood to one side of the vast marble-floored vestibule: a short man, balding, with – I noticed, as we drew nearer – grey hair protruding from his ears and his nostrils, and black hair coating the backs of his hands. I asked him how to obtain copies of birth certificates; explained that neither of the two I sought was actually my own.

"Then the first letter of the party's name?" he queried.

"M," I said. I winked at Sybella. "M for Martin."

"And the first letter of the second party's name?"

"M," I smiled. "Also M for Martin. Now you might reckon that's a bit of a coincidence – but, no, not really. A little like Alexandre Dumas, if you see what I mean: Dumas *père et* Dumas *fils*. Except that *those* two shared a given name and *these* two don't…unless in this instance you count the family name, which I suspect was a name not actually given until a month or so back – let's say, the end of March, the start of April? But I can see you think it's getting complicated."

Complicated? Plain crazy, more like! What *did* I suppose I was doing? (*You a bit cuckoo or summat? On leave from the loony bin?*) God in heaven. What a time for me to start to wonder.

I mean, to wonder why no one had yet turned up holding out that pair of handcuffs.

I couldn't have been mistaken, surely? Both the girl *and* the fellow? Innocent bystanders?

No. It wasn't possible. Just was *not* possible!

I had lost the hairy man's attention. His stare had transferred itself from me to Sybella. It seemed no less dazed, however.

Sybella was heading for the exit.

The attendant, of course, must have observed her departure with a lot more surprise than me. We heard the brisk tattoo of her heels striking the marble. It resonated throughout the lobby. It reminded me of the frenzied tapping of Blind Pew, on the highway, just seconds before he was mown down and trampled beneath the horse's hooves.

31

I went after her.

Thankfully I saw her, just across the road, starting to descend the stairs beside the bridge. These led to the Embankment. I didn't hurry. I kept some half-dozen yards behind and she didn't look back. She was heading in the direction of Charing Cross but when she reached a small public garden she went in. I stood near the gate and waited until she'd sat down. Then I followed the twisting path towards her bench…which may have taken me some thirty seconds. She didn't once glance up. Her face was obscured by her handkerchief.

"I truly am sorry," I said.

She didn't react.

"Please don't cry. Please don't." I sat beside her. "Unless you want me to join in. Might they commission us – two figures in a fountain?"

"Go away," she said.

"No."

"Then *I* shall."

But I pulled her back. "What's the point? You know I'd only follow. We haven't had our tea."

"Tea!"

"Yes. They tell me it's the cup that cheers. It seems you need a spot of cheering. I'm not too certain why."

"*What* did you say?"

"I said I'm not too certain why."

"Well, in that case…in that case…"

"What?"

"My God! It only shows me how insensitive you are."

"Why? Because I had to call your bluff?"

She didn't answer.

"And I bet Mata Hari never spoke like that. 'Oh, it only shows me how insensitive you are! When all the time I thought you were a gentleman!'"

She showed not the slightest tendency to smile.

I added: "'But no! Any *true* gentleman would have repulsed his suspicions!' I bet she never said that – or, at least, not very often."

"It's not the fact you had suspicions! It's the vile and gratuitous way in which you voiced them."

"Well, I didn't exactly enjoy that part of it myself. But if I was a bastard – and yes, all right, I was a bastard – perhaps I had good reason."

No acknowledgment of this.

"And anyway," I asked, "how *should* I have set about it? Sat down with you and had a nice illuminating chat across the buttered toast and scones? Well, in fact, isn't that what we're doing right now? Or could be doing right now? May I pass you the buttered toast?"

"Good reason?" she enquired, coolly – belatedly. "What good reason?"

"Oh, well. You yourself mightn't think it such a good one. And again I'm not convinced it's in the best traditions of Miss Hari. But I was hurt. Yes – *hurt*! Because you mightn't credit it: my biggest worry this morning on seeing you drive away from Waterloo was simply this. How on earth was I going to break it to you that the *Laura* thing was pure prefabrication?"

She didn't comment for a moment – and when she did, Franz Mannheim might have nodded his approval.

"Just fabrication," she corrected, wearily. "Someday someone ought to try to teach you English."

Although she still didn't smile, and her tone remained lifeless, I obviously saw this as a breakthrough. And took heart.

"It was easier for you," I said. "You knew from the beginning I was playing a role. But I hadn't the foggiest idea that you were. I believed every word you told me."

I remembered our walk back to camp; remembered the feeling of warmth which had so convincingly pervaded it. And remembering this – feeling further encouraged by it – I laid my hand upon her sleeve.

183

"Well, let's not exaggerate," I said. "Every other word you told me. But that turned out to be enough. More than enough, unfortunately."

She made no attempt to remove her arm. (Another memory surfaced – also, an encouraging one – the memory of when she had touched my wrist in The Tap and Tankard.) She seemed to look at me properly for the first time since we had arrived at Somerset House.

"More than enough for what?"

"Oh dear. Only somebody rather insensitive would have to ask me that."

She still didn't smile. She turned her gaze towards the river and waited maybe fifteen seconds before she brought it back.

"Why are you saying all this?"

"Because it's true. No other reason. And there's clearly no point in our lying to one another any more. Either about the big things or the little things. Though for the moment, please, don't ask me which is which."

A woman passed us with a pram and I smiled gravely at the infant who was sitting up inside it, as though she alone, in her fuzzy pink cardigan and pompommed pink hat, might be sufficiently qualified to pronounce.

"Do you honestly mean that?" Sybella asked.

"Yes, I honestly do mean that."

But I still didn't want to take anything for granted. I lacked the confidence. Seemed incapable of merely keeping quiet.

"Yes, I was playing a role – obviously. Yet at the same time, in spirit, I can swear that I never stopped being myself. And by far the greater part of what I told you was absolutely true."

"A minute ago you used the word *unfortunately*. Why?"

"Well, that's easy. Is there anything more unfortunate than somebody falling in love all by himself? And, besides, Capulets don't ever quite set out to fall in love with Montagues. Not if they possess one particle of common sense."

It struck me that those wretched Montagues got in everywhere. You might have thought Verona at least might be free of them.

184

"Although, on the other hand, I suppose I ought to qualify that a bit – I mean, if I'm being required to dot *all* the i's and cross *all* the t's, as apparently I am. You see, perhaps it's true that I don't possess one particle of common sense. Perhaps it's true that in a way I did set out to fall in love."

She waited.

"Though please don't ask me why. From the start there was something about your photograph which…oh, I don't know…"

I shrugged.

"In any case, your *photograph* was smiling."

"And you promise me," she repeated, "that you are now completely on the level?"

"Listen. How can I persuade you? No worthy German spy is ever supposed to leave himself exposed and vulnerable; the rulebook specifically forbids it. Yet this particular example of the species – *me*, in case you still need to have it spelt out – is right now feeling *so* exposed and vulnerable he might just as well be sitting here stark naked. My instructors would be furious. 'Put back your clothes on!'" I let them speak in English but supplied them with a weighty accent. "'That is not the manner in which any *true* gentleman ever likes to behave, no matter how repulsive!'"

Perhaps it was this final barb that toppled her defences.

"Well, at *last*!" I exclaimed. "At *last*!"

I shot one arm into the air.

"Oh, praise the Lord, Miss Standish! That is *far* more the way your photograph was looking!"

"How *can* you be a German spy? You must be the least likely German spy in history. Well, German or otherwise."

"And, if it could talk, far more the way it would have sounded, too! Yes, hallelujah! A hundred times – hallelujah! And incidentally yours is an assessment which those instructors would wholeheartedly agree with. In fact you seem to be so much one of them I fear you may be fighting on the wrong side."

This could have been quite hopelessly misjudged. I instantly regretted it.

185

She said: "And what actually made you assume that?"

"I was being crass. I'm sorry. It was nothing but a stupid joke."

"No, I don't mean *that*."

"You don't? What, then?" I tried to think back.

She gave a slightly crooked smile.

"That you might have fallen in love all by yourself."

I stared at her.

"You see," she added, after a pause, "perhaps most of the time my own role was no further from reflecting the truth than yours was."

"It wasn't?" I said at last, weakly.

"And do you know something? The ordinary man in the street might have thought we were both supposed to be at least of average intelligence."

"Then how about this?" I asked. "Just for the time being? The ordinary man in the street can go and take a running jump."

32

She had taken off her hat and put it in her lap. Her head was resting on my shoulder. She said, eventually:

"I suppose you wouldn't like to tell me something? The name of the person I've just been kissing?"

I did so. It turned out that she hadn't absorbed the half she had already heard. She didn't even remember she *had* heard it.

"Are you certain you told me?"

"Positive," I said.

"Oh, well, I suppose you were making so little sense then – overall – that it's scarcely surprising if I simply stopped listening. Anyone would have…I mean, anyone with the slightest claim to sanity."

"You sound like my grandmother."

"Thank you. She must be a very lovely person."

"She is."

"I can hardly wait to meet her."

Nevertheless, she spoke the name aloud and then repeated it more softly: Eric Anders.

Erich Anders.

"It's going to seem quite strange," she said, "getting to think of you as that."

"Yes, I'm sure. You knew me for so very long as something else."

"Precisely. But perhaps in time I'll grow used to it."

Her tone became bleak.

"Except that... I was forgetting, of course! Time isn't something we're going to have a lot of."

I stroked the top of her head. "You think this war is going to last forever?"

"Maybe not – but what will happen to us while it does? In particular...what will happen to *you*? They'll probably make you a prisoner of war, won't they? And when they do that...?"

Then she pulled away, abruptly. She sat up and gazed wide-eyed. As if in shock.

"Oh, my God! They don't shoot spies, do they?"

I gave a laugh that was probably as contrived as Heinrich's had been; but did my best to reassure her.

"Like our much-maligned Dutch friend whom we keep remembering? 'Acht, all these brutes, vhy are they *so* insensiteeve?' No," I said gently, "they don't shoot spies." I drew her down again. "Not this one, anyway. This one's allowed to roam at will." (My outlook had certainly undergone a change during the course of the afternoon. I now felt reasonably confident – although, I admit, not absolutely so – that I wouldn't have to face a firing squad.) "They pretend they haven't noticed him. Then they allow him – all in his own good time, of course – to go back to Germany."

"What?" she said.

Then, for a second time, she sat up. I realized why. She had to be able to see me.

"At least, that's up to you," I said. "What I mean is – he's allowed to roam at will so long as..."

But I could now see the look in her eye and that stopped me dead.

"So long as I don't tell anyone he knows the truth?" Her voice had grown as hard as her expression.

"No," I said. "That isn't what I'm saying."

Yet, again, she hadn't heard; or hadn't registered.

"So that explains all the sweet talk! Of course it does. I'm such an idiot. I should've realized."

"No, listen – please just listen! If that were true, what do you think I would have done? We'd have had our tea at the Corner House and I'd have let you go on sobbing your heart out over your tragically lost love. I'd have kept up that whole ridiculous charade, with never a hint of challenge, or of confrontation, to mar one tiny, magic moment. What I *wouldn't* have done was to allow my own juvenile emotions to clog up something which – oh, for pity's sake! – which most people would think fully important enough to transcend all that *personal* sort of guff."

I hoped it was a convincing argument; to myself it actually sounded unanswerable.

And thank God she *was* convinced. She leant back against me; gave a sigh.

"Yes, I'm sorry," she said. "Forgive me."

"I shall definitely consider it."

"And it isn't guff! Your emotions are not juvenile."

"Mixed up, then."

There was a lengthy silence. "But I shall *have* to tell them," she said, at last.

"Yes, of course you will! Of course you will! I was just getting round to that when you became Eleonora Duse and cried out you were an idiot."

"I am sorry," she said again.

"On the other hand, if I don't go back to Germany the Abwehr knows at once the letters were a hoax."

"Why?" she asked.

For a moment I had to give this question more attention than I might have thought.

"Well, I agree," I said, "the British *could* have taken me prisoner simply because my identity was rumbled – taken me prisoner without uncovering why I was over here, despite doing their utmost to find out. But my non-return would automatically renew every doubt the Abwehr ever had about the major."

I added, with a minuscule attempt at humour: "Renew more doubts than it ever had in the first place!"

"Yet equally," she said, "if you do go back to Germany, you immediately announce the truth."

A seagull had landed on the grass quite close to us. It didn't stay long. In silence we watched the unexpected grace with which this apparently ungainly bird took to the air again.

"No," I said, "I am not sure that I do. I am honestly not sure that I do."

I continued to watch the seagull. Its flight now took it back towards the south bank.

"Which isn't something I'm saying merely in order to string you along. You have got to believe that!"

After what was possibly no more than three or four seconds, yet appeared infinitely longer, she gave a nod.

"I do believe it."

"And just as importantly: you have to make *them* believe it."

I suddenly appreciated the immensity of my relief in being able to say all this. Of my relief and gratitude...gratitude for the things which only an hour ago I had been viewing as wholly catastrophic, but which had unforeseeably led to the present.

"I shall do my best," she promised. "I shall really do my best."

"And when I say 'them', you understand, I'm not necessarily referring to the Prime Minister and the whole of the War Cabinet."

"Thank you. I was rather scared you might be. Yet, in that case, whom are you referring to?"

"Come now. I'm sure you don't need *me* to tell you."

She responded with a slow and lazy smile...a teasing smile. "Don't I?" Once again she raised her head from my shoulder. "But I'm afraid I've suddenly been afflicted with memory loss,

189

and I was hoping you might be able to cure me, by supplying the right name."

"Oh, lady, lady, this won't do! I suppose you'll tell me next you've even forgotten his rank?"

She nodded, helplessly.

"Well, supposing we closed our eyes and stuck a pin in a paper and came up with…how about lieutenant, say? Or lieutenant commander? Would that bring anything back?"

"Army or navy?" she asked.

"Tut, tut, Miss Standish – and there you are, almost the toast of Aldershot! Applauded to the rafters! But didn't they tell you? They don't have lieutenant commanders in the army."

She looked impressed. "All right," she said. "We've got the rank. Let's have his name. I'll make it easy for you if you like: you need only supply the first letter."

"But you still don't think I can, do you?"

"No shilly-shallying, if you please! The first letter of the party's name?"

It was now my turn to be impressed. It couldn't be coincidence; I realized that she must be setting out actually to lay ghosts. I thought her almost as courageous – admittedly for slightly different reasons – as she had appeared to me yesterday, in Manor Park.

"Hmm," I said. "Shall we try M again? Yes, why *not* try M again? It worked for me before." Once more I gave her a wink – possibly a degree less repulsive than my previous one. "But, this time, not M for Martin. That would be too boringly repetitive and I feel we need to ring the changes. So this time, my love – well, what would you say to…yes, let me see, now…I think I'm feeling lucky…yes, what would you say to… M for Montague?"

33

"You may still be one of the most unlikely spies in all of recorded history. But I do have to say this. You're certainly not one of the least effective."

"Thank you. Mainly, though, I've just been lucky."

"No, I don't accept that."

"Why not? I ran into you, didn't I?"

"You're also," she said, "a most excellent debater."

"In that case then, as my reward, won't you tell me how it happened?"

"What – that you ran into me? It must have been written on the roll call of destiny. In letters ten feet high."

"That much I know. But now I'd like to hear about the small print."

"What part, exactly? There's a lot of it."

"Paragraph forty-seven. The one that deals with ENSA. You really are with ENSA?"

"Yes, I am."

"Not in counter-intelligence?"

She shook her head.

"So how did you get drawn in? Is the lieutenant commander a friend of yours?"

"Both a friend *and* a relative – well, in a way, that is, because I actually grew up calling him Uncle."

She explained.

"You see, the Manor House at Ogbourne St George belongs to Ewen Montague's brother-in-law. But my mother's been the housekeeper there, and my father the head gardener, ever since I was small. We had a cottage in the grounds. Right from the beginning we were treated like family – my sister and I, in particular."

For a moment she looked reminiscent but swiftly checked whatever digression might have occurred to her.

"Anyway, a bit earlier this year, I happened to be around one Sunday when Ewen paid us a flying and impromptu visit;

having belatedly decided that he liked the sound of the address! *The Manor House, Ogbourne St George.* Apparently its very Englishness was hard to beat; would prove, he said, practically irresistible to the Boche. (Meaning *you*, my darling, in case you still need to have all the i's dotted and all the t's crossed!) Of course, at that stage no one had a clue as to what he was on about; merely knew that he wanted to cadge some of the stationery. It was only as an afterthought that he looked at me and asked if he could have a snapshot. 'We might want to play a little trick on Jerry,' he said – I quote verbatim." She smiled. "And *that*, Mr Anders, is the story of how I came to be 'drawn in', as you so eloquently put it."

I myself didn't smile.

"But his asking for a snapshot – didn't that make your parents feel uneasy? (Your parents, at the very least.) A bona fide address? A bona fide occupant of that address?"

"Well, yes, I suppose it did, a little. But we wanted to help. And he assured us we had nothing to worry about. No one was ever going to call."

Sybella laughed.

"Uncle Ewen, the soothsayer!"

"No. Uncle Ewen the incredible optimist. Did he *honestly* imagine we wouldn't bother ourselves to check up?" I suddenly felt angry. Not only indignant – angry.

Yet, annoyingly, I also had a duty to be fair. I remembered Franz Mannheim's opinion – with which, actually, I had been partly in agreement. "*In fact, Anders, do you know what I think? That in sending you over to England we're wasting your time.*"

But even this couldn't soften my resentment.

"Check up on what, exactly?" Sybella's tone had become wistful. "The contents of those letters? Although Ewen told me many bits and pieces regarding the set-up in general, naturally he couldn't tell me anything of its underlying purpose. I've no idea who wrote those letters – nor to whom they were going or what they said. None whatsoever."

She made me chuckle.

"Oh Lord…my own, sweet, shameless little Mata Hari!"

"And I thought I was being so crafty."

"Only sweet. Only shameless."

"But I don't see why I shouldn't know."

"I'm not sure that I do. Even if careless talk *does* cost lives and clergymen who look like Friar Tuck are never to be trusted."

However, I swiftly returned to my study of the small print.

"Ewen Montague clearly confided all those 'bits and pieces' while he was priming you for Aldershot. He can't have had a *lot* of time in which to get you ready."

"I might say that's the understatement of the year!"

"I think I was hoping you might say a little more."

"All right, then. What? That last Friday we were playing at Biggin Hill? That when we arrived he was already waiting near the main gates? That when I saw him I felt not only flabbergasted but *scared*, guessing immediately what he was there for? That on Friday night Peggy went on as Freda but in spite of this Ewen kept me up until practically half past four."

"And I don't suppose you slept very much even after that."

"Well, that's something! I'm glad you understand at least a *fraction* of the inconvenience you've been putting us through."

I smiled. "But he must have been so quick off the mark!" I exclaimed. "What time did your coach arrive at Biggin Hill?"

"We'd come down from the north. Shortly after four?"

"You're pulling my leg!"

"No. Why?"

"Because I wasn't at the solicitor's till shortly after two!"

She didn't understand the reference.

"All I know is, you spoke to my mother on Thursday; the family happened to be out that evening. She alerted Ewen almost the minute you'd put down the phone."

I gave a whistle.

"Was your mother an actress, too?" I remembered how relaxed she had sounded. "In that case I'd say you could *easily* employ her as your understudy."

"I'll tell her. She'll be pleased. Shall I also pass on your apologies for having cut her off?"

"Oh, how could she possibly have thought that?"

"Search me. But there's one thing I *won't* let her think, not even as my understudy. That she could ever have learnt such an *incredibly* complex part half as swiftly as her daughter!"

"Could anyone – Ewen Montague included? Did he stay in touch with you over the weekend?"

"Oh, yes. On Saturday he phoned twice. First during one of the matinée intervals. Then back at camp, after the evening show. Seemed surprised that I hadn't heard anything. Was it you, though, waiting there opposite the stage door?"

"It was!"

"Oh, you poor love! How pathetic!"

"Utterly."

"Of course, I rang him on Sunday as soon as I'd received your card. He called straight back – spoke for nearly *two* hours. That's why I couldn't make it to the pub a little earlier."

She raised a hand, spread wide her fingers, pouted. "Scarcely had the time to paint my nails!"

"Well, from your own point of view it might have been better if you hadn't. Although I've got to say that they looked good. So – by the way – did the rest of you."

"Well, thank you. But *I've* got to say that Ewen thinks of everything – no matter how rushed he may have been. On Friday afternoon, would you believe, he even turned up with clothing coupons! So I had a lovely time, Saturday morning, taking my mind off scary thoughts of *you* and ransacking the shops for an outfit that would boost a nervous girl's morale."

She laughed.

"Well, thinks of *practically* everything…I couldn't get any silk stockings! *Why* might it have been better if I hadn't painted my nails?"

"Because Freda's weren't painted the night before. So, naturally, I had to put you down as a duplicitous little baggage right from the beginning."

"I don't see why."

"*Oh, alas and alack, I only got your note about an hour ago, while I still lay sleeping in my bed!*"

"In other words," she said, severely, "you're talking of nothing more than everyday, universally accepted, totally endearing feminine wiles?"

"Is *that* what I'm talking of? Mmm."

But, despite the grin I gave, I was still feeling peeved by her earlier comment: *Ewen thinks of everything!* (It had been qualified, of course, but not seriously.) Oh, no, he doesn't, I wanted to say. *Oh, no, he does not!*

Because – a case in point! He'd coached Sybella for roughly a dozen hours altogether. Why, then, hadn't he coached Mr Gwatkin in the same manner, even if he'd had only the Friday morning in which to do it?

Although – to be fair again, tediously fair – perhaps he had. As with Sybella, that later conversation might have been more in the nature of a refresher course, a last-minute pep talk. And if he *hadn't*, there could still have been a valid reason. That he had simply believed no sound purpose would be served by alarming Mr Gwatkin. He may have thought my investigations would confine themselves to Sybella.

Had he known, however, from where I had been telephoning his brother-in-law's housekeeper, things would no doubt have been different. But she was the only one who might have traced that call and presumably she hadn't thought of it in time. So Mr Gwatkin, who would surely have been supplied at some earlier stage with copies of any correspondence concerning McKenna & Co – as well as a codeword to use in the event of an emergency – had not been warned that a surprise visit could, just conceivably, be imminent. The thoroughness of any lone German spy had clearly been as underestimated as the thoroughness of the whole department which had sent him.

(Yet, on the other hand, *could* that call have been traced? If so, it would certainly explain the solicitor's pretentious rigmarole woven around *The Importance of Being Earnest*.)

195

"But anyhow," said Sybella, "moving on, if we *may*, from all that tiresome mockery, I seem to remember you asked me a question? The one about Ewen keeping in touch with me over the weekend."

"I know – I hadn't forgotten it."

"Well, I'm not convinced you even deserve to be answered, but never mind; I have a lovely and forgiving nature. After that very long top-up yesterday morning I spoke to him again last night. He seemed pleased by what he heard and thought everything appeared to be going well. How was I to know that you'd already had such very grave misgivings? *Duplicitous*, indeed!"

She glared at me accusingly. Took my hand and placed a kiss upon the back of it. Then asked:

"Had you, in fact, already had such very grave misgivings? Rising now above cosmetics – if you're capable."

"Yes, I'm afraid I had."

"Tell me."

"Well, those love letters, for example. I can't understand why they didn't get you to write them yourself, wholly in your own style."

She shrugged.

"I don't even think I could have done it. They were written by a woman working in one of Ewen's offices. He gave her complete freedom; only stipulated that the second of them should have a line or two relating to the theatre. In case – although he didn't think it likely – in case anyone should ever come making enquiries about that incredible young beauty in the snapshot. Oh, and I assume he also wanted some mention of the diamond ring."

"Of *course* you could have done it."

"Well, anyway, I wasn't asked. And this woman in the office was *there*. No messing about, you see."

"All the same. I think it was an astonishing oversight. There were such grave issues at stake and so many lives being risked and everything dependent on his getting every detail right."

"In theory," she said.

"What do you mean: in *theory*?"

"As I've said, I don't know anything at all about the issues involved, but I do know he never foresaw someone like yourself turning up. Turning up complete with bloodhound and magnifying glass and sweet little deerstalker! He never foresaw that it would get to be so complicated."

"Well, that's my point! He *should* have foreseen it; of course he should! That he didn't do so – to my mind that's not only arrogant but slapdash!"

She offered no reply; began to stroke my hair again.

"Arrogant and slapdash," I repeated. "That's how it appears to me."

"Oh, but it would, wouldn't it? You're so thoroughly German and pedantic and repressed."

Yet already I felt better. It had helped, being able to get all that out of my system. I turned my head and smiled.

"Why repressed?"

She answered airily: "No particular reason. I felt I needed a makeweight."

Then she went on stroking my hair whilst she returned, in an indirect way, to the championship of her adoptive uncle. "And in any case we British always seem to muddle through – don't ask me how!"

This sentiment, even on the lips of somebody I loved, didn't suddenly acquire an unsuspected charm. Added to which, it was the second time that I had heard it from her.

"Well, to me that sounds both woolly and fat-headed, *especially* in view of the circumstances. I hope you don't mind my being so frank?" Plainly, a good time for getting rid of all my grievances. Probably mentioned as such in that day's horoscope.

"Oh, no, it's a free country," she answered calmly. I wondered if she meant to draw comparisons.

"Thank you. As that's so, may I ask another question? When will you next be talking to Ewen?"

"Tonight," she said. "We've never been so close; I've already spoken to him once today."

"You have? And what did you tell him?"

"Simply that everything was fine. In fact, I didn't tell him just *how* fine! Didn't happen to mention that I'd gone and lost my heart. Nor about the man I'd lost it to being so pedantic and repressed. But perhaps I'll acquaint him with all of that this evening. I said I'd give him the latest update when I got home. After the show."

"After the show which you won't have seen."

"Not tonight; not ever. I know that's very slapdash."

"Not ever? Do you know – stupidly, that hadn't occurred to me?" I brought up my wrist. "Oh, but come on; we could easily make the second half!"

"Could we?"

"And what's more we'll now be in the mood for it! I mean, *really* in the mood for it!"

"*I* would have been in the mood for it, anyway. Until sometime around a quarter to five!"

Her tone might have sounded reproachful, but she was already standing up and putting on her hat.

"Tell me," she asked, "does that look okay? And – oh, God, I hadn't thought – how my mascara must have run! And my nose is probably all shiny. Why can I *never* find my compact when I'm most in need of it?"

I suggested she should empty her things out on the bench. She did so and the compact turned up. I also saw my fountain pen but didn't allude to it. She repaired her make-up without fuss, put a comb to the back of her hair, smoothed down her skirt and jacket. I brushed her possessions back into her handbag and snapped shut the heavy clasps.

"You look wonderful," I said.

"And so do you. By the bye, I was lying. I don't think you're so thoroughly German."

"Never mind. Don't give up hope. We'll work on it."

34

We cut up Villiers Street, where we stopped off briefly for our seriously delayed cup of tea and a very necessary – well, in my case, anyway – cheese-and-pickle sandwich (I had two; plus a cake). We then skirted Trafalgar Square, heading towards Coventry Street and the theatre. "By the way," I said casually. "Have you seen your flatmate Lucy since you got back?"

"Lucy? No-o-o! Now what the dickens do *you* know about Lucy?"

"Actually very little. Only that she has a boyfriend named Reggie who was somewhat out of favour when I spoke to her on Friday night. Oh, yes – and I suppose as well – that she's now fully aware of your being engaged to a fellow called Bill Martin. Major Bill Martin of the Royal Marines. I mention this simply because I feel you ought to be prepared."

"Oh, no!" She gave a groan. This groan was undoubtedly more genuine than the one she had given yesterday on hearing the name of the film now being shown at the Aldershot Ritz.

"I really am sorry," I said. "But can't you merely say you were asked to keep it secret? And just leave her to imagine it was Bill who did the asking." I realized I was again talking about him, and even thinking about him, as if indeed he had been real.

"But a man I never mentioned? Not even once?"

"Yes, she did suggest you'd been a little cagey."

"Hmm."

"Furthermore I'll bet Lieutenant Commander Ewen Montague, or someone, was also being a little cagey when enquiring where you'd be playing on Friday and Saturday and whether she'd recently had anybody else asking that same question. Which might also demand a spot of explanation."

"You're quite enjoying this, aren't you?"

"Oh, come now! Me? But in any case whoever was making those enquiries could easily have got the first of those answers from Drury Lane. Depending on whether Lucy was at home on Thursday night."

She looked at me as if to say: And do you really think *that* is going to make things better?

"Lucy or your other flatmate," I added, comprehensively.

"Anything else you feel I ought to know?"

"No. I believe that's it for the present. Though, naturally, if anything *does* spring to mind I shan't hesitate to pass it on." Momentarily I watched the excitement of a child in schoolcap, blazer and short trousers who'd just had a pigeon alight on his head; and the disappointment of his young friend who hadn't been similarly earmarked for distinction. "As a matter of fact, you know, a further thing *has* just sprung to mind. I am sorry."

"Oh, no!" she said again. "Please not."

"But what can I do?"

She sighed. "Well, I suppose you'd better break it to me. *Very* gently."

"All right. It won't be easy. And I shan't be saying this with Teutonic presumptuousness, you understand. More with Uriah Heep humility."

Despite a certain flippancy in the words the feeling which prompted them was very far from flippant.

"You see, I'm asking you to marry me."

She came to a standstill. We both did. But whereas, for the moment, the situation had clearly deprived Sybella of speech – one of those old platitudes that can so frequently prove true – my own problem (as usual) appeared to be precisely the opposite.

"Not that Uriah Heep was genuinely humble – I realize that. But *I* am. Right now I would willingly go down on one knee if you liked. I *would* say both knees, but being repressed only allows me to do things by halves."

"Oh, you idiot." At last she had found her voice. "But you surely weren't being serious, were you?"

"What do you mean…about marriage or about knees? About marriage, never more so. All right, about knees as well, if that would really make a difference. At least the pavement's dry."

We were now standing very close to one another. The evening crowd surged around us tolerantly. Well, for the most part tolerantly.

"Okay, then," I said. "Even if the pavement were wet. It seems to me you drive a hard bargain. *And* covered in birds' droppings...which actually, on closer inspection, I discover that it is. (Oh, *now* you should be happy!) And yes – very well, I give in, I give in – down on both knees...'all or nothing' is sometimes in my nature, too. Because I love you and I know for a fact that I shall never meet anybody half so wonderful. And because it would help me, help me immeasurably – oh, how self-centred can a person get? – if through all the months or years we've got to be apart I knew I truly had something to live for – *someone* to live for – a woman whose presence in my world would make the whole earth seem so beautifully radiant. Would send down a soft and cleansing rain and spread bluebells and daffodils and make the angels sing."

She said, "Darling, you *are* being serious, aren't you?"

I answered, "Darling, I am."

"You may be marginally unbalanced, too."

"Well, if that's so, I'm hoping you can match it."

"I'm very much afraid I can. Besides. I've always been a sucker for cheap poetry, flowery speeches, romantic gobbledegook."

"You can be cutting as you like. But does this mean we're engaged?"

"I rather think it does."

We kissed.

People still continued – by and large – to be tolerant. Even encouraging. "Go for it, mister! Don't be shy!"

At least spectators kept on walking. There was no smiling ring of onlookers, no small outburst of applause, as might well have happened in the movies.

"Therefore if we're engaged," I said, after we had finally drawn apart ("We're engaged!" I told a woman who was passing by at the moment we separated – at first I didn't notice she was dragging a reluctant child. "Bad *luck*!" she responded,

201

with a lot of feeling), "if we're engaged, then tomorrow we shall choose you the finest engagement ring in all of Britain. Of course, it might be scandalously extravagant, but I know how you adore diamonds."

"Stop it," she warned. We were now waiting by the traffic lights to cross onto the pavement alongside the National Gallery.

"All right," I said, "but I've got to make one small stipulation. Whatever the ring, you won't let Lucy see it, will you? You won't even tell her we're engaged? I fear I'm with the woman in the train on this: you've just got to be a little more discreet!"

She smiled and shook her head.

"You may think you're being very funny," she remarked, "but the damned thing is…! And how the hell shall I ever get through life without being able to talk about you? Somehow I never felt the same compulsion to burble on about my *last* fiancé."

"Poor old Bill," I said.

"Though that's beside the point. The point is they're never going to forgive me, those two, when eventually they do find out. And I know that I'll be feeling like a heel. I'm fond of both my flatmates; they've been good to me."

"But one day, of course, you'll be able to explain."

"Oh yes…one day…one day! And just now you spoke about *years*, not simply months. Oh, darling, do you really feel it's going to take that long? I'm not certain I can stand it. And we've only been engaged for three short minutes. I think we'd better call the whole thing off."

In place of which, we crossed the road.

"Listen, my love. Say at the worst we have to be apart for a couple of years. At the very worst. Well, then. By the time we're celebrating our golden wedding – or even just our silver – a mere two years won't seem like anything at all. I promise you that."

"Oh dear. So young and yet so wise."

"I know."

"But just don't go and die on me in the meantime!"

"Nor you on me."

"Well, I won't if you won't. Pact?"

"Done!"

We stopped for a further kiss with which to seal it. A poster over our heads advertised a series of lunchtime concerts featuring such soloists as Myra Hess and Harriet Cohen. Somehow, when we drew apart and happened to look up at it, our resolve was further strengthened by this juxtaposition of a Blitz-damaged art gallery with the call to come to listen to enduring music out of all the nations – with Germany most definitely not excluded, and with at least one Jewish pianist lovingly interpreting the splendour that transcended every barrier.

35

Poor old Bill.

I now asked more directly about this man who had died young before taking up his appointment in the Royal Marines. Sybella's claim, that she had been given information far exceeding the actual requirements of her job, was soon shown to be true.

She told me that one of the biggest problems facing Ewen Montagu and his team (I had by now discovered that the surname lacked an 'e') had been to do with locating a corpse. This might have seemed surprising during a war – or even during peacetime – but their needs had been specific; and of course they had not been able to advertise.

But at last their unflagging persistence had paid off: a Service doctor had known about a man who'd just died of pneumonia. And after pneumonia the lungs tended to contain liquid – which would also have been the case, most probably, if death had resulted from the struggle to survive in a rough sea.

The bereaved parents of this man had appeared not only trustworthy but taciturn. In addition, they had been willing, for the sake of their country, to renounce all rights in the body of their son – even though Montagu couldn't so much as hint at his plans for it. He could say only that it would be used to fulfil some potentially war-shortening function approved of at the very highest level, and that he could guarantee the young man a Christian burial, albeit not under his own name.

But the one thing, in fact, the parents had asked for – besides a photograph of the grave – was that the real name of their son should never be disclosed.

"Though talking of photographs," Sybella said, "don't you think this is interesting? The parents had no idea of the whereabouts of their son's identity card and couldn't provide anything that might have been suitable. So Ewen tried to take a photograph of the corpse. 'Well,' he asked me, 'have *you* ever tried to photograph a corpse?' I had to confess that, no, actually I hadn't, although I knew this was neglectful. 'Then I'd advise you never to try,' was all he said, 'not if you want to come up with anything showing even the smallest spark of life!' So what had happened, he told me, was that they'd had to conduct a search almost worthy of David O. Selznick; not only through all the government offices but also in the streets, in the shops, everywhere. Even in the parks. Yet even in the parks, apparently, *doppelgangers* don't grow on trees – it was nearly as hard to find someone resembling the body as it had been to find the body itself. Which I now pass on to you," she repeated, "because it's an interesting little detail that would probably never have occurred to most of us, don't you agree?"

But then she returned to the point about the parents not wishing their son's real name to be disclosed. She considered this bizarre.

"Wouldn't you suppose they'd want to see it firmly enshrined in the history books...if only as a footnote?"

"Yet this way," I answered, "perhaps it places him almost in the same category as the Unknown Soldier. He becomes a symbol of patriotism – heroism – self-sacrifice!"

She squeezed my hand. "Well, no one would ever set *you* down as a romantic."

We had now turned into Leicester Square.

"No, of course not. Why should they? For one thing, if I was, I'd never have been found at the Ritz Theatre in Aldershot last night exposing myself to a film so grittily hard-hitting and uniformly pessimistic as *Random Harvest*."

She laughed. I gave her a smile which was supposed to be satanic.

"Oh and by the way, my darling, just cast your eyes to the right and you will see before you yet another picture house – you could almost call it the *parent* picture house – but not one in which I believe you ever experienced that same starkly harrowing catharsis."

Hardly had I said it, however, than I forgot all thoughts of being either satanic or satiric. I remembered only how I'd needed to stand at the kerbside that morning, under the sardonically indulgent eye of airman John Wayne, believing, first, that I was about to throw up; second, that dozens would be disgusted witnesses to such an act; and third, that I should never again feel anything but hopeless.

Only five hours ago?

Now there were lengthy lines outside the Empire, a price-stand at the head of each, and a Groucho lookalike who wore a fez (with kettledrum, cymbals and other musical instruments attached to his back) performing a soft-shoe shuffle on the sprinkled sand.

Indeed, there was at least one busker entertaining the queues at every cinema that flanked the square. We were walking along its southern side. We stopped for a moment to listen to an organ-grinder whose cap was being passed round, not only to picture-goers but to the loitering world at large – passed round by a monkey in brown trousers and a maroon jumper. Sybella and I each put a sixpence in the chequered cap, but the monkey, although he smiled broadly, skittered away before either of us could stroke him.

"Well, anyway, I'd like you to know that I've seen *other* films there!" exclaimed Sybella, righteously, after we'd moved on again. She sounded like a woman who'd once been harshly judged in Puritan New England – but whose present testimony erased the scarlet letter from her brow and placed her back amongst the pure. I gave a whistle and professed surprise.

"You mean…in the company of Major Bill Martin?"

"No, I do *not* mean in the company of Major Bill Martin! Nor even – before you ask it – in the company of his drily humorous father, whom I think in time I might have grown quite fond of!"

But by now we had arrived at the theatre. In the distance the organ-grinder was still playing *Roses of Picardy*. We went inside to watch Sid Field striking a new note.

Field was a music-hall entertainer whose first West End show this was and for whom a starry future was foretold. We had, of course, missed several of his sketches but everything we did see was wonderful. We were indeed in the right mood – and so, it seemed, was the rest of the audience. Probably his best sketch (for us) was the one in which he impersonated a brash US Air Force officer: a type, Sybella told me, from whom everybody had suffered at some time or other during the past year; she said he hit it off just right; the satire wasn't that far-fetched. As it happened, there were many Americans around us in the stalls – maybe because Rainbow Corner was straight across from the theatre – but certainly the applause the skit received, and the applause which shortly afterwards rewarded the whole performance, betrayed not the slightest hint of umbrage. (When at one point someone had come on to the stage holding up a placard announcing that an air raid was in progress, nobody had appeared to take heed of the warning, preferring instead to delight in the stream of first-class jokes.) I was thankful we had been a part of the experience. Thankful I'd resisted the impulse to book for something else.

Thankful, above all, we'd been a part of *any* theatrical experience.

But at the end of the evening, in the taxi on our way to Knightsbridge, I returned to what we'd been discussing earlier. (At least over our meal in a pleasant Regent Street restaurant – a meal for which, true to her word, Sybella had tried her hardest to snatch the bill from my hand – I'd had the grace to speak only about personal, mainly peacetime things.) I asked whether the woman who had written Sybella's letters had also written Mr Martin's.

"Oh, good heavens, no. Ewen said that *those* seemed so redolent of Edwardian pomposity that they were practically beyond invention – no one but a father of the old school could possibly have written them. *Then* he told me that the officer who had in fact done so was only in his twenties!"

I spoke with some unwillingness.

"Well, Uncle E must be very talented at finding the right people. Between them they certainly transformed a corpse into a living individual."

I remembered the bills and the bus tickets and the pencil stub. I remembered the letter from Lloyds Bank: "I am given to understand that in spite of repeated application your overdraft amounting to £79.19s.2d. still outstands"; and even the envelope in which this letter had been sent, erroneously addressed (or so it had seemed) to the Army and Navy Club, Pall Mall, where the hall porter had written on it, "Not known at this address, try Naval and Military Club, 94 Piccadilly."

And yet! And yet! All the minutiae on the periphery – so carefully and even lovingly thought out – along with so much inattention to detail nearer the centre!

But now I honestly tried to shed the last of my irritation.

"They must really have enjoyed their work; must really have gone at it with a will!"

"Yes, I think so, too. Like writers collaborating on a play," she said. "Apparently the method they used to build up Bill's personality was to keep on discussing him, rather as if he were a friend they were pulling to pieces each time he stepped out of the office. And in fact Ewen said they talked about him so much they really did come to see him as a friend. They even felt a strong sense of loss when they had to let him go. Some part of them was truly missing him."

"Like sending off your son into the big wide world or seeing off your favourite brother. Incidentally – how *did* he go? By submarine?"

"And one of the toughest parts of the entire enterprise," she said, "was preparing him for his journey. Getting him into his uniform."

"Of course – yes, it must have been!" I hadn't thought of it before. "Because up till then, I suppose, the body had been kept on ice?"

She nodded. "And imagine trying to put on boots, where the feet were all frozen and inflexible! Imagine trying to coil those stiffened fingers around the handle of a briefcase!"

I did imagine it. "But presumably they only had to wait until the poor fellow had warmed up a bit?" I hadn't intended this to sound flip or disrespectful.

"It wasn't that easy. They couldn't just defrost the whole body meaning to refreeze it once they'd got him dressed."

"Why not?"

"Well, it seems it would have done something disastrous to the rate of decomposition, after he'd thawed out a second time. And he had to be kept cold right up to the last possible moment. Even in the submarine."

"Right."

"Therefore, you see, he was put into a specially designed canister, in which loads of dry ice were packed all about him."

She shuddered; though not only, I guessed, because her thoughts had been centred on refrigeration.

But in any case I pulled her close. We were by now at the further end of Piccadilly. If I had been really considerate I would have changed the subject, yet in the end – despite her shudder – curiosity won out over kindness.

"So what *did* they do, then, with his feet and his fingers?"

"They had to thaw them out in sections, using a small electric fire." As she said this, Sybella intensified her grip on my hand; probably pulled a face, as well. "It makes me think of

Grand Guignol! And, even when they'd eventually got his fingers wrapped around the handle, there was still a worry that the briefcase would simply float away…which is why they attached it to that chain, hoping to heaven that you lot wouldn't think this strange."

"What chain?" I asked at once.

"Why, the one looped through the belt of his trench coat!"

"*Really*? We never heard anything about a chain."

"Well, unless I've got it wrong, you most certainly should have."

"Then I suppose it must have been an oversight on the part of the Spaniards. I'm not sure if we'd have thought it strange or not. The only thing we did think strange was the non-existence of a rubber dinghy."

"Oh, but there *was* a dinghy! I know there was: Ewen told me they wanted to give the impression of accident and haste, and therefore it was suggested the dinghy should be launched upside down, with only one of its oars inside it. The oars are collapsible and made of aluminium and I'm so impressively knowledgeable about all this because he said he'd held on to the second oar himself, as a keepsake. And that's when he took the trouble to describe it to me."

Because of my innate hankering after tidiness I found this particularly satisfying: her confirmation that there actually had been a dinghy.

"I'd definitely believed that there *should* have been one – I couldn't understand why the drift hadn't washed it into shore, together with the body. But now it occurs to me that a body wouldn't have been of much value to a Spanish trawlerman, whereas a rubber dinghy, of course…"

"Oh, but that's so cynical," she said, reprovingly.

Yet, cynical or not, my customary dislike of loose ends was for the present taken care of – and now, indeed, the subject *could* be changed. In fact, needed to be…we were driving towards the Albert Hall, were already passing the boarded-up Albert Memorial – with its thriving allotments alongside – and I wasn't sure how much longer our journey might take.

(Added to which, I guessed that on arrival she wouldn't feel too easy if I were to hang around, not even if we remained only on the pavement. So I'd decided to do no more than see her into the building and then have the cabbie drive me back to Abbey Road – it was now too late to think about returning to Paradise Street.)

"And don't forget, my darling – tomorrow, the ring!"

"As though I ever *could* forget!"

But then she added more plaintively: "And as though I could ever forget something else! That tomorrow's your last full day in England."

"Only according to guesswork, that is."

"According to *educated* guesswork, that is."

"Well, anyway. If I do have to go back on Wednesday, at least this means you won't be getting tired of me."

"Perhaps I ought to make it plain. I have a marked antipathy to Pollyannas."

"Oh, that's a pity. Me, I'm all for them."

"I feel it's becoming increasingly clear, then. We haven't got a chance."

"No. You're probably right. In the restaurant, though, I had a pretty good idea."

"What?"

"I thought of a marvellous place where we might start to look for the engagement ring."

"Go on," she invited – slowly, even warily – as if expecting me to suggest breaking into the Tower of London, or wherever, for the Duration, the crown jewels might have been sent.

"Well," I smiled, "you honestly don't have to agree to this because it may not have been *that* good an idea. In fact, it may have been an absolutely lousy one. But I was wondering – how about Shrewsbury?"

36

We got to Shrewsbury shortly after two. The first thing we did was to book a room in a hotel and drop off our pieces of ridiculously mismatched luggage – Sybella's was merely an overnight bag. The hotel was certainly the oldest and reputedly the best in town. It was called the Lion.

"Oh dear! Lacks something of the inventiveness of the *Black* Lion, wouldn't you say?"

Moreover, the stone beast over the entrance wore such a soppy grin he looked quite gaga.

Our room also appeared somewhat lacking in nobility, although we'd been informed at reception that the guest list had included such luminaries as King William IV, Paganini, de Quincey and Jenny Lind. It was a further boast that Charles Dickens had written here about 'the strangest little rooms, the ceilings of which I can touch with my hands'. Which therefore disposed of all petty ideas regarding plain pokiness: we'd be able to remind ourselves that we slept with majesty and music, with opium-eaters and nightingales, with Pickwick and Copperfield and Pip; not simply in some old coaching-inn but in a house of well-known and most definitely appealing history. And, in that case, what modern guest would ever miss high ceilings, or space, or grandeur of design?

We had decided, though, that after we'd explored the room and unpacked it might be better not to dawdle. Dalliance, of course, could only lead in one direction and no matter how tempting that direction, neither of us wanted to anticipate the night – especially since this would have meant, inevitably, our having to stay mindful of the time. Even as it was, we realized we had better postpone until the following morning any search for an engagement ring.

However, on our way to the bus station we passed a jeweller's with a window display sufficiently striking to make us feel we *could* perhaps spare a couple of minutes; and having been shown something we both considered attractive – and having remembered it was so often the first thing to take your fancy which finally drew you back – we walked out of the shop half an hour later with Sybella proudly sporting our new purchase, and her thin white gloves now relegated to her handbag.

"So let the populace be dazzled!" she affirmed, in the manner of a town crier showing himself to be most generously disposed.

It felt strange to be in Shrewsbury again. Four years…but it could have been scarcely four months. How familiar the castle and the old town walls and all those spires rising up over the rooftops! How familiar the ten bridges thrown across the Severn; the mediaeval and Elizabethan alleyways; the sharp-pointed timber gables! The countless oak-beamed pubs! I pointed out the Hen and Chickens standing so perilously close to the Cross Foxes: a thing I could remember being endlessly amused by as a child – my grandfather had made up all sorts of wonderful stories about why the foxes were cross, including one involving a day-long wait at the bus station.

"Which was obviously prophetic," I announced now, when we found that, since my last visit into Shropshire, the bus service to Acton Burnell had been quite seriously curtailed. Nothing to take us there until five o'clock.

Five o'clock *tomorrow*!

So we enquired about taxis. Yet because of the petrol shortage there weren't any available – not for a journey of that distance…which was slightly over ten miles.

But I then remembered there used to be an interesting old shop which hired out bicycles. The woman at the taxi company told us it was still there.

"Well, just so long as you promise we shan't be landed with penny-farthings," remarked Sybella, the moment before we went in – having been impressed, not altogether favourably, by the distinctively Victorian shopfront, in need of renovation.

"Or a bicycle made for two…with me doing all the work."

Anyway, a tandem might have been difficult to manoeuvre along some of the narrow and twisty lanes awaiting us – for although Acton Burnell lay roughly in the path of Watling Street, which was obviously as dead straight as any other Roman road, I encouraged Sybella to choose the much prettier route of my boyhood, even in spite of knowing that our bikes were neither lightweight nor modern and that all of those alluring byways must add considerably to the length of our journey. I hoped I wasn't being selfish.

But what I'd failed to take into account was the quantity of dried mud we would encounter, much of it forming deep ruts; also, the fact that the afternoon had been growing increasingly oppressive, the sky murky.

"I trust you're good at mending punctures in the pouring rain!" shouted Sybella, behind me. I surmised she might have meant to mutter this lugubriously. But of course it was hard to mutter lugubriously over a gap of some seven or eight feet.

Yet the banks we rode between were full of violets and forget-me-nots, cowslips, primroses and lady's-smock; the hedgerows were dotted with wild parsleys; and behind those hedgerows Friesians grazed in fields where the grass was thick with buttercups. There was no sunshine but in all other respects the scene was close to perfect.

And – besides – Sybella might secretly have welcomed that extra delay caused by one of us getting a puncture; although preferably, she was soon to acknowledge, *not* in the pouring rain. She made this confession whilst we each stood – hands on handlebars, left foot on pedal – on the summit of a hill just minutes from our destination.

For she had already mentioned that she felt nervous about meeting my grandparents. Chiefly, she was uncomfortable with the idea I hadn't warned them we were coming.

But although she couldn't be properly reassured, at least she might be temporarily distracted. The sensation of coasting downhill – a long and winding road, in places fairly steep – was something that even on our roadsters proved to be as good as I remembered.

"I hope you're truly enjoying this," I shouted. "I warn you! You'll find the ride back won't be so exhilarating."

"Oh, that's encouraging," she responded. "Thank you. Now I feel there's something I can *really* look forward to."

Acton Burnell was a picturesque and prosperous looking village set deep in the heart of a wooded valley. My grandparents lived in a black and white, timber-framed house with an overhanging first floor and a roof of Welsh slate. The front garden was still beautiful and still had flowers – despite having been turned over, in the main, to the cultivation of vegetables.

We dismounted and I took off my clips. But as I started to push my bike up the flagstoned path Sybella hung back.

"No," she said. "I'll wait here by the gate. How do I look?"

"You look adorable; and that's precisely what you're going to be – adored. Which you already are, anyway. But if it helps at all, I'm suddenly feeling nervous, too. So in the light of that…how do *I* look?"

"Adorable. Though come back here a moment." I thought she meant to remove a fleck of mud or a bit of twig or something; but instead she gave me a quick kiss. "And as a matter of fact it does help. But, even so, I still intend to stay here by the gate."

Yet her decision was rendered irrelevant. A woman in her mid-seventies came round the side of the house with a trug in one hand and a spade in the other. She was followed by a cocker spaniel.

The dog saw me before the woman did and instantly hurled himself towards us at a speed which belied his initial appearance of a sedate and ponderous old age. I swiftly cast aside the bike; the dog had barely time to spring up and fall back before I'd joyfully scooped him to my chest and was being covered in exuberant licks that randomly ranged from chin to forehead.

"Toby – you remember me! I've missed you, old thing. But, oh my word, haven't you put on weight!"

Nevertheless, I had been managing to move forward at the same time, and by then the woman had greatly shortened the distance. She had thrown down the trug and the spade.

214

"Am I seeing things? Eric! Is this right? Can it possibly be you?"

"Grandma, it can! It *can*!" I let the dog slip back to the ground then hastened towards her with my arms outstretched.

"But how...oh, *how*? Either I'm dreaming it or else I've finally gone potty!"

A hug that lasted fully a minute, because it kept on renewing itself, put an end to these speculations. Yet instantly gave rise to another. As she stood back and appraisingly held me at arm's length she murmured:

"Well, then, obviously the war is over. But how like them – they've completely forgotten to tell us!"

"Oh, how I wish that could be true!"

She turned her head slightly towards the house.

"Neville! Neville! Come out here and be astounded! Come out here and be *delighted*!" But at the same time her eyes seemed scarcely to leave my face, not for a second.

Until, that is, something made her step a little to one side and take a look behind me; and then for the first time she became fully conscious I hadn't arrived here on my own.

"But who's this?" she asked me, gently.

"Ah, Grandma, you must come and meet somebody very special. And she, too, must meet somebody very special." I took my grandmother by the hand and led her the few remaining yards to the gate, where Toby had long since rolled over, panting optimistically, to present his stomach for a tickle – and, despite the awkwardness of the bicycle, was being plentifully indulged. "Sybella and I are engaged to be married."

"What!"

"Oh, darling, you do spring things on people!" exclaimed Sybella, straightening up and now transferring her grip from the crossbar to the saddle. "Good afternoon, Mrs Baxter; I'm very pleased to meet you." They shook hands across the bike just as my grandmother was saying – but in a fashion decidedly dazed:

"I think he means to give me a heart attack!"

215

But then she added immediately: "Oh, no, that sounds rude! I really didn't mean…! You speak very good English, my dear."

"Grandma, that's because she *is* English. And being English she'd probably think that a nice cup of tea would go down a real treat right now."

Yet by this time my granddad was hurriedly advancing. He was of medium height and, just like Grandma, white-haired, blue-eyed and still amazingly youthful. Indeed, they had almost grown to look alike, as well as act alike – well, act alike for much of the time, anyway. And certainly on this particular afternoon their astonishment expressed itself in very similar phrases. Their hugs lasted every bit as long. The welcome each extended to Sybella was equally as warm.

But it was Grandma who broke the news to him, not I.

"She's going to be your new granddaughter-in-law. So try hard to make a good impression."

"Oh, he already has," said Sybella. "Before we arrived I was feeling slightly scared. Now I can see how foolish that was."

"That's because we're still standing at the gate and you believe you can make a rapid getaway. Neville, you take Sybella's bicycle, and I'll hold her firmly by the arm, and we'll all go and have our cup of tea – then you and I can hear what staggering events have brought about this joyous miracle."

"Oh, I forgot to tell you," I remarked to Sybella. "My grandmother can be a trifle overwhelming on occasion. She's not the type to brook any nonsense. You'd better do exactly as she says."

37

Well, first and foremost there was their admiration of the ring.

But then, of course, came all the questions. When and where had I arrived in England and why hadn't I got in touch much sooner – last Thursday, for instance, straight after disembarking at Holyhead – and what in the name of everything wonderful was I doing over here in the first place? And why hadn't I rung up yesterday, or even this morning, to say we were coming and ensure at least *some* faint chance of rounding up the family and preparing a meal that such a celebration so obviously deserved: a meal as worthy of the prodigal grandson, and of his bride-to-be, as wartime conditions were ever likely to permit?

"Whoa," I laughed. "Whoa there! Slow down. Take pity."

I had already answered the first question but now I decided to leapfrog the next two and concentrate upon the last.

"To begin with," I said, "I wasn't certain until last night that I'd be able to see you. And then, when I was, it would have been far too late to telephone. I mean, if I *had* phoned, I'd not only have woken you but probably have put paid to your getting back to sleep. Added to which, I knew you'd have gone to masses of trouble to make Sybella and me feel welcome – and that wasn't what I wanted at all. No, what I wanted was to be here and actually to *witness* your amazement. That's why I didn't even ring today. I hoped to keep the whole thing simple and I wanted you both to be as you usually are…not all at sixes and sevens and running around in circles feeling totally exhausted."

"Hmm," said my grandmother, gravely, to her husband. "Do we think that that stands up to close inspection?"

He considered the situation with matching gravity.

"Well, perhaps we should try to give it the benefit of the doubt, old girl?"

I smiled. "And it truly wouldn't have been such a good idea, either, having the whole family round when I introduced Sybella, because – well, like I say – you two are quite overpowering enough, without any reinforcements. Don't you think she's beautiful?"

I had added this on impulse, having just happened to look down at her as she knelt in front of the sitting-room fire and skewered another thick slice onto the toasting fork.

"Oh, Eric, don't," she said. "Now you're making me go all red!"

"Good. You deserve it. Spike your guns a bit when you're talking to Greer Garson."

"And, anyhow, why does it have to be my rear view that's being held up for everyone's assessment?"

("Everyone!" I said. "She *does* like to exaggerate!")

"Very beautiful," proclaimed my grandparents in unison. And then: "Sybella, do you know Greer Garson?" from the one, while from the other: "Well, if it's true you think I don't brook any nonsense, then I'd better live up to my reputation and demand to know precisely how you met and where and at what time and what both of you said and what both of you said immediately after *that*. And so on. And so on. I warn you – I intend to be relentless."

"Yet, Grandma, we've only got an hour or two. How can we possibly hope to do it justice in only an hour or two?"

"Oh, what nonsense! You'll be spending the night here! Even if it's no more than beans on toast that you'll be getting for your supper."

"But we can't," I said. "We've left all our things at the Lion. And remember we're on bicycles, so we oughtn't to – "

"Your grandfather and I can lend you everything you need. And you, darling, can have your old room and Sybella the guest room – you must be crazy if you think that after four long years we could ever be satisfied with just an hour or two!"

Sybella, who was sitting back on her heels, turned her head and smiled, first at myself and then at my grandmother.

"That would be wonderful," she said, "if you're sure it really isn't too much trouble."

And I thought that I might have read something else in the look which she had directed towards me: that my own room

218

and the guest room surely couldn't be so *very* many miles apart? Therefore I gave in with as good a grace as she herself had shown. (I hoped I would have done so, anyway.)

What's more, for the time being at least, the questions had stopped and the answer to that last demand for information could wait until my grandmother had poured the tea and my grandfather had collected the biscuit tin. ("We must have been warned in some strangely mystic way – only this morning your grandmother baked some Banbury Cakes; her first batch for weeks!") The answer could wait, indeed, until that last piece of toast, fresh off the fork and smelling faintly of wood ash, had been thickly spread with homemade raspberry jam.

Even Toby was treated to a Banbury Cake – which for the sake of his figure he shouldn't have been.

And what about that answer? Happily, it was a joint effort, Sybella providing it one minute, me the next, but often with the other butting in. When we had conferred on the train that morning, neither of us had seen any reason to depart too wildly from the externals of our meeting (my having seen her in the play; our subsequent encounter in a pub), nor be coy about the time which we had later spent together. What could there be in any of that to require concealment? Naturally there was no need to say anything of Major Martin nor of the major's mission. And of course, along with mythical fiancés, we made no reference to Somerset House; and, in fact, didn't even allude to the Victoria Embankment Gardens.

Which meant that in the end – despite our general faithfulness to the essential spirit of the story – our account was a little more fudged, perhaps, than factual.

Though, even so, not quite so fudged as common sense might have dictated.

"Then you're saying you've only known each other for three days?" My grandmother gazed at me in consternation.

"Three very full days," I said, without drawing her attention to the fact that it was actually more like two and a half. I was sitting with Sybella on a sofa which faced my grandparents' chairs and which was covered in the same chintz. "And I realized after only three *hours*, practically, that this was the girl with whom I wanted to spend the rest of my life."

"But what will your father say?" It was the first reference to my father since we had arrived.

"Oh..." I looked thoughtfully at the row of copper saucepans hanging in decreasing sizes from a beam above the mantel. "Oh, doubtless he's going to be a little old-fashioned about it. Or should I put it another way? Doubtless he's going to be *exceedingly* old-fashioned about it."

"And I imagine your other grandparents will certainly follow his lead?"

"Yes, bound to."

"Mmm. Hardly unexpected, one might say, from the little one knows of them."

Ironically, the one person she'd left out was the one person most likely to show genuine pleasure and excitement (even if these would probably be expressed only in the absence of my father). Which might well, indeed, have been the reason for her omission. Yet my stepmother had never been a great deal mentioned in this house – not so far as I knew – unless I myself had been the one to mention her.

Even so, I tried to be as fair as I could, to both my father and his parents.

"Of course, the fact of Sybella's being British would scarcely cause *anyone* back home to congratulate me at the moment."

(Excepting again – in all likelihood – Gretchen.)

But most of the other comments that immediately succeeded the story of our meeting weren't quite so happily disposed of. I mean, those addressed to me, rather than Sybella.

"What we just can't understand, though – what we shall never understand – isn't that right, Neville? – not even if we live to be a hundred – "

"Which only gives us another twenty-five years, my pet, so how about our now tottering off to the kitchen to put our hoary old heads together over this all-important question of the supper...?" My grandfather was already on his feet and offering both hands to my grandmother (which she didn't really need) to help her out of her chair.

She demurred, however.

"No, darling, you're very sweet and we can all admire your motives – no matter how thoroughly misguided – but this is still something that needs to be addressed."

Her gaze returned to me.

"What we can never understand, Eric, because in so many ways you once bade fair to be nearly as kind-hearted as your foolish old grandfather here…and although we haven't seen you in the past four years, we're sure you can't *altogether* have changed…"

But it seemed that even my normally outspoken grandmother might never get around to finishing her sentence. I myself had to help her out.

"What we can never understand," I said, "is how on earth you could ever be over here, in England, on a spying mission for Germany?"

"Yes. And there's no need to smile as you say it. It isn't – it isn't in the *least* bit – a smiling matter."

"But Grandma. I'm a German citizen. Germany is my country."

"And England is ours. It's also Sybella's. And it used to be your mother's. And…well, shall I tell you something, my sweetheart? Something we thought we'd never have to tell you? Your mother didn't even *like* Germany. Yes, that's perfectly true. Over the years she came to feel less and less at home there. She'd never admit it until you were about five – before then had always claimed that it was only natural for a daughter to become a little tearful when saying goodbye to her parents – but every time she brought you here on holiday she found it harder to go back. Much! Towards the end she absolutely hated having to do so; it made her feel desperately miserable and, of course, it made your grandfather and me feel miserable as well."

I could remember some of the anguish of those departures: how my mother had hugged me extra tightly on the train; how

221

she had kept telling me that it was only a naughty little piece of grit which had flown into her eye.

I pursed my lips.

"In that case," I said, "why *did* she go back?"

"She went back for your sake. Purely for your sake."

And once more I felt that old familiar mix. Guilt and longing. Guilt and longing.

(I had asked my father: "Was it *my* fault that she died?" "No, of course not," he had said. "If it was anybody's fault it was mine." Yet certainly as a ten-year-old I had never quite believed him.)

Sybella squeezed my hand again – during the past few minutes she had been regularly showing her support in this manner.

"But that's ridiculous," I said. "If she had decided to stay here, clearly I'd have stayed here, too."

"You mightn't have been allowed to, Eric You were by far the most important thing in your mother's life; if she was ever afraid of anything, that fear was of losing you. Yet the point is…although she no longer felt a lot for your father, your father wasn't a bad man. A little cold, maybe, but that's the worst she would ever say of him. And cold or not he undoubtedly loved you, loved you devotedly; and if she'd taken you away, she knew he'd have moved heaven and earth to get you back. What's more, there isn't a court in the world which wouldn't have supported him. Your mother realized that; she couldn't have lied about his being unfit. And so she had to remain with him. Purely for your sake. In a country that she hated."

"I had no idea," I said, slowly. "I hadn't the *least* idea."

"Well, how could you? A little boy of five or six or seven? And naturally – *naturally* – you weren't in any way to blame. But this doesn't alter the fact that England was your mother's true home, or that she came to care for it more deeply with every year that passed, both for England and for all the values England stood for. She'd died, of course, long before that filthy little man became Chancellor but even in the twenties she could see the way that Germany was going."

I said: "Grandma, if you're going to use expressions like that, Sybella and I will have to leave."

"Come on, Carrie, my dearest. You've made your point. That's fine! But now let's go and think about the supper. We haven't seen this lad of ours for such an age and whatever the circumstances it's just like you yourself were claiming earlier – a lovely, shining miracle! So is there any miracle which *we* can now accomplish in the hope of doing it honour?"

"And may *I* help?" Sybella gave my hand a final squeeze and sprang up from the sofa. "Peel potatoes or something? Bring in some vegetables? I'd love to take a closer look at your garden."

"Thank you, Sybella." My grandfather had been standing by the hearth ever since trying to coax his wife out of her chair. "By the way, my dear, I expect you know that Eric's mother was very nearly a Sybil. Just before the christening, Carrie and I still hadn't decided between that and Penelope. Even in the trap on our way to the church! I fear we were almost thinking of divorce by the time we got there – glowering at one another across the font!"

"Which of you wanted which?"

"Oh, you'd have known the answer to that by the sheer sulkiness of my expression!"

"But I'm sure that by the time she'd been Penelope for just a week you must have wondered how any other name could possibly have suited her."

"A week? More like a day. An *hour*!"

"And to tell the truth *I'm* actually a Sybil. But when I decided I wanted to act...well, comparisons are odious, aren't they?...and then too, to my mind, it seemed practically presumptuous." For some reason, this hadn't yet come up between us, and she glanced at me with a smile that bordered on apology. "Also, as a girl, I had always wanted people to call me Sybella. It was the name of the heroine in one of my favourite stories and I found it dashing and romantic."

Yet it was no good. None of it was any good. My grandmother's attention was still rigidly focused on myself and although she prefaced her next question with a soft endearment it wasn't at all a question likely to improve matters. She gave a long, regretful sigh.

"But, darling, you can't refuse to recognize the fitness of that adjective – after all, filthy is as filthy does – surely your eyes have been opened a smidgen since 1939? We vividly recall your ostrich-like behaviour *then*, when at last we prevailed on you to read about the wholesale slaughter of the Jews! But for a sensitive and intelligent young man *still* to be trying to bury his head so deep…no, I simply can't accept it, not of any grandson of mine nor of any child a loving mother once saw as being the very *raison d'être* of her whole tragically cut-short and disappointing existence – "

But, in fact, just at this point it was my grandmother herself who was cut short.

"Carrie! *Shut up*! For God's sake, woman, for the sweet love of heaven itself, won't you just put an end to all of this, *right now*!"

I had never heard my grandfather speak to her like that. Shout at her like that.

And during the stunned silence which ensued, reminiscent of the sudden hush that had yesterday succeeded the hurling of a whisky tumbler to the floor, Sybella turned to me awkwardly.

"Oh, please, darling," she said, "I should so much like to see the garden – won't you take me out on a short tour, before the light goes, or the rain starts?"

And, during that same stunned silence Toby pulled himself to his feet and slunk behind the sofa, whining.

I said a short prayer; abandoned the retort I had been intending to come out with: "It wasn't *the wholesale slaughter of the Jews*!"

Instead I asked – though not very graciously:

"Have you still got that file of newspaper cuttings? The one you collected back in '39?"

It was not only ungracious. It was unpremeditated – possibly almost in the same category as my grandfather's outburst. But, in some strange way, it may have been this second instance of

224

complete unexpectedness which threw us both a lifeline: my grandmother and me.

"I certainly haven't kept it up to date," she answered, coldly. "After your reaction to it that last time, there didn't seem much point."

"Yet you've still got it?"

"I really couldn't say. Who knows? Perhaps."

"But where?"

"If anywhere – on top of that cupboard in your room."

I stood up. Now, out of the four of us, only my grandmother remained seated. She looked small.

"Well, if it's there, I'll read it…so that we can afterwards talk a little more intelligently, maybe, about ostriches and biased journalism and other such related issues. Speaking of which, *Kristallnacht* was immensely horrible, yes – but it was *not* the wholesale slaughter of the Jews. If the report made out that it was…well, there you are then, I think I've proved my case."

I didn't think any such thing, of course, but whilst delivering this line I had managed to get as far as the door.

I shouted back: "And for heaven's sake, Sybella, won't somebody please do *something* about that poor frightened little dog!"

Though that, as a secondary exit line, was both unnecessary and deplorable and one for which I later on – but not a moment too soon – wholeheartedly apologized.

38

That dismally contentious report retained its pride of place: still the top one in the folder. But otherwise the clippings were in strictly chronological order.

The first lot related to the Jewish question.

For instance:

Dec 16, 1937.

A full-scale attack on modern art – 'a decadent by-product of Bolshevik Jewish corruption' – was launched by Hitler when he opened a new art gallery, the Haus der Kunst, in Munich. A crowd of 30,000 heard him blame the decadence of German art, before the Nazis, on Jewish art dealers and critics, who promoted 'something new at any price'.

He added: "We had Futurism, Expressionism, Realism, Cubism, even Dadaism. Could insanity go further? There were pictures with green skies and purple seas. There were paintings which could only be due to abnormal eyesight."

Herr Hitler, himself a one-time painter of conventional street scenes, went on to threaten that people who see things in such ways should be dealt with under the programme for sterilizing the insane.

March 18, 1938.

A pogrom, called 'the great spring cleaning' by the Nazi newspapers, is being carried out at great speed in Austria. Jews are being excluded from their professions, Jewish judges have been dismissed, shops have been forced to put up placards saying 'Jewish concern'. Theatres and music halls have been 'spring cleaned' and among the artists Vienna will know no more are Richard Tauber and Max Reinhardt.

June 19, 1938.

German children have been recruited for the Nazis' anti-Jewish campaign. Boys of 13 and younger, armed with brushes and buckets of white paint, marched along the Frankfurterallee in a Jewish neighbourhood of east Berlin today and daubed the Star of David on shops pointed out to them by adults.

In schools, children are asked where their parents buy school clothing, and those who admit that it comes from a Jewish shop are made to stand in a corner. Playing with or even speaking to Jewish children is forbidden.

Dec 12, 1938.

Walther Funk, a one-time financial journalist and now Economics Minister, has found a way to ban Jews from any kind of business activity (while avoiding, he claims, disruption of the German economy). Jews are forbidden to deal in property, jewellery or precious metals, or freely operate bank accounts. Any securities they own will be disposed of as the Minister judges to be in the national interest. Jewish businesses will be closed down by specially appointed executors.

January 17, 1939.

Jews are banned from being dentists, vets, and pharmacists, also banned from driving, going to cinemas, theatres, or concerts.

*

But the second lot of cuttings – under a different paperclip – was concerned with resistance to the Nazis.

Non-Jewish resistance.

For instance:

Feb 10, 1938.

Adolf Hitler has crushed opposition among the officer corps of the German army by sacking two leading generals and appointing himself Supreme Commander of the armed forces. The two army chiefs have each been smeared by sexual innuendoes. It is said that the Field Marshal Werner von

Blomberg married a former prostitute and that General Werner von Fritsch is a homosexual.

March 4, 1938.

Pastor Niemoeller, the German Confessional Church leader, was today sent to the Sachsenhausen concentration camp for 're-education'. There he will join 3,000 inmates under the 'Death's Head' battalion of the SS (Schutzstaffel, protection squad). The pastor, a former U-boat commander, has become a focus of resistance to Nazi ideas.

The Nazi regime has been using concentration camps during the last five years for the confinement in primitive conditions of Jews, Communists and other political suspects.

Each of these camps is under the control of Heinrich Himmler, Reichsführer of the SS and chief of German police, and every camp is guarded by 1,500 troopers, serving in the elite SS security force.

*

I sat on the bed I had slept in each time I came to Acton Burnell; at least, the one I had used after outgrowing the crib which Gramps, some fifty years ago, had made for my mother.

And I considered those reports.

Most of them were both short on detail and unsupported by a photo. Even *with* a photo the text was often unconvincing. For example, one purported to show two Nazi bureaucrats measuring a man's nose; they suspected him of being a Jew. *If* the photograph were genuine then perhaps its most disturbing feature was the sheer ordinariness of those three individuals. They all looked perfectly pleasant, like people you might happily have chatted to on the train – the alleged persecutors as much as the alleged suspect. 'Alleged' being once again the operative word here, since there was obviously a much surer way of discovering whether any man were Jewish. For the purposes of this photograph, indeed, I wondered why they hadn't chosen a female.

228

In any case, who were 'they'? German propagandists? Non-German propagandists?

And why weren't there any pictures of Pastor Niemoeller or of those two sacked army officers? I either hadn't known about this latter pair or else had totally forgotten. Which I imagined was possible – having been only twenty at the time. And not a particularly mature twenty at that.

(I had known about Niemoeller, of course; had regarded him merely as a crank.)

But if I was making excuses for myself – 'only twenty' – did this mean I was now partly accepting what I read? (More than *partly*, perhaps; I supposed that if in fact I had read those extracts back in 1939, I might *partly* have accepted them even then.) Therefore – possibly a better way of expressing it – could this mean I was now a little less *obdurate* than before, a little less hostile, a little less in denial of a steadily encroaching idea? That the education to which I had been insidiously exposed, especially throughout my adolescent years, might always have been slightly slanted?

I wasn't sure about 'insidiously'.

Nor about 'slightly'.

(And I wondered suddenly if such a belated discovery as this – or acknowledgment or whatever one might choose to call it – could actually have been crystallized in some strange fashion by Buchholz's telling me about the admiral.)

There were other clippings in the file. A score of them.

And while I retained my concentration I read about German parents who risked having their children taken away from them if they weren't sufficiently rigorous about instilling the precepts of Nazism.

Then I read about Hitler's bombing of Guernica in 1937.

Guernica had been a communications centre. In addition, it had possessed an important munitions factory. But the report claimed the complete avoidance of military targets; claimed the bombs had been unloaded instead over the town's main square and the streets surrounding this. And since it was market day, the square had been packed with country people, mostly women and children. ('In the city, soldiers were collecting charred bodies. They were sobbing like infants. There were flames and smoke and grit, and the smell of burning human flesh was nauseating. Houses were collapsing into the inferno. Debris was piled high. The shocked survivors all had the same story to tell: Heinkels, Junkers, incendiary bombs, machine-gun fire. "*Aviones…bombas…mucho, mucho.*"')

After Guernica I read again about *Kristallnacht*. Perhaps the elapse of four years had altered me more than I knew. I had been equally appalled – at least equally appalled – in 1939; but in 1939 I had not felt satiated. I had still been moved by rhetoric. Had still been moved (and I realized that this was vile, I realized that this was totally contemptible) by the prospect of adventure. In 1939 I had been far readier to rationalize. (Except when I'd been arguing with my father!) And since then, too, I had actually come across people who had *boasted* of taking part in the debased proceedings of that night. No women as it happened; but I supposed it could be true that women *had* been caught up in the hysteria. Even their infants. Even their babies. I closed the file and flung it to the bottom of the bed.

But I mustn't get depressed, I told myself. Absolutely must *not*! This present time was much too precious, *much* too precious.

And I had only twenty hours left. Less! In twenty hours from now I'd be far away from Acton Burnell; far away from Sybella. I would be standing on a beach in Anglesey…on Amlwch beach in Anglesey. Last night – while she and I had still been laughing at Sid Field and feeling integrated, insulated, safe – Heinrich's letter had been left for me at Abbey Road. Tomorrow, at fifteen hundred hours, I had an appointment with a rowing boat.

And roughly ten minutes after that I had an appointment with a submarine.

Of course it was by submarine that – figuratively speaking – Bill Martin had been delivered to the Fatherland.

Somehow it seemed appropriate that the tracker of Bill Martin should be delivered in the same way.

39

So – quite determined that I *wasn't* going to be depressed; that I wasn't going to spoil what little time remained, either for myself or for anyone – I passed no comment on the clippings. Not one word. And Sybella, quick to empathize, instinctively refrained from asking me about them.

If she'd been hoping – as of course she had – that, when we all convened again, my grandmother would be equally reticent …well, in that case, she saw her hopes abundantly fulfilled. What had happened less than an hour ago might never have happened at all. Grandma came back into the sitting room carrying a tray with a bottle and four glasses.

"This important occasion calls for a toast!" was the first thing she said.

Gramps, also smiling – he, possibly, out of sheer pride at such a spectacular recovery – followed behind her holding an armful of precariously balanced logs. I jumped up and unloaded them. As I was brushing chips of bark off his cardigan, I caught Sybella's look of unmistakable relief.

"Well, what *do* you think of her?" I cried.

"Oh, darling, not again, please!" said Sybella. "And besides… If you were bent on making such a fool of yourself you could at least have done it in the kitchen."

"Why? Do you feel an answer in the kitchen would have been in any way different?"

"Perhaps a *degree* less constrained."

I made no reply, not verbally, but somehow – suddenly – we were all laughing.

"Yes, that's absolutely right," my grandmother told her. "Eric didn't need to pull that face. Some of us in this family have acquired a reputation for being truthful in any room in the house…I'm sure *I* don't know why! So in the light of that, Sybella, when I say we think you're charming and delightful you can rest assured that it's the truth."

"Oh," stuttered Sybella, "thank you, that's very kind, I – "

231

"You note, though, how Grandma phrased it? *When I say.* That doesn't mean she *has* said."

"Oh, that boy! Sybella, will you teach him, please, not to split hairs?" By now the sherry had been handed round. "Does everyone who has a second language strive to speak it quite so perfectly? How tiresome! What are they trying to prove, I wonder. Still," she conceded, "considering he has only *two* such aggravating faults, perhaps you'll tell me next it's almost churlish to complain."

Sybella said: "I'll tell you when I've heard about the *other* aggravating fault."

But it was only after she had spoken, I knew, that she would have realized the nature of the risk she had taken.

"Why, naturally, that he doesn't listen sufficiently to his elders and betters. Or to *one* of his elders and betters, at any rate. What else could it be?" (I imagined Sybella casting around for some appropriately light-hearted response.) "But in fact there may still be grounds for hope. At least he's made himself a choice of wife that even his grandmother couldn't have improved upon."

So it seemed an evening of real harmony lay ahead of us. There occurred only one short exchange that might have proved disruptive. After we'd virtually finished off the sherry between the four of us – and the bottle had been a new one – my grandmother said to me:

"Darling, do you really have to go back?"

"Yes. Unfortunately, I do."

"But is there no way you could conceivably see yourself – just conceivably – remaining over here with your wonderful grandparents who love you, and your wonderful fiancée who loves you, and your marginally less wonderful but by no means wholly negligible aunts and uncles and cousins and things who quite naturally love you, too? Is there absolutely no possible way?"

I was arguably a little less affected by the sherry than she was.

"Grandma, no possible way in the world. If I could stay, I would – surely you know that? But there are certain ramifications. I can't talk about them, yet they mean I don't have any choice. Truly."

"And, darling, has that got to be your final word?"

"Completely. I only wish it hadn't."

But, even so, it all appeared okay. Grandma went off to put the finishing touches to the supper and the supper was delicious and we had a bottle of French wine – in common with the sherry, a long time hoarded – and then the telephone rang (surprisingly without incurring a rebuke, although admittedly we'd been a little late in coming to the table). The caller was my Aunt Connie, and Grandma asked me to go into the hall and be congratulated in person. Then she made a telephone call herself, presumably to Uncle Jack, but this time I wasn't called upon to go to speak. And only a short while after that – a period during which she seemed more than usually distrait, not passing on what Uncle Jack had said, but disconnectedly telling us about his recent and supposedly amusing stay in the cottage hospital…only a short while after that, there came a heavy and insistent knocking on the front door. And when an incredulous and considerably shaken Gramps, with Toby at his heels, returned into the dining room, he had a couple of hefty policemen walking close behind. And the policemen had come at his wife's urgent instigation to take into custody their German grandson, on suspicion of his having illegally entered the British Isles upon a spying mission for the Hun.

40

First, I had expected to spend the night in a hotel. The hotel room, though not large, had dwindled into a guest room. The guest room, though not large, had dwindled into a police cell.

And that initial double bed had diminished into separate single beds, which in turn had diminished into a solitary hard cot, offering nothing but a thin and scratchy blanket for its covering.

And Sybella, as the person I had naturally expected to remain the closest to, had changed into Sergeant Leighton. And Sergeant Leighton wasn't even female.

Oh, what a comedown!

How are the mighty fallen!

Yea. How are the mighty fallen in the midst of the battle!

And yet, oddly enough, apart from certain obvious factors, I didn't really care. Plainly, I wouldn't have chosen for any of it to happen but now that it had – and happened due to forces entirely beyond my control – it felt almost relaxing. My own part in the war was over.

I no longer had to agonize about having to come to a decision.

In point of fact, would I *ever* have come to one? I might well have gone straight to Admiral Canaris and abandoned all responsibility. (Though even that, I supposed, would have represented a decision of some sort.) Abandoned? No, perhaps I was being too hard on myself. Delegated.

And if the man was truly the turncoat they appeared to be saying…? Well, then, okay. So be it.

Amen.

But the slur was far from proven. The admiral could still turn out to be a hugely committed supporter of the Third Reich.

Therefore, whilst I realized that millions would have decried such an act of abandonment (or delegation) as tantamount to simply the tossing of a coin, I believed that it would, in fact, have been quite different.

Altogether different.

And if my trust in Providence had been misplaced…well, in that case, what was the point of even caring? One path would be fully as meaningless as any other.

So then…

Relinquishment of responsibility.

Directly to Canaris. Indirectly to God.

Maybe I hadn't *unalterably* made up my mind about this but it felt pretty much as though I had.

Nor did this line of reasoning seem, of itself, irresponsible. For how could someone like me have either the wisdom or the foresight to determine which was going to be the better course: to endorse the integrity of Major William Martin or to expose him as a complete and utter fraud? (And if at times I suspected that this 'better course' was more likely to involve a victory for the Allies, at least I kept shying away from it.) I tried to think coolly and analytically of what it was about Germany that had made my mother come to hate it so.

I tried to think coolly and analytically of what it was about the admiral that I particularly admired; and of what it was about my father that I found dissatisfying.

In truth, however, there wasn't much room in any of my present thinking for either cool *or* analytical. I was lying on the bed fully clothed; hadn't even bothered to remove my shoes, although they had now had the laces taken out of them. The light had been turned off. But I hadn't been left in total darkness: a low-wattage bulb burned in the passageway and my cell door had a fanlight. The bolster I'd been given was a soft one. My pallet wasn't soft, yet so far it hadn't proved uncomfortable. I wasn't in a bad way, really. Just couldn't think too straight.

But I had no real fears concerning my future. What were the authorities likely to do: attempt to feed false information back to Berlin, using myself as a conduit? No; far too optimistic if they were hoping they could ever get away with that.

Yet otherwise? Perhaps I myself was being unduly optimistic; but, despite the Treachery Act introduced over here three years before, I still didn't think that I'd be shot; and the prisoner-of-war camps in Britain were probably neither a whole lot better nor a whole lot worse than their counterparts in Germany – wasn't there even a good chance I might be put to work on the land? Which would actually be *fine* with me…even during the thick of winter or in the coldest part of the country. At least I'd be getting fresh air and vigorous exercise and have the satisfaction of knowing that I was doing something useful.

And if I were working on the land, I might even be able, on occasion, to see Sybella.

Not that I would actually have opted for *any* form of detention. (My thoughts were confused and circular and probably contradictory.) But if life was truly a matter of making the most of whatever got thrown in your direction, and if this was truly what God and my grandmother, between them, had decided to throw in mine…?

My grandmother…!

My grandmother, who would naturally have known nothing whatever about the Treachery Act…!

At first, certainly, I had been angry with her. Furious. Had ignored her every attempt at explanation; had even felt gratified to see the hint of tears. Yet now, of course, I had calmed down and could easily accept that she had been looking out for my own best interests as much as she had for those of England.

She would have declared the two were indivisible.

But, in any case, I myself was now out of it.

Yes. How are the lowly fallen, fallen in the midst of the battle. How are the lowly stretched out on a hard palliasse, in a police cell in the centre of Shrewsbury, with hands clasped beneath the head, legs crossed at the ankle, eyes either closed or staring up at the darkened ceiling.

I probably wouldn't have slept much anyway; yet around midnight the storm began: that long-awaited storm.

High up in the wall there was a small barred window. At times the rain rattled against it like gunfire and the gusting wind sounded powerful enough to lift the whole building and deposit it in Oz. Sometimes the lightning appeared to be coming straight at you – at *you*, I mean, personally – and the crash of the thunder was as deafening as a bomb coming down on the house next door. I kept imagining what it must be like to be at sea. In a fishing smack or lifeboat.

So at least if the storm kept me awake it also kept my mind off my own troubles; or reduced them by comparison.

But it must have been nearly dawn by the time it blew itself out; after which I managed to doze a little; until – wouldn't you know it! – I fell into a heavy sleep roughly ten minutes before being woken. I was awoken when a special constable brought me in some breakfast.

This man was naturally uncommunicative, perhaps, but added to that, he was tired and ready to go off duty and, added to *that*, he clearly felt a deep resentment at being told to feed a German. All he said was, "My father was killed in the last war and my two brothers have died in this. If they asked *me*, simple hanging would be too easy for the likes of you!" I didn't worry right then about the possibility of any lynch mob. I merely hoped that, in the interim, its potential leader hadn't spat into my tea.

But later on – at around nine – Sergeant Leighton reappeared; and showed himself just as amiable as before.

"Streuth, son, I shouldn't think you got much shut-eye in the midst of all that! Slates blown off roofs, branches torn off trees; in some places the whole ruddy tree brought down as well! Telegraph poles – telephone lines – the lot! *We* knew it was coming…yet the Met Office (and I'm really not having you on about this!) hadn't said a single word." He laughed, grimly humorous. "This morning they're trying to claim it was a freak."

He was a gaunt man with shadows under his eyes, with pallid skin and thinning hair. In more normal times he might have been beyond retirement age: pottering about on his allotment by now, or fitting schooners into bottles, or walking in the mountains with his wife.

"But even apart from that," he said, "I've got a bit of news for you."

I suddenly felt hopeful. Eager.

"Your girlfriend came. My deputy wouldn't let her see you but she brought your suitcase, so you'd have some shaving things and all the rest. I'll fetch it through as soon as I've checked she hasn't stowed a Mauser in your underwear."

I smiled. "Not just my girlfriend," I said. "My fiancée."

I paused.

"But I wonder how she made it into Shrewsbury?"

"Search me, mate. I find it hard to understand that you're a German."

"Why?"

"Well – if only to kick off with – your English sounds as good as mine does, any day."

I explained about my mother having been born in Acton Burnell.

"And are you honestly a spy?"

"Yes."

"And spying on what?" he asked. "Or who?"

"I was sent here to investigate one of your own agents. Somebody who was doing his best to misinform us."

"So what you're saying then – tit for tat?"

"Sort of."

"Well, I don't mind spies. What most people really can't stomach are the traitors. Take that Lord Haw-Haw, for example. Have you met him?"

"No."

"He broadcast on the wireless about our clock in the town square being four and a half minutes fast."

"And was it?"

"Still is. You don't think we'd take any notice of what a squirt like him says?"

But I wondered less about Lord Haw-Haw than about the sort of person who would pass on to Berlin such a worthless scrap of information in the first place. I wondered, sourly, if they could ever, possibly, derive any satisfaction out of their work.

Yet this was merely an extension of my irritation about the word 'traitor': that it could be applied to a man like William Joyce, who was the current Lord Haw-Haw, and at the same time to a man like Willy Canaris. It seemed almost as undiscriminating as having Barabbas, in the eyes of the crowd, being viewed as an equal of Jesus.

Yet despite all this, I became aware I'd only been half-listening. Half-listening, at best. Basically I was still wondering how Sybella had got into Shrewsbury.

I was still picturing the struggle she must have had with my suitcase.

And I was remembering, too, her outcry at the moment she had actually realized why those policemen had come to the house. Remembering how she had tried to reason with them; and how she had afterwards tried to place herself defensively in front of me, almost clinging to my arm when they had ordered me into the car.

Nor was this all. On one level my disorganized brain was wondering (as it must have wondered some fifty times before) what sort of night she would have passed; and whether she had even bothered to undress and go to bed. It was also wondering how Ewen Montagu would have reacted on receiving her SOS…because presumably she'd have managed to send one before all those telegraph poles and telephone lines had got blown down.

Her confusion must have been overwhelming. I only hoped the shock she'd sustained wouldn't permanently influence her attitude towards my grandmother. Nor towards me, come to that. I hadn't behaved well.

Still, there wasn't much that I could now do, other than pray about it and ask for pen and paper. When I'd shaved, then had a fairly decent wash, Sergeant Leighton brought me a copy of the *News Chronicle*. He handed it over with a grin.

"We've just received a telegram about you. I'd say you've got some crafty old friends out there, haven't you? Fair made me chuckle, don't mind admitting it."

I forgot about pen and paper.

"Instructed me to get to a telephone that worked – and get there pronto! Then to ring up the Admiralty. Ask for some bloke and use the word *mincemeat* before I did so! (Is that what you're going to make of us, my son, mincemeat?) But I repeat – all highly entertaining. Nearly as good as them Falcon pictures you can see at the Odeon."

He pulled one of his unusually long earlobes, pensively.

"Yes, you and your mates! Some cheek! Ring the blinking Admiralty, indeed! The very thing, so I'm told, your girlfriend was going on about last night – I hear she even tried to ring the number herself but kept on being connected to the news theatre at Victoria Station! Sorry, not your girlfriend, your *fiancée*! So she was trying it on even then – quick-thinking young woman, I'd say! Resourceful. That's something I admire!"

"There," I said, "you see! Right from the beginning she was telling them to ring the Admiralty! Doesn't that convince you?"

"Oh, nice try, my son. Nice try. I know *you're* not a crackpot." He laughed. "Can't quite speak for your girlfriend yet."

"Yet?"

"That's right – we're hoping to interview both her and your grandparents before the day is out."

He gave a cheerful nod and left the cell.

And left me, as he locked the door, with something new to think about.

Montagu obviously wanted to have me released; his telegram couldn't mean anything less.

But it was nearly half past ten, and if I missed that train at 11.23, I shouldn't get to Anglesey on time. And if I didn't get to Anglesey on time, then Operation Mincemeat was kaput. (Whatever my report concerning it. Whatever the reaction of the admiral on reading my report concerning it.) Because I didn't see what explanation I could possibly give for not being on Amlwch beach by 15.00 hours.

Especially if I hadn't first notified Heinrich. And given him the time to notify Germany and alert that U-boat.

Yes, but! Wait a second! Stop!

Trains were cancelled in wartime, weren't they? Or frequently ran late, didn't they? (Probably in peacetime, too, since here they hadn't got their Mussolini.) And the freak weather could certainly be held accountable; even back home they would know about that storm. And just so long as I'd be able to get in touch with Heinrich over the next couple of hours…? I began to feel that all was not necessarily lost. I blamed my tiredness for having enfeebled me.

Although – again – hold on! Wouldn't Buchholz be inclined to check my story, enquire from Paddington or somewhere? Buchholz was a man to be reckoned with. I suspected that he didn't quite trust me. What he mistrusted might be nothing more than just my reverence for Canaris, coupled with a certain ambivalence of attitude, but these two things could easily be enough to damn me.

And then might he not regard it as his duty – since even as it was he was being obliged to break radio silence – to safeguard against any element of risk and slightly to expand on his message to Berlin? *Anders claims his findings contrary to general expectation.*

And I'd have no idea, of course, what signal he was sending. That was the frightening part. Or, at least, it could become the frightening part if there were any chance that, after all, I might decide *not* to delegate. Any chance that, after all, I might decide *not* to reveal the truth, not even to the admiral himself. (Yet I was here presented with a different worry: what would Canaris *do* with the information I delivered, whether delivered honestly or, indeed, falsely?) For I had now come to see that – just possibly – I had not made up my mind as unequivocally as I'd thought.

Another difficulty. It had been on Monday night, hadn't it, that I'd received notice of my rendezvous on Amlwch beach? Notice of some forty hours, in other words. So why, then, hadn't I allowed for the probable late running of the trains? Why hadn't I chosen to spend Tuesday night somewhere considerably closer to the meeting point?

241

Like any *true* son of the Fatherland would unfailingly have chosen.

And what, for the love of Mike, had I ever been doing in Shrewsbury?

So perhaps it wasn't merely tiredness which had been enfeebling me. Perhaps it was a clear awareness of the way things were.

Or was I now being overly pessimistic? Maybe Sergeant Leighton *was* intending to contact Whitehall; maybe that problematical train journey *could* still be achieved?

I looked at my watch again.

Two minutes short of eleven.

No, dear God. It couldn't be achieved. Not with just twenty-five minutes to get to the station.

Overly pessimistic? Huh!

And for the first time since being put in my cell I began to grow agitated. Or, rather, to let people realize I was growing agitated. I started to bang on the door. (And, in the process, hurt my fist.)

Leighton came to see what I wanted. He probably thought he was anticipating me. "There's a cup of tea brewing," he announced.

I almost shouted.

"Oh, for God's sake! There must be *something* you can do! What about the hospitals? What about the nursing homes?"

"Eh?"

"When telephone lines are down, aren't those the sorts of places which receive priority?"

"You think the nursing homes get preference over the *police*?" Leighton spoke sardonically, then spread his hands. "Friend, I'm busy. And the joke is wearing thin."

"How can it be a joke? They gave you the bloody phone number, didn't they? Then test it! *Test* it! And if you don't…well, all I can say is, Sergeant, I wouldn't want to be in your shoes afterwards! You can't imagine what trouble you'll be in!"

"There, now. Is that a fact?"

"Why even take the risk? What can you possibly lose by making *one* phone call?"

"Oh, nothing, except for time, perhaps? Dignity? Things of that sort? I'll fetch your tea."

"Or forget the Admiralty, then – ring the War Office, direct!" How logical was that? "Demand to speak to Churchill."

Oh, but that blessed storm, I thought. Despite all the achievements and advances of mankind, wasn't it amazing the whole of civilization could simply grind to a standstill, purely on account of a few odd flashes of lightning or a few strong gusts of wind?

"And tell me," said Sergeant Leighton. "Supposing I did just like you say, what interesting suggestion do you think Mr Churchill might want to whisper in my ear?"

"I don't think. I *know*. You'd be ordered to release me."

"Oh, I would, would I?" Despite the joke's now wearing thin he still appeared good-humoured. "But I thought you were one of their lot, not ours."

"It's more complicated than that." Luckily, I had recovered some of my composure. "To be honest, I'm not even sure *whose* lot I belong to."

"Difficult," he said.

"In fact, I'm beginning to suspect…"

But I couldn't finish the sentence. It would have felt too drastic. Too extreme. I said in its place:

"And your releasing me – your releasing me *right now* – could make such a vital difference! If only I could get you to understand! It might make all the difference in the world!"

"To yourself, yes. I do understand that. But to anyone else?"

"To everyone. *Everyone*! To the whole outcome of this crazy war."

Again the sergeant laughed.

"Well, naturally, when you lay it on the line like that, son, what can I do but believe you? Kind of a double agent, then – is that how you might see it? Sort of Bulldog Drummond, like? Or Captain Bigglesworth?"

Oh, that blessed storm, I thought again. That blessed, blessed storm.

But then I hesitated.

It was the adjective which gave me pause.

A storm of such far-reaching magnitude? A storm arriving at that particular time out of all others? Could it be nothing but coincidence? (And actually I was never quite sure if I wholly believed in coincidence.) Didn't it almost seem as if God were willing me to miss that train?

Willing me to miss that submarine?

Then prove it, God. Won't you please provide me – just this once, I'll never ask again – provide me with some form of unmistakable proof?

I mean, if it's your plan for me to stay in England then make it clear to me. Incontestably clear.

Please.

And even before I had articulated this – well, *practically* before I had articulated this – I knew what needed to be done. Other than in the boxing ring, or during some hand-to-hand training session, I had never set out to disable anyone.

Therefore it appeared both incongruous and awful that now, when for the first time it was no mere exercise, I should have to pit my strength against somebody so much older. Not to mention somebody so obviously well-disposed.

Nevertheless, I clenched my fist.

And swung out.

<u>41</u>

And missed.

I *missed.*

My action hadn't been instinctive; I must have thought about it half a second too long.

And so the instinctive action (*reaction*) had turned out to be his. He'd received sufficient warning to enable him to sidestep.

He almost laughed.

"Oh, no, you don't, my son! *Oh, no, you don't!*"

Yet, even then, he didn't become vengeful or in any way unpleasant. He simply spoke those words and backed out through the doorway. Fast.

But he needn't have worried.

I wouldn't have tried again. Why? Because I knew I hadn't pulled my punches. Because I knew the force behind my blow, connecting, would almost certainly have floored him.

And because I knew I had received my answer.

I felt satisfied then. Even thankful. Events from now on must simply take their course. It clearly wasn't meant for me to get away. It wasn't meant for me to get in touch with Ewen Montagu.

Nor – come to that – with Heinrich Buchholz.

Sicily wouldn't be left undefended…virtually undefended. That just wasn't going to be the way of it. I had to accept this.

Or did I?

I was fully aware that most people – presumably the same who'd earlier have decried the element of coin-tossing – that most people would have seen my easy acceptance as showing a weakness of character: a shocking and pathetic weakness of character. But at least I had tried. I had really meant to knock the sergeant unconscious. I could derive encouragement from that.

So – slowly – I went back to my cot; sat down; opened the newspaper.

Of course, there was nothing there about the storm.

In fact, there was nothing much about anything. The Prime Minister had arrived in Washington yesterday for talks with Mr Roosevelt. (So much for my instructions to the sergeant…*demand to speak to Mr Churchill*!) On Monday the Allies had bombed Sicily: presumably part of their elaborate double bluff, part of their campaign to establish it was still through Sicily they were meaning to come.

But I found that often I couldn't concentrate. I was reading whole columns without afterwards being clear as to what they had told me. In truth, I just couldn't be bothered. I felt no interest. It all seemed so absurd.

There was a short and very familiar Bible quote – bottom of the second page, obviously a daily feature. This quote was so much my favourite that for a second or two I saw it as a message of encouragement sent expressly to myself...until I remembered that at this particular moment there must be literally thousands of others equally in need – *at least* equally in need, if not a great deal more so. 'All things work together for good, to them that love God.' The Epistle of Paul to the Romans. chapter eight, verse twenty-eight.

Just above this, an article on concentration camps. Mainly those which had been used in South Africa forty-odd years ago during the Boer War. I only scanned it but it made me think of Pastor Niemoeller in Sachsenhausen and of all those 'Jews, Communists and other political suspects confined in primitive conditions,' whom I had read about the previous evening. (Yet St Paul had lived in violent times, as well. No one could say St Paul hadn't known about brutality.) And indeed there were currently rumours in Berlin about whole trainloads of Jews now being transported east – and to what? – no longer merely to concentration camps, whispered the few, but to actual *death* camps; although there was as little real evidence for *that* as for all those tales I'd been subjected to on Monday afternoon concerning the perfidy of the admiral. And surely on occasion, I thought, there *could* exist smoke without fire?

Couldn't there?

For only look at some of those other rumours in circulation: to do with the Gestapo and the methods they used in interrogation; methods condoned, it was said, or even encouraged, by the great Führer himself. But if only ten per cent of what was hinted at was true…!

Which, of course, it wasn't. Couldn't be.

Yet, on the other hand.

Why simply in the matter of Canaris are you now prepared to believe there could be substance in the rumours? As quite obviously you are.

Why not in the matter of the concentration camps? The *extermination* camps? And in the matter of the secret state police and their activities?

You're twenty-five years old. You belonged to the Hitler Youth. You've heard things; you've seen things…

Are you an ostrich?

I folded the paper; let it fall to the floor. Lay down again and stared up at the ceiling.

11.23 came. I pictured the train slowly leaving the station, its heavy plume of smoke blown back above the carriages, my erstwhile future powerfully picking up speed and steaming away without me.

A definitive fork in time.

From now on, I should definitely be walking down a different road.

42

At about 12.45, coinciding with the arrival of lunch – which was heralded by Sergeant Leighton, who remained standing in the doorway with a truncheon in his hand and an ironic expression on his face, but which was actually brought in by another man whom I hadn't met up to this point – at about 12.45, and in fact coinciding with the very moment at which I reached out to take the tray onto my lap, there came the sounds of abrupt and unexpected activity.

My cell was at the back of the police station but, even from there, we could hear the damp pulling-up of more than just one vehicle and the almost instant tread of more than just one pair of feet; the opening and closing of swing doors that seemed more purposeful than swing doors usually sound.

Soon, moreover, the push-button bell on the counter wasn't merely being pinged to announce someone hopeful of attention; an imperious finger was lodged on it, inflexibly. And, simultaneously, a loud but well-bred voice was calling out for service.

"Your chums, I wonder?" enquired Sergeant Leighton – and symbolically, yet still with wryly pointed irony, raised his truncheon. Like a war club.

The large tin tray had practically been dropped; as much by the sergeant's backup as by me. It was left on the bed with one of its metal domes half sliding off the plate and releasing quantities of steam. Both the deputy and I now headed for the open door, which the sergeant had just hurried away from – no one appeared to have thought about closing it, let alone turning the key. The jailbird followed his jailers down the corridor.

There were four sturdy men wearing motorcyclists' gear; and a fifth, more slender, wearing naval uniform.

This fifth man – in his early forties, thin-faced, with dark eyebrows and determined green eyes – ignored both Sergeant Leighton and Sergeant Leighton's colleague.

"Herr Anders?"

"Lieutenant-Commander Montagu?"

Swiftly – even brusquely – we shook hands.

"*There* is all the paperwork you need," said the naval officer to the policeman, indicating a letter and two other documents spread across the desk. "You've five seconds flat in which to read it. If you try to detain us after that, we shall have to use force. We're taking this man away on a matter of national importance and there's not one moment to be wasted."

"But, sir, are you aware that he entered this country under a false name and on a forged passport –?"

"Sergeant, have you read those papers yet? Are you now prepared to sign his release form?"

I felt sorry for the sergeant. I sent him a small, apologetic smile – although he probably didn't see it. Even as I gave it, he turned to ask his subordinate to fetch my suitcase from the cell.

And, at the same time, was pulling a fountain pen from his tunic pocket. Less than a minute later, we were out on the pavement.

Parked at the kerbside – and receiving a good deal of interest from a growing cluster of pedestrians – was a grey Rolls Royce. In the front of it sat a chauffeur in rating's uniform.

Immediately behind him sat Sybella.

Yet I scarcely had time to take my place beside her, and Leighton scarcely had time to close the rear door after myself, and the front one after Montagu, before we were already moving away from the kerb and beeping at people to get out of our path. Then we were purring along the centre of the road, with two of the motorcyclists several yards in front, and the other two bringing up the rear. The early afternoon was shrill with the sound of sirens.

Montagu sat for the most part in silence. I felt grateful, both for this and for the fact he wasn't sitting next to me. No last-ditch bids for cooperation; no eleventh-hour form of emotional blackmail, subtly involving Sybella. Whenever he did speak it was only to the driver, and pertained to consideration of detours we could take in order to avoid possible holdups; advice on how best to circumvent a flock of Welsh sheep that at one point was herded across our route; and questions and comments as to whether we might be keeping to our target regarding speed. He was more often occupied in gazing out of his nearside window and didn't appear to be listening to any of the murmurings which took place behind him. As a matter of fact even *we*, Sybella and I, weren't talking all that much. We were content merely to be sitting close to one another; to be discreetly holding hands.

But I still hadn't come yet – not *completely* – to tolerate loose ends.

"How did you get into Shrewsbury this morning? Did Gramps bring you?"

"No, I cycled."

"Cycled!"

I paused in the act of rethreading my shoelaces.

"Yes! It may surprise you, Liebchen, but I couldn't sleep. So I finally gave up trying – and for an hour or two just sat in the kitchen with the back door open, flicking through magazines and waiting for that storm to finish. It was light by the time it did. Then I set out practically at once."

"I hope you had some breakfast."

"You sound like my mother. No, good heavens, I did not have any breakfast – couldn't have felt *less* like having any breakfast! But your grandfather had come down after my third or fourth *Picture Post* and we drank two cups of coffee together. As a matter of fact, he did want to drive me into Shrewsbury; seemed disappointed when I decided against it. Yet the thing was – their little Austin hasn't any roof rack and there wouldn't have been room for even one of the bikes inside, let alone two. So eventually we worked it out that Gramps could cycle in later, riding yours, at the right sort of time to catch the bus back after he'd spent an hour or so in paying you a visit – though fat chance of *that* ever happening, judging from my own experience! But in the end I was really glad to have the bike ride. It made me feel as if I was actually *doing* something. The air was wonderfully fresh after the storm, and instead of

250

choosing the Watling Street route, I even decided to take a sentimental journey, along those very same roads the two of us had travelled yesterday."

"And were you able to remember the way, even without signposts?"

"Yes, you patronizing man! Even without signposts."

"No, I didn't mean to sound patronizing. I meant to sound incredibly admiring."

"Although if you *must* know, damn it, I did have to ask directions from one very charming old gentleman who was out walking his dog. But in fact I almost enjoyed the journey…I mean, insofar as I could have enjoyed *anything*. Except, of course, for that long uphill trudge near the beginning which – well, just exactly as you predicted – I do have to admit wasn't *too* much fun. You must be thrilled, delighted, to be told you nearly rank with Nostradamus."

"That is – you're implying? – more so than *some* people."

I said this totally without rancour. Sybella nudged me in smiling reproof (even if, despite her bravery, her smile was growing gradually more tremulous – her voice, as well). But when I glanced at the back of Montagu's head it seemed clear he was still more intent on looking out for landmarks than on listening to anything which she and I might be discussing.

It appeared that our driver was making good progress.

By ten past one we were racing through Oswestry.

Half an hour later, we were awakening all those sleepy hills and valleys round Llangollen.

Another twenty-five minutes and we were passing down the main street of greystone cottages that was Betws-y-Coed.

And at two-thirty on the dot we were just departing from Bangor and about to drive along the wooded shoreline of the Menai Strait. We were now only minutes away from the suspension bridge, where, at its entrance, we should leave behind our four outriders. No further need of their path-clearing duties or the barrier of protection they bestowed (the mark of honour they conferred, Sybella now explained it, jokily – jerkily), services which must have been more essential on the

251

road up from Whitehall than they were on the road on from Shrewsbury. I waved goodbye to them, a gesture I felt to be slightly farcical, practically a royal acknowledgment – yet it also expressed a depth of gratitude I knew they couldn't be aware of.

Sybella and Ewen would shortly pick them up again…as somewhat needless escorts for their rather more leisurely return.

We crossed the bridge and saw Parys Mountain rising up before us. And at last we knew we could relax – not least of all the young and fresh-faced sailor at the wheel. We had completed the journey in just under two hours and were nearly in sight of our objective.

At Amlwch we stopped behind a man-made hillock: a reminder of the days when – in consequence of copper ore, discovered in the mountain – this little place had been a boom town.

The time was barely a quarter to three.

Plainly I should now need to travel the rest of the way on my own. I shook hands with the driver – again, I thought, one of the many ships that maybe only passed in the night but made both the night and the sea-lanes much better worth the passage – and then walked to the other side of the car, where the lieutenant commander was standing.

"Well, anyway," he said, "no matter how this turns out, I'm glad you and Sybella are going to marry. And when I say that, I know I'm speaking very much for your future parents-in-law, also."

Here, I thought, there *might* have been just a glimmer of emotional blackmail. Yet, if so, it was assuredly the kind to which I couldn't take objection.

"Actually," he said, "this possibility only occurred to me in the car, but I think we'll presently be seeing Sybella's parents. Making a short detour – well, not exactly *short* – that'll enable me to drop her off for a day or two of well-deserved rest if she feels like it, and a day or two of hard-to-beat home cooking.

252

We should both envy her. Nothing like the tranquillity of Ogbourne St George!"

"And, besides that, such an irresistible address," I murmured, drily.

"Strange," he smiled, "I always thought the same."

"So please give them my regards," I said. I didn't believe – not for an instant – that Sybella's parents would yet know the first thing about their daughter's engagement, but it was nice of him to imply they did and that they actually felt happy about it. "And thank you, sir. Thank you for everything."

"Thank *you*, Erich."

We shook hands and I turned away.

But then immediately turned back.

"Sir...why do you think Admiral Canaris sent somebody like me?"

He hesitated. "You mean – somebody still reasonably new to all this kind of thing?"

I nodded.

Montagu spoke slowly. "I really think you'd have to ask *him* that."

It was an exchange which might have sounded utterly banal to practically anyone else, but I'd been taking a chance that it wouldn't do so to him.

And I realized that it hadn't.

"Yes, I really think you *should* ask him," he said. "In fact, I know I have no right to do this...but I ask you very humbly to make it your priority."

I nodded again and said goodbye. If I'd been in a mood to find anything even remotely comic, I might have felt mildly diverted by the notion of placing 'very humbly' alongside Lieutenant Commander Ewen Montagu.

Then I rejoined Sybella – who, for the past three or four minutes, had been standing out of earshot.

While the lieutenant commander got back in the car she and I walked a short distance from where it was parked. Only a dozen yards or so, but there was a bend in the track which conveniently hid us from view.

"Oh, darling," she said. "I can't stand it! Not being able to write. Not having any idea, ever, of what may be happening to you."

Up until now her voice, her manner, had both appeared more under control.

"I know, I know, my sweetheart! Oh, God, *how* I know! I can't stand it, either."

"A week ago, I'd never met you. Now my whole life has been turned upside down; there'll never be a waking moment when you aren't in my thoughts. I ought to be sending you off with a cheery smile – I know I should – and I don't want you remembering me all tear-stained and red-eyed and ugly. But I can't go on pretending."

"Listen, Sybella. You *must* go on pretending. Both of us must. For if we don't, what can I possibly tell the captain of the submarine when he looks at me and says, 'But why are you all tear-stained and red-eyed and ugly? *Achtung*! What is the meaning of such blotchiness?'"

"Darling, you are…" She was having difficulty. "Oh, you are…you're such a…"

"Fool? That's very true but even so. What if the captain reports back to his superiors? *He loves that country so much he blubbers when he has to leave it.*"

Her screwed-up handkerchief was already in her hand.

"Yes, you're right," she said. "You – are – absolutely – and definitely – "

She wiped away her tears and blew her nose.

"There's something else," I told her. "Will you apologize to my grandmother for me? And my granddad? I was childish and I behaved badly. Will you phone them for me?"

"Yes…yes…but nobody thought that you…behaved badly." She wiped her eyes again.

"I can see exactly why she did it. Will you try to make her understand that?"

She nodded.

"And one last thing. Sergeant Leighton. I wish you'd write to him for me…or telephone…tell him how much I appreciated all his kindness."

She gave another silent nod.

"In fact, weren't you supposed to be seeing him today? He spoke about needing to interview you."

"I'll…I'll telephone him, then."

"Oh – and here – I haven't paid you yet for the hotel!"

But she pulled back my hand even as I was reaching for my wallet and – as she did so – the car horn sounded.

Only a gentle beep. Reminding; apologetic. But it made us hold on to one another all the more fiercely.

"We've still got a minute!" I said.

"Oh, yes – please – we've still got a minute!"

"But then I walk away, my darling – and when I do I shan't look back. Only remember that we love each other and that we're going to have a marvellous life together. Twelve or fifteen children, at the very least. Only hold onto that, Sybella! And remember, too, that not for nothing do they call me Nostradamus."

But my voice caught slightly on those final four syllables.

So for that final minute – *two* minutes – we struggled to draw whatever comfort we could from each other's closeness.

But naturally it wasn't as easy as I'd said…just to break away. I forced myself to think about the awfulness of what had happened in Guernica, and of what had happened in the London Blitz, and of what was still happening everywhere about us. I had to ask myself what comment anyone caught up in the physical agony and mental anguish inseparable from maiming, say, or torture or bereavement, what comment they'd have made on the sadness of two lovers merely faced with saying goodbye.

Did this seem exploitative? Yet I knew I had to do something to try to put it into context, the way I felt, if only for the sake of the impression I should soon be making on the oarsman in the rowing boat, the crew of the submarine and – well, yes, of course – that all-too-readily suspicious captain.

But inevitably – *inevitably* – I did look back.

Just couldn't help it.

And she was continuing to stand there, arm upraised, hair blown back by the stiff breeze coming in off the sea.

Yet at last I came to the dunes and to the steep and bracken-bordered path descending to the beach. And in one sense, when I sank below her line of vision, it was almost a relief. But I found I'd been gripping my suitcase so tightly that my fingers and the handle felt practically welded. I transferred the suitcase to my other side.

It was two minutes to three.

I saw the man waiting by the shoreline, with his rowing boat drawn up a short way on the sand.